Cover Design: Jay Aheer
Editing done by Jenny Sims Editing4Indies
Proofing Julie Deaton by Deaton Author Services
Interior Design by CP Smith

Titles by Natasha Madison

The Only One Series
Only One Kiss
Only One Chance
Only One Night
Only One Touch
Only One Regret
Only One Mistake
Only One Love
Only One Forever

Southern Series
Southern Chance
Southern Comfort
Southern Storm
Southern Sunrise
Southern Heart
Southern Heat
Southern Secrets
Southern Sunshine

This Is
This is Crazy
This Is Wild
This Is Love
This Is Forever

Hollywood Royalty
Hollywood Playboy
Hollywood Princess
Hollywood Prince

Something So Series
Something Series
Something So Right
Something So Perfect
Something So Irresistible
Something So Unscripted
Something So BOX SET

Tempt Series
Tempt The Boss
Tempt The Playboy
Tempt The Ex
Tempt The Hookup
Heaven & Hell Series
Hell And Back
Pieces Of Heaven

Love Series
Perfect Love Story
Unexpected Love Story
Broken Love Story

Faux Pas
Mixed Up Love
Until Brandon

Dedication

To my family who supported me through this journey
every step of the way.

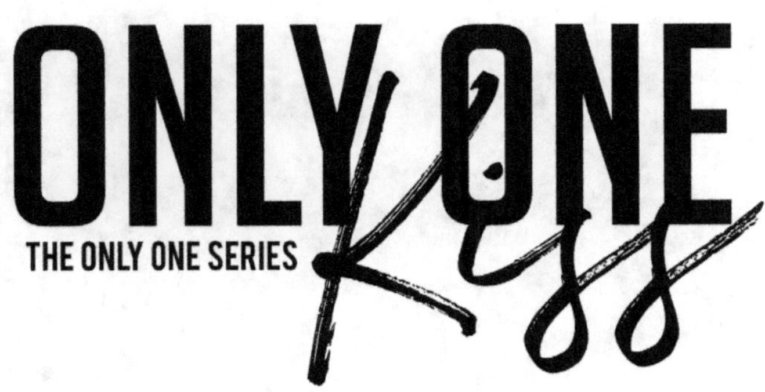

NATASHA MADISON

ONE

CANDACE

"Aaron, please explain to me how you ended up 'balls deep' in the Stanley Cup?" *You fucking idiot,* I say in my head instead of out loud, pinching the bridge of my nose as I lean back in my chair.

I close my eyes as I listen to him. "Can." He groans my nickname. "It was a private party. I'm allowed to be naked at my house. Fuck, I just won the Stanley Cup," he snaps.

"There were over one hundred people there. Did you know all one hundred?" I ask but then don't wait for an answer before I continue. "I wake up this morning to phone notifications through the roof, and then I open it, and there you are. Swinging your dick like you're fucking Tarzan."

"You looked at my dick?" He chuckles, and now it's my turn to groan. "I always thought you liked me. But now that you see I'm a shower and a grower…?"

"Can you for one second shut up?" I ask, trying to stay professional by not telling him that I wouldn't touch him with a ten-foot pole. "How do you want me to spin this?"

"How about you say that I was celebrating on my own private property, and that being said, I was having fun." He almost groans out. "It's not that big of a deal."

"Actually," I start. "It's a huge deal, considering we spent the past year pushing you as a family man."

"How do you think I got the family?" He laughs at his stupid joke, and I know that this conversation isn't going nowhere.

"Auntie Can!" Hearing my name, I look up from my laptop toward the doorway and see my three-year-old niece, Zoey, running toward me. She climbs onto my lap, and I kiss her head as she leans forward to grab the pen next to my agenda. I reach for her book and open it so she can doodle on it.

I hang up with Aaron and look at my niece. "Don't ever date hockey players," I say and then hear my brother, Evan.

"Don't ever date anyone," he says, and I look over at him as he leans against the doorframe watching us. He and his wife, Zara, are in town from New York, visiting for the week. I'm in Dallas because Evan got drafted here when he was eighteen. When he turned twenty, his career really started to take off, so he began to work on his image and his branding, and that is where I as his little sister came into the picture. I took over his social media accounts, posting things each day, and the bigger he got on Twitter and Facebook, the more his jersey flew off the shelves. He brought me out to visit him, and the visit lasted longer than anyone expected. It started with him telling one person, and then the other person told another one, and I now manage the social media accounts of over fifty NHL players. I speak with each of them or their assistants once a month, and we go over everything they need. I also have a waitlist for the ones I can't take on right now.

"What are you complaining about now?" Zara asks, hugging his waist. The story of the two of them is rather funny. She tweeted him, and before I had a chance to answer her, he agreed to be her plus one to crash her ex's wedding. Well, I wasn't the nicest person to her when she first came into the picture. To be completely honest with you, I was a bitch. I hated her before I'd even met her, but then I slowly got to know her. When he got traded to New York, he tried to get me to go with him, but my home was here in Dallas now. This is where I wanted to be.

"He's complaining that Zoey can't date," I say, and she just shakes her head as I hug Zoey close to me. I kiss her head, and she looks up at me with big eyes and a huge smile.

"Did everything work out okay?" Zara asks, coming into my home office and sitting on my new loveseat. I smile when I look around because it's decorated in my favorite color pink and everything I love from the throw pillows on the cream-colored couch to the furry pink leopard blanket that Zoey usually uses as a cape.

"I mean, define okay?" I say and then look down at Zoey who squirms in my lap to get down. Grabbing her pen and book, she walks over to the loveseat and climbs up next to Zara.

"I saw the video," Zara says, looking down to make sure that Zoey doesn't color on the cushion.

"You saw the video?" Evan asks in shock, coming in and scooting Zara over so he can sit next to her and pull her closer to him. "Why would you look at the video?"

"I didn't mean to," she says, laughing, "but it's trending on Twitter."

I close my eyes. "Of course it is," I say and then look over to see that Zoey has laid down and asked for Zara to cover her.

Evan leans over and kisses Zara's neck. "Sweetness," he says softly, using her nickname and then burying his face in her neck.

"Barf," I say, getting up. "Go to your room," I say. "And cover Zoey's eyes before you scar her."

"She's used to me loving on my wife," he says, "so nothing will scar her, but I do have some news for you." He looks over at me. "Everyone is coming here tomorrow for a pool party." My mouth opens and then closes, and he just continues to talk as my eyes bulge out of my head. "What else was I supposed to do? You have the pool."

"Who is everyone?" I ask, folding my hands over my chest. I know exactly who everyone is, but I want to see him squirm.

"Well, my in-laws," he says and then puts his hand

up to stop me from talking. "It's not my fault no one can travel without each other. This is Zara's fault." He looks at Zara, who glares at him. "No one can be alone."

"Your in-laws are a hundred people." I look at Zara. "No offense but they can be a bit . . ." I try to be as polite as I can.

"Overwhelming," she finishes the sentence for me. "And I get it, but I promise it's not a hundred people. It's actually only Justin and his family who are down this time." I don't listen to anything else she says, thankful we're only talking about a couple of people and not the whole family.

I don't have a chance to say anything before my phone rings, and I see that it's another client of mine. "What is with today?" I mumble to myself, picking up the phone. "Hello?"

"Hey, Candace, it's Jeremy."

"Hey, Jeremy," I say, grabbing my calendar and flipping it to his page. "How are you?"

"I'm okay," he says, and I hear the waves crashing in the background. "Sitting out on the patio in Malibu."

"Sounds divine," I say, smiling. "Are you enjoying summer so far?"

"Yeah," he says. "I'm still in the middle of training." I nod my head. What people don't realize is that the summer break isn't really a break for the athlete; it's when they actually get ready for the next year. Their training is sometimes even more intense during the off-season than when they play during the year. "I was actually calling to schedule a couple of things to promote."

"I can definitely get those on the calendar," I say.

"I wonder if you can add me to your calendar," he says, laughing, and I ignore it.

"What were you planning on doing?" I ask.

"My foundation is having their annual celebration," he says. "You should come down."

"Oh, I think you told me that," I say, looking at my calendar and see the notes that he gave me yesterday. "Yup, I have it down. I'm going to start posting about it tomorrow. I even set up a special link for people to follow via your website."

"That is perfect, just like you," he says, and I remain quiet, not sure what to say. "I might be in Dallas in a couple of weeks."

"Are you coming here for business?" I ask. Looking at my notes, I don't have anything about him coming to Dallas.

"Just coming down to check things out, and I was wondering if you'd like to get dinner while I'm there," he says, and I stop, looking at the paper. "Maybe we can have dinner and then who knows . . ."

"Um . . ." I start. "I would have to check. Evan is in town, so I'm spending some much-needed family time with them." When I look over at Evan, he's looking at me, almost glaring.

"Oh, yeah?" he says. "Then why don't we meet for lunch? Or what if I flew you out here, and you can stay at the beach house?"

"Jeremy," I say, my voice going low. "That sounds amazing but . . ." I say, and he laughs.

"That but gets me every time," he says. "One of these days, Candace, I'm going to fire you, and then you will have no other excuse."

I laugh. "Good to know. Now, are we still okay with everything we discussed earlier?"

"Yeah," he says. "Talk soon."

I put the phone down after I end the call and shake my head. "Was that Wagner?" Evan asks, and I nod. "What did he want?"

"That's confidential." I look at him and wink, and Zara laughs.

"That's code for he wanted to take your sister out," she says, and Evan whips his head to look at me.

I put up my hand before he can open his mouth. "I said no." Evan lets out a deep sigh of relief. "Besides, you know my rule," I say. "I never get involved with a client."

"That's interesting," Zara says. "I used to say the same thing and look at what happened to me."

I laugh when they start to fight about how and when they got together.

"I don't know about you," I say, getting up from my chair, "but I can say that I will never ever get involved with one of my clients." Little did I know, the universe had other plans for me!

TWO

RALPH

THE SOUND OF ringing startles me, and I sit up in bed because I'm not sure where the sound is coming from. Picking up the baby monitor from the side of the bed, I put it to my ear and say hello. I blink two more times, then snatch the phone off the side table to stop the ringing by swiping right.

"Hello?" I say, trying to sound awake, but my voice comes out groggy.

"Shit," Becca says, her voice almost a whisper. "Did I wake you?"

"Why are you whispering?" I chuckle. When I got the contract and was traded from Edmonton to Dallas, I hired Becca as my agent. She came highly recommended and is cutthroat with her deals. She always has her clients' best interest at heart and hasn't let me down once. She helped tremendously after everything went down with Cassie.

"I'm whispering because I thought you were sleeping, but I have no idea why. It's a reflex thing," she says, sounding a touch out of breath.

"Where are you?" I ask, and she huffs out a bit harder now.

"I'm on the treadmill," she says. I lie back down in bed and look over at the video monitor on the nightstand. Ariella sleeps in the middle of her crib without a care in the world. "Is Ari up?"

Ariella Cassandra Weber. We call her Ari or Princess, and we baptized her the same day we buried Cassie, but it's all a blur for me. Being in the delivery room, then Cassie being rushed to the operating room, and then in the blink of an eye what was supposed to be the best day of our lives turned out to be one of the worst days. Yet I couldn't just break down and drown my sorrows. No, I had a little girl to take care of. I was all that she had.

Becca begged me to hire someone to help with Ari, but I refused. I went through two months of almost zero sleep, but I was there every second of every day. I went back on the ice a week after Ariella was born. Becca stayed with her in one of the rooms while I played. I was so out of it on the ice, wondering if Ari was okay, that I didn't see the hit coming my way. Before I knew it, my ass was on the ice, and I'd banged my head hard enough that I suffered a concussion.

Watching every game with her lying on my chest, I would tell her all about hockey. After a month, the doctor still hadn't cleared me, and when we didn't make it to the playoffs, I took the time to heal.

To say raising her was hard is the understatement of the year. I asked Siri everything. Sometimes, I called her pediatrician four times a day. With her first diaper blowout, I stripped her naked and took a shower with her. I would spend my days talking to Cassie about Ari. I would crave the dreams when I saw her hold Ari in her arms and sing to her. But then Ari would wake, and the crying would start. I'd be up again, and the nightmare would be real.

"Not yet," I say into the phone, "but she will be soon. What's up?" I get up now and walk slowly to the kitchen to start my coffee.

"I was wondering if you had time to talk about some sponsorships." She blows out a breath. "I know I'm going to sound like a broken record, but you need to get on social media."

I groan. "Seriously, Becca, I don't have any time for that." Grabbing my cup of coffee, I walk to the bottle maker and press the button, then wait for it to spit out a heated bottle.

"You haven't updated your Facebook page in three months," she says. "And I was the one who did it. These sponsors look for a presence on social media."

"I hate it," I say. Taking a sip of the hot coffee, I lean against the counter and look out into the backyard.

"So you need to hire someone to do it for you," she says, and I put my head back.

"I'm already trying to hire someone who I'm comfortable with to stay with Ari. That has taken me four months now, and I've gone through seven people."

"You need Candace Richards." She mentions a name that sounds familiar. "She's the one you want. I know her, but I also know she has a waiting list."

"That name sounds familiar," I say, trying to think.

"Her brother is Evan Richards," she says, panting faster. "She started doing his social media, and she has the best client list out there. She has people begging her to take them on."

"That's why," I say. "Evan is one of my best friend's brother-in-law."

"Yeah, well, I didn't tell you this," she says, her voice going low, and I hear Ari starting to babble in her crib. Looking over at the hand monitor, I see the little red lines jumping, indicating she's getting restless in her bed.

"Ari is waking up," I say, knowing that I have about a minute or two before her patience runs out, and she screams bloody murder. She's the perfect baby if she's in your arms or she sees you, but the minute she doesn't, well, let's just say she can shake the house down.

"Okay, I'll make it fast. Call in a favor if you have to and get Candace to take you on as a client. I can't believe I'm going to say this," she says, "but do whatever you need to do."

"Jesus, Becca," I say, laughing and putting down my coffee. "I'm sure she's not the only one out there."

"Nope," she says, and I hear the beep of her machine. "But if you want to be the best, you need the best." I close my eyes. "I'll call you later with backup choices, but . . ." I know what she's going to say.

"Okay, I'll talk to you later. The new nanny starts today," I say, and she laughs.

"You didn't like the last one because of her eye-brows," she jokes, and I shake my head.

"They didn't move," I say. "I have to go." After hanging up, I walk down the carpeted hallway from the kitchen to Ari's bedroom. I can hear her get louder. The rising sun lights her room up just a touch, and when I'm finally close enough, I see her hands moving up and down the same time as her feet. My feet sink into the plush carpet as I make my way over to the crib. Everything is arranged the exact way Cassie wanted it. I look at the picture of Cassie smiling with her hand on her big stomach in the built-in armoire she had made. It was taken at her baby shower a month before she left us. The pain in my chest is just as raw now as it was five months ago.

I stare down at our baby who looks exactly like Cassie. Her big blue eyes shimmer, and when she finally sees me, she smiles so big. "Good morning, my princess." Bending down to pick her up, I slide my hand under her back and feel that it's wet. "Did we leak again?" I ask her as if she is going to answer me, but all she says, "Da-da-da-da."

When I lay her down on her changing table, she fusses and squirms, letting me know she doesn't want to do this whole changing diaper thing. I hand her one of her teething rings, and she grips it and brings it straight to her mouth while I change her diaper and put on a clean onesie. "Now don't you feel better, princess?" I ask, and she just smiles. "Let's go get you a bottle." I lift her to me and toss the teething ring back on the changing table, then walk out into the huge family room. I press the button on the automatic shades, and the sun slowly fills the room. In three minutes, we are both sitting on the big couch with her in the crook of my arm as we watch *SportsCenter*.

Holding her bottle for her, I kiss the top of her head, then look up. The day after the funeral, I put up pictures of Cassie all around the house. I lay my head back and think back to that bleak day five months ago. How I sat in the hospital room with tears running down my face while I held our daughter in my arms. We were chest to chest, doing skin to skin, something that Cassie should have been doing. The nurses tried to sound upbeat, but they all had the same tone and look of pity on their faces. It was supposed to be the best day of my life, and it turned out to be the worst.

"Da-da-da-da." I hear and look down to see her chewing on her bottle. Once she sees me look at her, she smiles at me. "Da-da-da-da."

"Did you sleep okay?" I ask, and she just kicks her feet. "Did Mommy come visit you?" I ask, and her hands and feet start moving fast. I'm about to ask her another question when I hear the front door open. "Miranda is here," I say, and she looks around when she hears Miranda's voice.

"Good morning, pretty girl," Miranda says when she drops her bags on the counter and then comes over to us. I knew I had to get a nanny the minute the playoffs ended. I had to get in shape, and I had to get my head back in the game. So I interviewed what felt like a thousand people. Something was always wrong with them, but when Miranda came in, there was absolutely nothing that I could pick at. She is a thirty-year-old single woman who came from Denmark and has raised two other children. Plus, Ari didn't scream when Miranda held her. I mean, Ari didn't like it because I was there, but she didn't cry bloody murder, so I hired Miranda on the spot. "Good morning, Ralph." She smiles at me and then walks to the kitchen and washes her hands.

Getting up, I walk over to the corner where I have all of Ari's toys laid out. My house is basically just barely furnished. Cassie was waiting for me to do it with her, but with being on the road and all that, I just didn't have the time, nor did I want to. This house wasn't even my first choice, but Cassie wanted it, and well, I just gave in.

I put Ari down on her stomach, and she lets me know with a whine that she is not happy, so I pick her back up, and she lays her head on my shoulder. Yup, totally whipped by a fourteen pound, twenty-five-inch baby girl.

"Aw, she loves her daddy," Miranda says with a smile. She reaches out to take Ari, but Ari buries her hand under her chest that is pressed to mine. "That's okay, baby girl," she says, rubbing her head, then she looks at me. "Did she sleep last night?"

"Yes," I say. "She woke up twice and then went right back to sleep. She was drinking her bottle when you came in." I look down at Ari who just watches Miranda. "I will be gone for four hours today. She naps in about three hours, and she likes to—"

"Go to sleep being rocked," Miranda finishes, and

then I smile at her. "She'll be fine, I promise." My heart pounds for a couple of seconds at the thought that I'm going to leave her, and she is going to cry. Miranda walks over to the couch and gets her bottle. She walks back to us and holds out the bottle for Ari, who tries to reach for it, but Miranda takes advantage of her arms out to take her away from me. She wants to cry, but instead, Miranda walks away from me, and I want to yell at her and tell her to come back. I want to kick Miranda out of my house and just stay the two of us, but instead, I hear Cassie's voice telling me it's going to be okay. I wait for Ari to scream when Miranda sits down, but she starts to talk to Ari as she gives her the bottle. She waits a bit, then looks at me and nods, giving me the okay to walk out. As I leave, I swear you would think I was missing a limb. I make my way out to the truck, and it's so odd not to open the back door and have to buckle her in.

Once I pull up to the training place, I get out and stretch my legs. Grabbing my phone, I see that Miranda has sent me a video of Ari sitting on her blanket as she sings to her, and Ari shakes her hands and her feet. I walk into the rink with a smile, smelling the ice right away, and my feet are getting antsy to get back on the ice. I started skating when I was three years old, and from then, I never left. I used to skate indoors and then come home and beg to go to the outdoor rinks in the winter. Even when it was freezing, I would be out there until I couldn't feel my toes anymore. Then once I got into high school, I just got better and better, earning an invitation to the try-out camps. It was tough, but I made it, and every single year, I had to fight to keep my place on the team. Luckily, I have a contract this year, but I also know someone is always ready to take my place.

Turning, I walk down toward the changing room, I stop when I hear someone call my name. When I turn, I'm shocked to see Justin Stone walking to me. "Holy shit," I say to him as he comes closer, and we hug. "I was not expecting you."

"Yeah," he says, laughing. Justin and I played together in Edmonton before we both got traded to different teams. It was thanks to him and his brother Matthew, who is GM for New York, that I even got a call from Nico. I owe them a lot.

"Wanted to show Caroline Texas," he says to me and then looks down. "Sorry, man." Everyone says the same thing to me once they mention their own spouse, then remember I don't have mine anymore.

I laugh. "No worries." I shrug, knowing he didn't mean any disrespect by it. "Is Dylan with you also?" I ask of his stepson.

"Nah, not today. He's having a rest day with his cousins. It's just me and Evan." He motions his head. "What are you doing here?"

"Training," I say. "Got to get ready for the season. I was chasing your record last year." I push his shoulder, and he shakes his head.

"You want to get on the ice with us?" he asks, rubbing the back of his neck. "Like old times' sake."

"Yeah," I say. "Nothing better than getting my ass kicked by the Stone family." I laugh and then hear a woman calling his name. I look over to see his wife, Caroline, approaching, and her face spreads into a huge smile when she sees me.

"Oh my God, Ralph." She walks up to us, dropping her blue bag by Justin, and gives me a short hug. "Where is she?" She looks around. "Is she here?"

"No," I say. "She's at home with the sitter." I look down. "It's killing me."

"I keep checking your Instagram for pictures, but you are the worst." She pushes me now.

"You sound like Becca." I shake my head. "I really need to start the social media thing."

"You should hire Candace. She's great," Caroline says. "But more importantly, when can I finally meet her?"

"Um, how long are you guys in town for?" I ask, and she looks over at Justin.

"I think for the week, but we are having a huge barbecue at Candace's house tonight. Do you want to come?" she asks, and then Justin answers for me.

"Count him in," he says, and I just look at him. "Do you know what my sister would do to me if I didn't force you to come with a new baby? It's like coming home with a puppy."

Caroline smacks his arm. "Did you just compare Ariella to a puppy?"

"No," he says, shaking his head. "But at the same time, you can meet Candace and beg her to take you on as a client. She said no to the last ten people I sent to her, but if you can bribe her with Ari, she might just say yes."

I shake my head and laugh, and it's at that moment I realize that this is the first time I've had an adult conversation in the past five months. I've spoken to Becca and my coach and shit, but to be joking and free? It's been a long time.

"Why not?" I say, my heartbeat starting to pick up a bit. "But are you sure it's going to be okay?"

"Evan!" Justin yells down the hall, and he pokes his head out and smiles when he sees me walking over.

"Hey." He puts out his hand, and I shake it. We've been cordial to each other on the ice, and he was very nice to me last year when we met officially.

"Is it okay if Ralph comes to the barbecue today?" Justin asks, and Evan doesn't even wait for him to finish.

"The more, the merrier," Evan says, and I don't have a choice. By the time I walk out of the arena three hours later, I'm rushing home to get my girl ready for a barbecue.

THREE

CANDACE

"Do you have any red Solo cups?" someone asks me. Looking up from the sink, I see Caroline standing there in shorts and a white halter top that Justin, her husband, grumbled about. "There are maybe ten more left outside."

"There should be another bag over there by the table." I point at the four white bags right next to the door. "I told my brother to take those outside." I walk over to them and then hear Caroline laugh.

"Was that before or after he saw your shirt?" she asks, and I look down and smirk to myself. I knew it was going to be a hot day, so I put on jean shorts and a Dallas hockey shirt, tying it in a knot at my side. "You have a backyard with New York Stingers players, and you're going to come out here and wear a Dallas shirt." She shakes her head, then looks around. "Do you have an extra one?"

"What?" I laugh, bending down and picking up the cups. I look over when the back door opens, and Justin walks in wearing shorts and a tank top with a baseball hat on his head with the New York logo. He's carrying a bottle of water.

"What's going on?" he asks me and then looks at Caroline. He tries to assess the situation as he walks over to her and kisses her lips.

"I was asking her for more cups," Caroline says.

"By the way, I invited a friend over," he says, and I look over his shoulder to my backyard.

"I mean, there are about twenty people here," I joke. "What's one more? I seriously didn't know that my brother still had friends here."

"Two," he says, taking a sip of water. "He's bringing his daughter."

"That's fine," I say as we both walk outside. Soft music fills the air, but it's drowned out by the kids screaming and jumping into the pool. I am about to sit down in a chair at the table next to the girls when my phone beeps in my pocket, telling me someone is at my door.

"Do you need help?" Zara yells from the table, and I shake my head as I turn and walk back into the house.

My phone beeps again with a text this time from Layla. Layla and I have been best friends for about four years now. We met at an event for the hockey team when Evan was here. She is a sports radio show host, and the two of us struck up a conversation, and we just clicked. Ever since then, we've been best friends. There is nothing I wouldn't do for her, and I know that if I was arrested or stranded somewhere, I couldn't and wouldn't be able to call her because she'd most likely be with me.

Layla: Hope you are having fun with the family. Text me when they leave. Also, I borrowed your black heels.

Shaking my head, I want to answer her right away, but the doorbell rings, so I tuck my phone into my pocket. I open the door, expecting a food delivery, but what I'm not expecting is the biggest crystal blue eyes. She garbles out da-da-da-da while waving her hand and giving me the biggest gummy smile I have ever seen in my life. My heart fills, and the need to bend over and just take her in my arms is so great that I have to grip the door handle so hard I'm sure my knuckles are now white.

"Sorry, I didn't know if I should go around the back or not." My eyes fly up to the man holding the little girl. His brown hair looks like he just ran his fingers through it, and his blue eyes light up with the sun. The scruff on his face is perfectly groomed to show off his plump lips. "I'm Ralph," he says, my tongue still tied, "and this is Ariella." I look back at the little girl who is wearing a pink short onesie with a pink hat, her almost brown hair sticking out a bit in the front. A pacifier clipped on the front of her onesie that says Daddy's Girl as he bounces her up and down on his hip.

I shake my head and smile. "I'm so sorry," I say, moving aside so he can walk in, then closing the door behind them. He's dressed in shorts, and we are wearing the same shirt. "Come in please. You must be Justin's friend?"

"Guilty," he says, turning to look at me. My mouth

gets dry when I hear the back door open and then hear little feet running.

"Auntie CanCan." We both look down the hallway as Zoey runs to me, hugging my leg. "Can I have a popsicle?"

Bending down, I pick her up, then kiss her nose. "Where is Mommy?"

"She is right here," Zara says from the hallway and then looks over. "Oh my God, Ralph." She walks over to him, and I just stand here as she hugs him and kisses his cheek. "And, oh my God." She takes her hand and rubs her finger up and down the baby's cheek. "This must be baby girl Ariella?"

"This is her," he says, leaning over and kissing Ariella's cheek as she giggles and then looks at me, saying da da over and over again.

"She is the prettiest and look at those eyes," Zara says. "If you want to go into the back, everyone is waiting for her." Zara points down the hallway. "I'll bring you there while Candace gets some p-o-p. . . " She starts to spell it when Zoey throws her hands in the air.

"Popsicles." And then she claps her hands, making everyone laugh. Ralph walks in front of me, and I totally check him out. Though I'm about to kick myself when he stops, and I almost run into him.

"Can I leave the diaper bag inside?" He looks over at me, waiting for an answer, and again, I'm standing here tongue-tied, not sure what to say. What the fuck is wrong with me? "I have her milk that needs to stay cold."

"Oh, yeah," I say, trying to put Zoey down, but she just hugs me tight. "If you want a popsicle, you have to let me go."

"No," she says softly and then plays with my hair. "I love you." She bats her eyes at me.

"Okay, fine." I kiss her neck and walk around Ralph to the kitchen. Going straight for the freezer, I take out one of her favorite frozen yogurt ones. She claps her hands. "Give me love." Grabbing my face in her hands, Zoey kisses me on the lips. "Love you," I say as she squirms out of my arms and then skips over to Zara who scoops her up.

"I'll go tell Justin that you're here," Zara tells Ralph and walks out. I look back over at Ralph, and my heart speeds up a bit. I put my hand on my head, seeing if maybe I have a temperature. Maybe I'm having a sunstroke, and I don't know it.

"Are you sick?" Ralph asks and turns just a touch so I can't see Ariella, shielding her from the crazy lady who doesn't say anything.

"No," I say, laughing nervously. "I'm fine. Do you need me to help you with that?" I point at the big diaper bag hanging off his arm. "I can hold her if you like," I ask, walking over to them and holding out my arms to her. He looks at me and then down at Ariella.

"She usually doesn't go to strangers," he says. Right before I put my hands down, Ariella reaches out and grabs my finger.

I smile at her. "Hi, pretty girl," I say. She smiles at me, and I take a step forward, smiling at Ralph. "I can try to hold her, and if she fusses, we can make a swap. The kid for the bag." I try to make a joke of it. "Can I?" I lean forward, opening my hands, and he slowly hands her over.

"Yeah." He waits for her to cry once I take her. Instead, she smiles and then looks around.

"Five." I start counting. "Four." Ralph looks at me once I finish counting down to zero. "Usually, if they don't cry in the matter of five seconds, it's safe to say she isn't going to cry."

His eyebrows bunch together. "Really?" He looks at me and then looks at Ariella, who looks from him to me and then smiles.

"No clue," I say, shrugging, "but I'm going with it." I look at Ariella, really hoping that she doesn't cry. "You can put whatever you want in the fridge." I point over at the fridge, and he grabs the bag and pulls out six bottles. I have to roll my lips and not laugh at him. "How long were you planning on staying?"

He laughs, and it's somehow light as he puts the bottles in the fridge. "I've been stuck without a bottle once, and I'll never make that mistake again." After he closes the fridge, he comes over and kisses his girl on her neck, and just the smell of him has me off kilter. It's a clean smell, which sounds weird. I wish I could explain it better.

"Does she have sunscreen on?" I ask when the haze of his smell leaves me.

"Yes, I put it on her just before we left the house." He takes his hat off, scratching his head, and then places his hat back down. He looks at Ariella and smiles. "Are you ready to go outside and meet everyone, beautiful girl?" he asks her, and I swear my ovaries just combusted. He reaches for her as she calls his name. "Are you coming out?" he asks me, and all I can do is smile and nod my head.

He walks past me and goes outside just as Zara comes back inside. "What are you doing in here?"

"Who the fuck is that?" I ask, pointing at the door, then putting my hands on the counter. She looks at me as I try to get my head back on straight.

"That's Ralph," she says, then she looks out the door and then turns to look back at me. "Oh, no, no, no, no."

"What?" I ask her, not sure what the hell she is going on about.

"You can't go there, especially not with him." She points at the door.

"Oh, God, is he still with the mother?" I put my hand in front of my mouth. "I would never."

"Candace." She says my name, and I don't know what I'm expecting her to say, but what I definitely was not expecting was the next sentence. "His wife died in child-birth," she says softly and leaves me here in the middle of my kitchen looking outside at him. My heart just sinks thinking about the baby girl in his arms without a mom. I watch as Justin sees him and comes over right away with Zara and Caroline following suit.

Swallowing down the lump in my throat, I walk out of the house. "Look at the big guy with a baby," Justin says. "Shit, have you met Candace?" He motions to me.

I smile at Ralph. "We met when she answered the door," he says, and then I watch Caroline take Ariella and then pass her to Zara. I walk over to the table to sit down and take a sip of water. *Maybe I'm just dehydrated,* I think to myself.

"You three should take a picture," I say, looking over at Justin as he stands with Evan and Ralph.

"Put Ralph in the middle and somehow make a joke about 'turf war.'" I pop a strawberry in my mouth.

Evan shakes his head. "My sister's always working." He looks at Ralph. "She's a social media expert."

"Really?" Ralph says, then looks over at me.

"Oh, yeah," Justin says. "She's the best. You should hire her." He slaps Ralph on the shoulder. Ralph looks at me like he wants to say something, but instead, he turns back and starts talking to Justin.

Zara comes over and sits next to me at the table. "I know that look," she says softly, grabbing a water bottle and bringing it to her mouth for a drink. Looking out into the backyard, I wish I had shades on to shield how I'm watching Ralph. He's holding Ariella again, as she just looks around, taking in all the commotion.

I turn to look at Zara. "I don't know what you mean."

"I mean you are looking at him in a way that you're curious, and that can only lead down a road and path I don't think you want to go down." She puts her hand on my arm and squeezes it. "It's just . . ."

I swallow over the lump in my throat and get up. "I need to go to the bathroom." I walk away from her and step into the house. "She's right," I say to myself. "Nothing good can come of this."

FOUR

Ralph

ARI SMILES ALMOST the whole day as she gets passed from one person to the next until she's over it, and now she just wants me. She starts to get a bit cranky, and then she goes from zero to a hundred in point three seconds. I shake my head and look around to ask Candace if I can go inside, but I can't find her anywhere, and Ari's cries are only going to get louder.

Getting up, I walk into the cool house and come face-to-face with Candace standing in the middle of the kitchen writing something on a piece of paper. When she looks up, I try not to stare at her too much. Fuck, she's so fucking gorgeous. She took my breath away the minute I walked in, and just having that reaction to her made me feel uneasy.

"Hey," she says. Flipping her ash blond hair over, she stands up straight, and her shirt rises just a bit, showing a sliver of her stomach. "Is everything okay?" She drops her pen, and her blue eyes just pop even more. Walking around the counter, she comes to us as Ari screams bloody murder. She brings her hand to Ari's cheek. "What is all this fuss, pretty girl?" she asks her softly, and Ari stops crying, just looking at her. Ari looks at me and then back at Candace, forgetting she is hungry.

"She wants a bottle," I say to Candace. Her eyes come to mine, and I quickly look at Ari. "Do you think you can hold her while I get the bottle going?"

"Hold this little angel?" she says, grabbing Ari from me who then decides this is a bad idea and wails at the top of her lungs. I'm waiting for her to pitch Ari back to me, but instead, she starts bouncing her up and down and walking away from me.

Looking over her shoulder, she says, "I'll try to keep her busy by walking around the house and showing her things." I don't say anything to her as she walks away. Instead, I stand here for a good three seconds, wondering what the fuck is going on. I also listen to see if Ari is going to continue her fit, but she's settled substantially, and all I hear are whimpers of irritation. Walking to the fridge, I grab a bottle, then head to the sink and run the bottle under the hot water. I continue to listen for her, but I don't hear her, and when the milk is warm enough, I go looking for them.

Heading down the hallway, I'm not sure where I'm going and don't want to walk into a room I shouldn't. "And this, right here is my second client I ever got." I hear Candace's voice. "He was a hard one, but I finally got him on track," she continues, and I stand in the doorway of what is an office. Her back is to me, so she doesn't see me standing here. Ari has her head on her shoulder as she chews on her pacifier, listening to everything that Candace says. "This is my girl Zoey." She points at the picture of baby Zoey smiling at the camera. "She's my favorite," she whispers to Ari. "Don't tell anyone." She leans down and kisses her cheek. It's then that she looks over and sees me. "Hey there, is the bottle ready?" When she turns, I can't say anything to her, so I just hold up the bottle in my hand.

She walks over to me. "I was going to use the bathroom if that's okay before I feed her." She holds out her hand for the bottle.

"I can start feeding her, and then you can take over," she says, tilting her head to lay her cheek on Ari's head. "I mean, if that's okay." She waits for me to answer, and I just stand here watching her and wondering if this is how Cassie would have been. After I hand her the bottle, I turn to walk away before I say something to make her think I'm a fucking creep.

Turning, I walk down the hallway, peeking in doorways until I find a bathroom. I go in and sit down and close my eyes. Fuck, what the hell is going on? I take my hat off and toss it on the bathroom counter, putting my head down. I wait for my heart to slow down before getting up and turning on the cold water. Maybe I'm having a heatstroke. I cup my hands under the water and splash it on my face three times. Grabbing the towel, I dab my face with it and ignore looking at myself in the mirror. I can't even stand myself right now. The last thing I need is to look at any woman that way or even want anyone. This was not for me. Picking up my hat, I open the door, going straight to the family room where I expect Candace and Ari to be. When I don't see her on the couch, I look outside where the party is still in full mode. The men are all in the pool supervising the kids as they jump in while the women sit together talking and laughing. Turning, I walk back into the house, trying again not to look around where I shouldn't when I hear her voice again. I walk back to the office, but she isn't there, and when I hear her voice again, and I walk to the other room, I'm shocked that it's a room for a baby. A white crib is pushed against a white wall, and huge pink flowers painted on the right wall look so real. I look around and see that she's sitting in a rocking chair as she holds the bottle. She watches Ari while she rocks, and then she must feel me looking at her because she looks up. "Hey," she says softly. "She's out like a light."

"Is she still drinking?" I ask, walking into the room and feeling my feet sink into the white plush rug. "This carpet is so soft."

"I had three layers of padding added," she says. "In case Zoey decided to climb out of the crib and fall." I look around the room and see that there are pictures of Zoey everywhere.

"I have a confession to make," I finally say awkwardly, and she just looks at me as she rocks my child in her arms.

"Okay," she says softly, her voice probably staying low in order not to startle Ari.

"I know who you are." The words come out a little bit harsh, and the look on her face is confusion and shock. "I mean, not like I know who you are I'm secretly stalking you," I say, and when her face still doesn't change, I know I literally sound like a creep. I take my hat off and laugh as I scratch my head and pull my hair. "Okay, I'm going to start over."

She chuckles now. "Okay." She smiles. "Why don't you go back out and then come back in again, and we can start over?" I don't know if she's joking or not, and I already fucked this up more than I should have, so I turn and start to walk out of the room, and she laughs louder now. "Stop. I was kidding." I turn around as she takes the empty bottle out of Ari's mouth and holds it in her hands. "So you know who I am?"

"No." I think of the words to say. "I mean, I've heard of you." She stares at me still. "I seriously am going to stop talking right now. I just want to say I've heard of you through a couple of people. All good."

"Well, thank you," she says. "I think."

I look down at them, and my head is just swimming right now. "Do you want me to take her?"

"Nah." She looks down and rubs her cheek with her finger. "I love this."

"You're a natural," I say, and she looks up.

"I can't wait until it's my time," she says, her whole face lighting up, and it's at that point I know that I can never ever do anything with her. "I just need to fall in love, and you know, get married and all that jazz."

"So, traditionalist?" I scratch the scruff on my face,

ignoring the burning in my stomach.

She shrugs. "Not really, but I want the white dress and the whole wedding. I want to have a house with a white picket fence. I want the fairy tale that I've always read about." Her eyes glitter, and then she stops talking. "I'm so sorry. I didn't mean . . ."

I hold up my hand to stop her. "Please don't." I shrug, not saying another word. "I was actually going to get going," I say, lying. "I want to make sure that she takes a bath and sticks to her routine." I wonder what story she heard, and who she heard it from. I mean, it's not a secret that Cassie died in childbirth since it was all over the media. I just know from one person to the other, stories change, and I wonder what story she heard. I swallow down the lump in my throat, thinking to myself that no one knows the real story. No one knows me, for that matter.

She gets up, holding Ari to her chest. "Do you want to go say goodbye before you take her?" she asks, and I wonder why I didn't think of that before I said I was leaving.

"Yeah, that sounds good," I say and turn around, leaving her. I walk outside, hearing someone laugh and then suddenly see Zara try to hide behind Evan who just looks at someone else. I walk over to Justin who stands with his arm around Caroline as she slips her arms around his waist as they talk to his parents. "Hey," I say, and they look at me. "I'm going to get going. Candace has Ari, and she's sleeping so . . ."

"Aw, man, already?" Justin says. "How about we

meet up before I leave town?"

"I'd love it," I say, and five minutes later, I've said goodbye to everyone. I walk in, getting the diaper bag. I find Candace walking back and forth at the front door, and she looks up.

"I can take her," I offer.

"I don't want to wake her," she says and opens the door. "I can put her in the car seat, but you should start the truck beforehand, so she doesn't sweat," she suggests. I walk out of the house to the truck and start it, opening the door to air out the interior. After a minute, Candace comes out and smiles at me.

"Do you know how to put her in?" I ask, and she looks at the seat and nods.

"I have the same one in my car." She leans in and holds Ari's head while she places her gently in the seat. Ari's eyes open and then close again as she straps her in and brings the seat belt up to the middle of her chest. She shuts the door. "She should be out for a while since she finished the whole bottle," she says, handing me the empty bottle.

"Thank you," I say, grabbing the bottle from her. "For having us and for putting her to sleep."

"It was my pleasure." She smiles and then nods her head and walks back into her house, leaving me in the middle of her street watching her. She gets to her door, then turns around and waves before walking into the house. I hop in my truck, put my glasses on, and take myself home.

I don't think of her again for the rest of the night.

That's a lie. I think about her when I'm giving Ari a bath, and when I ask her how she liked meeting everyone. She plays with her brush as I blow raspberries on her stomach. "Did you like all the kids? Did you like meeting Justin and Caroline?" I ask, skipping Candace as Ari moves her hands up and down, and yells at me with a gummy smile.

After putting her pjs on and combing her brown hair to the side, I ask, "Are you ready for your bottle?" Walking to the kitchen with her on my hip, I warm her bottle and then head back to her room to read her a book. We have the same routine every night. I grab the book and notice the pages are already starting to fray. When I finish the last word in the story, I look down and see the bottle is coming out of her mouth. I get up and place her on her back in the middle of the crib. Her head falls to the side, and ignoring the voice in the back of my head, I count my blessings that I have her in my life.

"Good night, Angel," I say, and then right before I walk out of the room, I look over at the wall where Cassie's picture is. "I'm sorry, Cass," I whisper, walking away.

FIVE

CANDACE

I LOCK THE door behind Evan and Zara, then walk back to the bedroom to make sure that Zoey is still sleeping. I wish I could crawl into bed after a nice shower, but I know that if I do that, I'll only be thinking about the mess waiting for me in the kitchen.

Walking back into the kitchen, I see that Caroline and Zara put away as much as they could, so I clean up the rest of the mess. As I'm putting the stuff away, I notice the baby bottles in the fridge. I smile as I pick up a bottle, then walk over to my phone and send Justin a text.

Me: Hey, by any chance do you have Ralph's number? He forgot his baby bottles here.

Pressing send, I walk back to Zoey's room and hear her soft snore. I turn on the baby monitor and carry it with me into my room. I take a quick shower, and when I'm drying off, my phone beeps. Looking down, I see that it's a text from Justin.

Justin: I just texted him so I'll let you know what he says.

Me: Sounds good.

I put the phone down and slide into my big bed, and I'm about to fall asleep when I hear Zoey call for me. I get up and walk to her room, seeing her standing in her crib. "What's the matter, Angel?" I ask, picking her up. "Do you want to sleep in my big bed?"

"Yeah," she says, putting her head on my shoulder. When I walk back into my room, I make a whole pillow wall on the side of the bed and then get the kid rail from my closet and slip it on to make sure she doesn't fall off. She sleeps all over the bed, and when I get kicked in the face, I groan and open my eyes. Looking over, I see the sun starting to peek in, so I lie still for a bit, wondering if I'm going to go back to sleep. But I know I won't, so I get up and quietly make my way down to the kitchen. Starting the coffee, I open all the blinds, then walk to my office and grab my laptop and agenda. I peek in to make sure Zoey is still okay and put pillows on the other side of her where I was sleeping, and she doesn't budge. Once I make my cup of coffee, I open my laptop and start going down my list one by one, doing my posts for the week.

When I hear a thud and then the sound of feet running, I look up and see that Zoey is up. "Auntie CanCan." She runs over to me, and I open my arms for her to crawl into my lap. "You working?" she asks, pushing the hair away from her face as she leans into me.

"I am." I kiss her head. "Did you sleep okay?" I tuck

her hair behind her ears as she nods. "Are you hungry?"

"Can we have pancakes?" She smiles. "Banana and strawberry." I kiss her cheek and bring her to me getting up. "Can I help?" She runs over to her step stool that I had made for her when she was here last time. She drags it over to the counter and places it against it. Stepping up on the stool now putting her hands on the counter. "I'm ready."

"Okay," I say, walking and getting the stuff ready for her. I stand with her and we make pancakes and I put bacon in the oven. "I'm going to put on your show and cook your pancakes."

"Okay," she says, turning round, and I hold her hand as she climbs down. I wipe her hands and then carry her to the couch.

"Can I have some milk?" she asks after I put her on the couch and turn on her show. I walk to the kitchen, grabbing her sippy cup, and then head to the fridge. I smile when I see the baby bottles right in front of where Zoey's whole milk is. I pour some milk in her cup and then take it to her. She grabs it and then watches her show while lying down. I make her pancakes, and when she finishes them, she has sticky hands, and I laugh when her tongue comes out to lick the syrup from her face. The doorbell rings. "Don't move," I say, grabbing a wet cloth and cleaning her hands and face. Then there is a knock on the door. "Go sit on the couch," I say, walking to the front door. I unlock the front door, pulling it open and never expecting the sight in front of me.

Ralph stands there wearing shorts and a T-shirt, his

hair falling on to his forehead. My mouth opens, and then I see he's holding Ariella and she's hanging onto his shirt with one hand. "Well, hello there, pretty girl," I say, smiling at her, and she gets all excited and moves her hands and her feet.

"I am so sorry to come by so early, but we were in the neighborhood. I didn't have your number, so I texted Justin, but he didn't answer." He starts to fumble, so I move aside.

"It's more than okay. Come on in." I wait for him to walk into the house, and then I hear Zoey.

"Is it Daddy?" she yells from the living room.

"We had a sleepover," I say. "Come on in, please."

"I don't want to intrude," he says as he follows me into the kitchen and then looks at all the dirty dishes and the flour everywhere. "Whoa."

I shrug. "She asks me for pancakes," I say. "I couldn't say no." I walk over to the fridge and grab the bottles. "Would you like something to drink?"

"Um." He looks around, not sure. "I have a chair for her." I walk past him and go into Zoey's bedroom, bringing out the activity chair. "It's a good thing I didn't throw out any of this stuff," I say, opening it and then grabbing Ariella from him and kissing her neck. I didn't even ask if it was okay before I grabbed her. *I'm such an idiot*, I think as I put her into it. She squeals, and Zoey looks over.

"That's mine," she says, and I put my hands on my hips.

"That's my television," I say, pointing at the television she was just watching. "And I'm sharing it with you. That is what we do; we share."

"Wow," Ralph says. "You just went for it."

"She can handle it," I say and then look at him, and as soon as I do, there is the flutter in my stomach again. "What can I get you to drink?"

"Coffee, if you are going to have one also," he says, and I walk around the counter, pulling the coffee cups out.

"Have a seat," I say, looking at him as he looks around the kitchen. "Anywhere really that you think will not dirty you." I laugh. "That stool looks like it's in a safe zone. You can push my agenda aside." Turning around, I make him coffee. My hands shake with anticipation and nervousness, and I want to throw my head back and laugh at how silly I'm being.

"Do you work every day?" I look over at him as he points at the book I was writing in. He pulls out a stool right next to Ariella, who is banging on the bell.

I slip onto the stool next to him and hand him his coffee. "Usually, I have everything set up the week before. I usually get on the phone with all my clients at the end of the month, and we talk about what we want to focus on in the months coming up." I try to explain a little of what I do. I don't know why I get nervous around him and just word vomit things. "My big workday is really on Sunday as I schedule everything I have. But then sometimes," I say, taking a sip of my coffee, "things come up like yesterday."

"Yesterday?" he asks. I grab my phone and pull up

the picture that I posted for Justin of the three of them and then another one that is just him and Justin with the caption.

Off-season we are on the same team.

"I tagged you on it so you should see it on your side as well." He smiles and looks down at his coffee, picking up the mug to take a drink.

"I'm social media dumb." He looks over at me, and I swear his eyes just got a touch more golden.

"I doubt that," I say and look over to see Zoey lying on the couch watching television.

"My agent, Becca," he says, "was the one who mentioned you." He starts to talk. "She is pushing me to get my 'social media presence.'" He uses quotation marks at that, and I laugh, making him shake his head. "I swear that is exactly what she said."

"Why, though?" I ask, wanting to know everything. "Why now?"

He takes a huge breath. "I want to get sponsorships," he tells me, "and in order to do that . . ."

"You need to be 'in demand.'" I use the quotations now, and he just nods.

"Yeah, all that." He takes another sip of coffee. "So lets brainstorming about where to start in order to reach out to companies." His thumb hits the coffee cup at the same time as Ari starts to whine, and I get up, walking over to the fridge.

"Should I warm up a bottle?" I ask, not sure if she ate or not, and he nods. I take a bottle out of the fridge, then walk over and place it under the hot water. She gets louder and louder, and he picks her up and then gets off his stool. I test the milk and walk over to him. "If she wants it warmer, just let me know." He places her in his arms and feeds her the bottle.

"I did also have a reason for coming over," he says, looking at Ariella and then looking at me.

I sit back down on my stool and wait for it. My heart starts to speed up, my palms get sweaty, and I can swear I'm going to be sick. "What?" I ask in a whisper.

"I need your help," he says, and I bring my hand up that now holds a coffee cup. "And I was hoping that if I came, you would feel sorry for me." *Jesus, he wants me to babysit his kid,* I think to myself.

"Um." It's my turn to stumble. "If I can help, I will."

"Good," he says, smiling. "I need you to work for me."

SIX

RALPH

I WATCH HER face after I say the words as she looks at me and then the baby. "I don't know how to tell you this," she starts to say, looking back at Ari smiling, "but I'm not a babysitter."

Closing my eyes, I think about how bad this is going even though I practiced my speech in the car. A speech that went out the window the minute she opened the door and I saw her. I could barely get anything out. I wanted to get in, get the bottles, beg her to take me as a client, and then get out. But what did I do? I sat down and watched her in her home as I drank a cup of coffee.

"Oh my God," I say, opening my eyes. "God, I am such an idiot. I don't want you to be a babysitter." I shake my head, sitting next to her. "I practiced this in the car."

She smiles at me, and our shoulders touch as I look over at her. "What did you practice in the car?" she asks, her voice going soft, and I have no control of myself as I slowly move toward her. She sits there, her eyes looking soft and beautiful and mesmerizing. *This is crazy*, I think to myself.

"Ralph." She says my name, and I don't know if she's asking me a question or telling me to stop.

I'm about to say something else and maybe kiss her when the front door opens and then closes, and I hear a man's voice. "Honey, I'm home!"

I'm shocked that I almost just kissed this woman who I met yesterday. Shocked that I even had a thought about it, I take the bottle out of Ari's mouth. Is that her boyfriend? Is he going to think I'm putting the moves on his girlfriend? Is he going to know that I jerked off to her this morning in the shower? I'm ready to grab Ari in that circle thing and just run out of the house with her still in it.

When I got the text from Justin last night about leaving the bottles at Candace's house, I smacked my head with the palm of my hand because . . . rookie mistake. I texted Justin and asked for her number, and he never got back to me. Then instead of waiting for him to get back with me like a normal person would do, I showed up at her house. Like a crazy stalker!

I rang the doorbell, thinking it was going to be fine and telling myself I didn't really find her that pretty. *It's all in your head, you've been deprived of being around women. She's not that pretty*, I kept repeating to myself over and over again until she opened the door, and I just stood frozen with my mouth dry as she stood there with pink shorts that showed off her long legs and a matching tank top. I didn't even let my eyes linger on the little part that showed her stomach. The only thing going through my mind was she's hot as fuck.

I look at her now as she looks down the hall and doesn't move when her brother comes into view with Zara next to him. "Well, this is a surprise," Zara says when she spots me and then turns to the couch when she hears her daughter call her name.

I watch as Zoey gets off the couch and runs over to her yelling, "Mama! Mama!" She bends down and catches her daughter in her arms and kisses her, and my heart suddenly hurts when I look back at Ari who watches, not knowing that she will never do that. She will never know what it's like to have a woman's love. I will give her all the love I have, but I wonder if it's going to be good enough. "You're all sticky."

"Auntie CanCan made pancakes," she says, playing with her hair. "I helped."

"I can see that." She looks past us and into the messy kitchen, and I have to say this is what a home is supposed to be.

I suddenly feel out of place. "I just stopped by to pick up the bottles," I say to Evan, who is glaring at me for some reason. "Thank you for keeping them for me," I say to Candace, who looks taken aback that I'm leaving since we were in the middle of a conversation. I put one bottle in my left pocket, another bottle in the right one, and I carry two in my hand. "Have a great day, everyone." I nod to them and walk out of the house, feeling like a fucking idiot. I get to my truck and buckle Ari in as she smiles at me and slaps her hands up and down.

"I'm sorry, baby girl," I say, kissing her, blinking away the tears in my eyes.

"What was that?" I hear from behind me and make the mistake of turning around and seeing Candace standing in the middle of her driveway naked. Okay, fine, she has her shorts and top on, but it's almost as if she's naked. I look around to see if any of her neighbors are out looking at her. The Texas heat starting to get hotter and hotter as we stand here, I spot no one out of their house because of this.

"I didn't want to intrude on family time," I say, looking back at Ari as she smiles at Candace.

"You were not intruding on anything," she says. "Would you like to come back in?"

"Not really," I say and then look at the side, trying not to kick myself when I see her face.

"Okay, then," she says, her voice going just a touch lower than it was before. "Have a great day." She turns and walks away from me and instead of going after her, I get into my truck and drive back to my house. When I get home, I put a sleeping Ari in her crib, then go to the kitchen and clean out the bottles. I'm about to start a load of her clothes when the phone rings, and I see it's Nico, the owner of the team.

"Hello?" I answer after the second ring.

"Hey, Ralph," he says. "What's up?"

"I just put Ari down for a nap, and I was going to go and run on the treadmill until she woke up," I say.

"Keeping in shape. I love it," he says. He's been the owner of the team for two years now. His father used to own the team and was tired of having to deal with it, so he handed it over to Nico. I am not going to lie, the team sucked so bad when he took it over, they hadn't made the playoffs in four years at that point. The GM was tits on a bull and was making the dumbest trades of his life. His scouting agent was arrested for having underage sex with a girl he met while getting prospects. It was crazy. I'm sure that his father thought the team wouldn't thrive, but instead, Nico hit the ground running. First thing he did was fire everyone, and I mean everyone, right down to the coach.

Last July was a war zone. We didn't know who was going to stay and who was going to go. I was shocked when I got a call from my agent that Nico wanted to have a word with me. Unlike other owners who let the GM handle things, Nico was doing the bidding himself. He got me on the phone and offered me a three-year contract. He told me it would be a rocky year, but he wanted to win the Stanley Cup. I thought he was crazy, but then I saw all the kids he brought on and realized we were a brand-new team. He brought on the coach, John, that no one wanted to hire because he would call out his players if they sucked. I'm not going to lie; I was scared every time I got on the ice. I was waiting for the coach to tell me that he's benching me, but if you did your job the way you were supposed to, he had nothing to say. Now I'm not saying that everything I did was okay—it definitely was not—and I had made my share of mistakes during the year. I couldn't even argue or be pissed when he yelled my name because he was right each time. When

Cassie passed away, Nico was the first one to come and help me, besides Becca and Miller. He took care of everything that needed to be looked after, and I know that I owe him everything. Which is why I will do whatever he needs me to do to bring the cup back to Dallas.

"I got on the ice for the first time two days ago," I say, sitting down. "It felt so fucking good to lace up those skates again."

He laughs. "Well, I, for one, am glad you are back on the ice," he says. "How's Ari?"

"She's good. She's getting so big," I say, my heart filling with pride. "I also am going to need to get in for some target practicing."

"I saw the picture you put up last month," he says, laughing. "She's going to be a stunner."

"I'm afraid of that," I say. "She looks like Cassie."

"She has some of you," he says. "I saw her scowl at you once."

I laugh. "She also has zero patience. Totally me."

"Well, I was calling to invite you over for a barbecue. I'm inviting the whole team and whoever is still is town, and I'm not taking no for an answer," he says of the players who usually go back to their hometowns when the season is over. "So far, we are a good ten plus their guests."

"Sure," I say, not even thinking about it. "That sounds like fun. When?"

"This weekend," he says. "I'll see you then."

"Looking forward to it," I say and hang up the phone seeing that I got a text while I was on the phone. I open it up and see it's from Justin.

Justin: Hey, sorry I just got your message. I just sent you her contact information.

It was great seeing you! Also, your daughter is stunning.

I smile at that last sentence and then see he shared a contact with me. I answer him back.

Me: Great seeing you, too. Let me know when you're in town again.

I press send and then delete the message thread along with her number. There is no way she is going to work with me after this morning's debacle. I rub my face and try not to think about how massively of an asshole I was. I suddenly feel like just sending her an I'm sorry for being a dick message, but I deleted her number.

"It's better this way," I say aloud to just myself. "Besides, how can you work with someone you can't even talk to? Plus, she wants the white picket fence, and you can't even think about giving her that." I'm about to tell myself that I'm an idiot when I hear Ari wail out. Tossing my phone on the couch, I stand and head to get my girl, putting Candace Richards out of my head. Or at least in the back of my head and only letting her out when I'm in the shower or falling asleep, or even when I look around my house and hate everything I see.

Everything is back to normal the next day when Miranda shows up to watch Ari. I go train on the ice and then go home where I take her into the home gym so she can watch me while I train, or until she gets fed up and starts fussing. Whatever comes first. When she sleeps, I hit the gym again. I'm just winding down my run when my phone rings. I'm not going to lie; I keep hoping it's going to be someone I'm not supposed to be thinking about. I look at the phone and see it's Becca.

"This must be a record," I say, stopping the treadmill and grabbing the towel and water bottle. I sit on the weight bench to catch my breath while I wipe the sweat from my face. "Twice in one day."

"Twice in one day so I can light a fire under your ass," she huffs out. "You were supposed to call me back," she reminds me.

"Call you back if I had an answer," I remind her. "I don't."

"Listen, I'm going to be frank with you," she says, and I roll my eyes at her.

"When are you not frank with me?" I ask, and she groans.

"You want to get a shot with the big sponsors, then you have to step up your game. I told you this. You need to give me an answer, or I'm not even going to bother trying to help you."

"An answer to what?" I say, frustrated with myself and the situation. "I don't have an answer, and you know that. Can you get me a list of names and I'll call them?"

"I got you a list," she says. "I emailed you this morning. Did you not check your email?"

"I do," I say. "I just do it at night."

"You're killing me, smalls," she says, and I laugh. "Look at the list and get back to me. I'll call them for you."

"See, now that is a plan," I say, taking a sip of water.

"Well, if I had to be in charge of the plan, I would call Candace and beg her, but . . ." She stops talking when I groan.

"Fine," I say. "I have the barbecue tomorrow at Nico's, but after that, I'll get in touch with Candace and see if she will take me on as a client."

The minute I say the words, my stomach gets all upset, and Becca cheers out loud. "Good. Fuck, it's about time."

"Yeah, yeah," I say. "I'll let you know what she says, but let's get a backup plan ready just in case."

She laughs now. "You silly, silly boy." I can even picture her sitting in her office, leaning back in her chair. "I've already got plan B, C, D, and even E in place."

"Why am I not surprised?" I ask her.

"It's why you pay me the big bucks," she says and hangs up.

The next day, I try not to think of her as I dress Ari in a one-piece shorts outfit that looks like jeans and has little white hearts on it. I look at the headband that comes with it. "What do you think, Ari?" I ask, holding it up on my finger. "Do you want a big bow in the middle of your head?"

She moves her hands up and down and kicks her feet. "Okay, you asked for it," I say, putting it on her head and then looking at her. She just looks at me smiling, and I have to wonder if it's too tight on her head. "Is that on tight?" I bend down and kiss her feeling her soft skin. "Let's go." I pick her up and snap a selfie of the two of us and finally put it on my Instagram.

Me and my only girl.

I caption it and then turn it off, tucking the phone into my pocket. Only then do I see how we are dressed almost alike. I'm wearing navy blue shorts and a light blue V-neck T-shirt with white sneakers. I grab the Babybjorn and her pacifier as we walk out the door. "Are you ready to go make all the boys jealous?" I ask her as I buckle her into her seat and kiss her right before sticking the pacifier in her mouth. If everything goes the way it should, she should sleep until we get there since Nico's house is about an hour from mine. I stop at Starbucks on the way there to kill more time so she can nap longer. I also drive way under the speed limit.

When I pull up to his house, I see a bunch of cars all in his massive driveway. I park on the street so if I have to leave, it'll be easier. I grab the whole seat this time to let her sleep, and when I get there, I'm about to walk into the backyard when I see her walking up the driveway. Her head is down so she doesn't see me, and it gives me a minute to look at her. She's wearing a one-piece tank dress that is shorter on one side and shows her leg. Her long blond hair is loose. She finally looks up, and I see that she's wearing aviator glasses. She smiles but then looks down, stopping when she gets to me. It's fucking awkward, or maybe it's just me. "Hey," I say, and I'm about to say something else when I see one of my teammates and my good friend Miller walking up the driveway dressed in almost the same outfit as me.

He looks up and smiles and then stops next to Candace, bending and kissing her cheek. "Hey, beautiful." Then he looks at me. "Hey there, big guy," he says and puts his arm around her shoulder.

SEVEN

CANDACE

"HEY THERE, BIG guy." I stand here with Miller's arm around me, and my heart is speeding up just a touch, but it has nothing to do with Miller. It has to do with the man who smiled at me and looked like he was in pain or maybe upset I was even here. He looks at me and then at Miller, and then his eyes go to Miller's hand that is draped over my shoulder.

When Miller called me two days ago to invite me to this barbecue, I wasn't going to come. I don't usually mix business and pleasure, but he told me that some of my other clients would be there, and it would be a great time to just see them. I started working with Miller two years ago, and to say he's the biggest player in Dallas is an understatement. It also doesn't help that he's drop-dead gorgeous and has been on *GQ* twice.

"I'm good, man," Ralph says, avoiding eye contact with both of us. "I'm going to get in there and get Ari out of the sun," he says and walks away from us. I take a second to watch him and then shrug off Miller's hand, and he laughs.

"We should date," he says.

"We should not. Ever." I laugh at him and push him. He tries to put his hand over my shoulder again, and I push it away, scrunching my face. "I don't know where that hand has been." We walk behind the house, and I see that people are scattered all around the huge backyard. I want to pretend I'm not looking for where Ralph went, but I'd be lying. I spot his back to me as he puts the baby chair by his feet under the huge awning near the door.

Nico, the team owner, comes out wearing shorts with pineapples on them and a button-down shirt opened all the way down, showing you his defined abs. He's one of the youngest owners out there, and I heard he's a bitch to work for. But isn't anyone who is running a business? He walks over to Ralph, smiling, and they shake hands and then go in for a side hug. I see him put out his hand and smile at the both of them. He uses his index finger to tap Ariella on the nose. I turn my head to the right when I hear my name being called.

I walk up to a couple of people and say hello as I make my rounds to greet everyone I know. By the time I get to the awning where I last saw Ralph, I'm dying for something cold to drink. This Texas heat is too much for me. Nico spots me and walks over. "Hey there," he says, kissing me on my cheek. "It's so great to see you."

"Thank you," I say, smiling at him. "I came with Miller." I want him to know that I didn't just show up randomly.

"You are always welcome," he says, grabbing a water bottle and handing it to me. "I heard your brother was in town."

"Yeah," I say, smiling, and my heart hurts a bit now knowing that he's gone, and I won't see Zoey for a couple of weeks. Which is another reason I said yes to coming to this thing. I always get depressed when she goes home. "They left two days ago."

"I saw him when he was down and tried to get him to come back to us," he says, smiling, and I see that his blue eyes light up just thinking about it.

"I don't know if Matthew would allow that to happen." I laugh now. "We all know he wants the Cup back in New York."

"I hate to say it, but he has the team to do it. Especially now with Justin there, that team is a powerhouse," he admits. "I have to go check and make sure my guests are okay." He nods. "I'll catch you later. Please make yourself at home."

After he walks away, I turn to go inside to the cool air and to also use the bathroom. I hear wailing as soon as I open the door and walk into the house, which leads directly to the kitchen. "I know." I hear Ralph saying, and then I spot him standing in front of the sink as he warms up her bottle. "You're hungry. I get it." He bounces her up and down, and then he must feel my eyes on him because he looks up.

"Hey," I say, putting down my bag on the table and then walking to them. "Do you want me to take her?" I ask, and he looks at me and then looks down at Ariella, who is just screaming as loud as she can.

"I don't know if it will help," he says, and I reach out and grab her from him.

"Hey there, pretty girl," I say softly and look down to see big tears coming out of her eyes. "What is all this crying about?" I ask her as I lay her down in my arms and put the pacifier in her mouth. She stops crying to suck on it, and she looks at me. "You know that your dad won't let you cry if he could help it." I bounce her and walk away from Ralph.

"What is this pretty headband?" I ask her as her chest trembles up and down as she sucks on the pacifier. "Now that's better," I say, and she just blinks her eyes at me. Then she kicks her feet, fed up with the pacifier, and starts crying again.

"Shh, shhh, shhh, shhh," I say, picking her up straight now and putting her on my hip, bouncing her up and down as I walk around the house with her. "Look at the colors," I say, pointing at one of the paintings on the wall. She turns her head and looks and then wails. I feel Ralph beside me, and I look at the bottle in his hand. "Do you want her?"

"I actually need to go to the bathroom," he says, handing me the bottle. "Can you try to feed her? I'll take her as soon as I come out."

"Of course," I say, grabbing the bottle from him and ignore the goose bumps that run up my arm when he touches me. Turning around, I walk over to a chair and take a seat. Then I hold up the bottle. "Is this what you want?" I ask, ignoring the eyes watching me. I offer her the bottle, and she opens her mouth and sighs as she drinks it. My hand holds up the bottle as I rub her chubby soft cheek with my finger.

"You are so beautiful," I say, and she wraps her hand around my finger. "You got my finger," I say, and she kicks her foot now. Looking up, I see Ralph standing there.

"Do you want me to take her?" he asks, and I shrug.

"I'm good, but do you think you can get me some water?" Nodding, he walks over to the fridge, takes out a bottle of water, and then opens it for me. I take a sip and Ariella lets go of her bottle to squeal. "Is that so?" I ask, and she smiles and kicks her feet while finishing her bottle. Ralph comes over and sits in front of us, waiting for her to finish, and when she does, I put the bottle on the table and then stand her up on my legs as she grabs my hair as she smiles and yells. "Well, you are a happy baby once your stomach is full," I say, and she bounces on my legs.

"You sure you don't want me to take her?" he asks, and for the first time, I look over at him, and he is smiling at me genuinely.

"I'm good," I say. "Why don't you go out and hang with the boys, and I can hang with the girl."

"I couldn't do that," he says, and I get up now, putting her on my hip.

"Fine, then I'll come outside with her and just keep taking her from you," I say and then look over at Ariella. "Do you want to go and play on the grass with me?"

"Play on the grass?" he asks. I see him taking his phone out of his pocket. "Is that safe? I'm going to google."

I throw my head back and laugh. "Okay, let me know what it says," I say and turn to walk out of the door with her. "I'm going to get a huge towel, and we are going to go sit on the grass and sing about the wheels going round and round on the bus," I say as I walk out of the house seeing Miller standing there with a beer in his hand. The minute he sees me, he walks over to me hurriedly.

"There you are," he says once he gets close enough. Ralph stands at my back, then comes to stand at my side. "I have a situation."

"Oh, good God, Miller." I roll my eyes and shake my head. "What now?"

"Well, what if by accident I sent out a picture of a certain area of myself?" He looks at Ralph with a smirk. "And by accident or maybe even a glitch, it got sent to all my contacts?" He stands there, moving his head back and forth.

"You didn't." I laugh at him. "Did you tell Nico?" I ask.

"I was going to do that next," he says. "I just want to know what I should do. Like what is your professional opinion on how to handle this?"

"Did you delete it?" I ask, and he rolls his eyes at me like I'm an idiot.

"Obviously," he says. "As soon as I got a message from my sister asking me what was wrong with me. And that I'm gross."

"You sent a picture of your dick to another woman and you're telling your girlfriend that?" Ralph says from beside me and I just look at him. "And you're okay with this?" He turns to asks me.

"My girlfriend?" Miller says the same time I say, "He wishes."

"Dude, she is my social media advisor," Miller says, and I laugh now and then look at Ariella.

"He's so funny because if I was his advisor, he would have deleted the app when I told him to since he doesn't know how social media works." I look at Miller. "Delete the app."

"Can we say that someone hacked my phone?" he asks, taking his phone out, and I shake my head.

"How many contacts do you have?" Ralph asks and then takes out his own phone. "And I wonder if I got the picture."

"Oh, yeah, can you check?" Miller asks, and I shake my head, walking around them to the chair where I find a folded towel.

"Are we going to go and play in the grass?" I ask, and Ari slaps my boob with her hand. "Are we going to sing?" I ask as I find a spot on the grass underneath one of the big trees. I open the towel on the grass and then sit with her between my legs, making sure I don't flash everyone. "Look at all those people, Ariella."

I look over and spot Miller putting his head back and then shouting over at me. "I just deleted it again." Shaking my head, I roll Ariella over onto her back. Her hands and feet move as she laughs at me. I grab her feet and start to sing "The Wheels on the Bus," and when I'm almost finished, I look up at Ralph who just stands there watching us.

"Do I want to know what else he did?" I ask, and he smirks and sits down beside me.

"Um, let's just say Nico got the picture also," Ralph says. When I look over at him, I don't think I've ever felt as settled as I do when I'm next to him.

EIGHT

RALPH

S**HE LOOKS OVER** at me smiling, and all I can do is look at her and then down at Ari, who is kicking her feet at her. She bends over and tickles her stomach and then picks her up. "You are such a happy baby," she says, and then Ari puts her hands in her mouth as she chews on her fingers.

"So what do you think is going to happen?" I ask her about Miller's situation.

"Well," she says, and I look at her now. "I'm going to go home and change all his passwords so I can fuck with him." She smirks now. "Then I'm going to post a picture of him covering his face and admitting he's not sure what happened, but he's sorry."

"What else do you do for him?" I ask, and she looks at me with a weird look on her face. I look down at the grass, trying to wonder why I was so jealous of them. Why did it bother me so much that they were together? They are both two single, consenting adults, so why should it bother me? I don't know any of the answers, but what I do know is that I fucking hate it.

"I don't even know what you mean with that question?" She laughs at me.

"I didn't mean that," I say, holding up my hands and my stomach sinks thinking about her like that with him. "I mean not that I judge you or anything like that."

"Good to know." She sounds annoyed with me now.

"I just mean what other services do you perform?" I ask, and her eyebrow shoots up. "Oh, Jesus, I don't mean that. I mean professionally."

"Wow, I didn't think it could get worse," she says, throwing her head back and laughing, and if I could, I would grab her hair in my hand and pull her to me to kiss the laughter off her face. But I can't ever be the one who does that. She shakes her head and then looks at Ari. "Your dad can dig a deep hole." Then she looks at me as she bounces Ari on her legs. "I take care of all his social media platforms except his Snapchat, obviously." She shakes her head. "I go onto his page every single day and keep it active for the fans. I usually only take care of Twitter and Facebook and their websites."

"What about Instagram?" I ask her.

"I usually recommend that they do their own, but if they don't want to, I do it. Most of my clients take care of Instagram because they can post stories and whatnot." She mentions Evan and the Stone family members. "The only one who refuses to do anything with social media is Matthew and Max." I laugh. "Evan says you can't teach an old dog new tricks." She laughs now. "But they just have no interest in it."

"How do you decide what to post?" I ask. Suddenly, I want to ask all the questions and think of a way to beg her to work for me.

"Well, I go over their account with them, and we pick five topics that they want to be known for or want to post," she says.

"What would you do if it was me?" I ask. She leans forward now when Ari squeals and kisses her.

"I don't usually do this on the spot," she says, "but since I get to play with Ariella while I talk, I'll make an exception."

"No," I say, shaking my head. Getting up, I look around and wonder how I'm going to take Ari away from her without being an asshole. She looks up at me. "It's fine. Don't worry about it. I don't want you bending your rules to do me a favor," I say, my tone tighter than it should be. She looks at me, not sure if she heard me right. She then looks back at Ari and smiles at her, then gets up with her, and she hands Ari to me.

"I wasn't doing you any favors," she says, staring daggers at me. "I was being genuine." She doesn't wait for me to answer. Instead, she turns and walks away from me. Ari and I just watch her go.

Ari just looks at me and then back again, and I'm sure she's saying dude what the fuck did you do? I watch her walk around everyone and go to her purse and picks it up. She walks over to Miller and tells him something. He smiles at her, nods, then kisses her on the cheek, and a pit forms in my stomach again as she quietly walks out of the backyard with no one the wiser. I don't know how long I stand here, but when I finally do walk back to the covered awning, I spot Nico walking out of his house. "Hey, are you good?"

"Um, yeah," I say and then look down. "I think I need to hire someone to help me out."

He takes his beer and brings it to his mouth, taking a pull. "What were you thinking?"

"I was talking to Becca," I start telling him. "I have a couple of sponsors I'd like to get with, but I need to get a better handle on my social media. Someone to help me with my social media platform," I say, hoping to fuck he doesn't mention Candace.

He stops and looks around the backyard. "Have you met Candace? She is the best there is out there, and if she would, I would hire her to do the team's social media along with every single player."

"Yeah," I say to him as Ari whines now, no doubt pissed that no one is playing with her. "I heard about her."

"I can ask around," Nico says. "But if you can pull strings, I would get Candace. She is hands on and"—he looks around—"she knows her shit."

"Good to know," I say, and then Ari starts to whine. "I think I'm going to head out and get her home," I say, bouncing her up and down. Nico looks at Ari, then back at me.

"Why don't I call you tomorrow, and we can talk about things a bit?" he says, and I nod at him.

"Yeah, that sounds like a plan," I say, and grab my stuff and say bye to everyone. I put Ari into the seat and then clip her in the car. She fusses, but I stick the pacifier in her mouth and she looks at me as she kicks her hands and her feet.

She looks exactly like Cassie when she gets mad, not that I was around much when she used to get mad. To be honest, I wasn't even sure Cassie and I were going to be forever. We just clashed way too much, and when she told me she was pregnant, it threw me since she was on the pill. I never questioned her, never doubted her, but I would sometimes sit and wonder if she did it on purpose because I was pulling away from her. It's not that I didn't love her—I did—but she and I were together on and off for more than six years, and it was just the same cycle over and over again. But once she got pregnant, it got a bit better.

I swallow down the lump in my throat that comes to me every single time I think of the words I never said to her. Ari decides it's not the time to just chill until we get home, and she wails the whole time. I try talking to her and telling her we're almost home, but she doesn't give a shit.

When I finally pull into the driveway, she is having a full-blown crying fit. I open the back door to see her face red and stained with tears. The big headband had slipped down on her face, so I move it up, expecting her to stop crying, but she doesn't. When I pick her up, she cries even harder than she was.

"It's okay, baby girl," I say softly, grabbing her bag

and making my way inside. Dumping the bag on the counter, I head to make her a bottle. Maybe she's hungry again, so I start the bottle while bouncing her, and nothing stops her from crying. I walk into her room, undressing her, and change her diaper. She kicks her feet harder than before.

"Baby girl," I say, and she just screams. When I get back into the kitchen, I grab the bottle and my iPad and walk over to the couch. Placing her on her side of my chest, I give her the bottle. She takes the bottle for a couple of seconds and then wails as she chokes on her milk. I put the bottle down and grab a rag to wipe her chin.

"Hey," I say softly, holding her head in one hand as I move her softly side to side. "What is going on?" I say, and she blinks now as her chest trembles from the cries she just did. "There she is," I say to her and she blinks now looking at me. "Do you want your bottle?" I ask. Picking up her bottle, I then put it next to her lips, but she turns her head, arching her back. "Okay, so no to the bottle," I say. I get up and walk around with her in my arms as she settles down and her crying stops. "There is my girl," I say, and she smiles. "The attitude," I say as my phone beeps in my pocket. I walk over to the bag, grabbing the Babybjorn one. I slip her into it, facing out, and decide to go walk on the treadmill with her. I grab the iPad, putting it onto *Baby Einstein* as I start walking slowing as her feet kick my legs as I walk.

I take my phone out and see a text from Nico

Nico: Just spoke with Candace, and she said to give her a call. You're welcome. Here is her number. She's

waiting for your phone call.

"Fuck," I say, trying to forget about being a fucking idiot to her, and not sure of what to say when I call her. Instead of stewing on it and making it worse by not calling, I call her number, and she answers after two rings.

"Hello," she says, and I wonder if she's home. I wonder if she's in her office or sitting at the island with her calendar in front of her. Or does she take the weekends off?

"Hey, Candace, it's Ralph," I say, closing my eyes and hoping she doesn't hang up on me.

"Hey," she says, her voice staying the same. I can't tell if she's pissed or not, and that gets me even more nervous.

"Listen, about before," I say. "I'm sorry."

She stays quiet for a minute. "What are you sorry for?"

"Well," I say. "For one, being an ass."

"That's a start," she says.

"Can I come over to you, or maybe you can come over here?" I say the words before I can stop myself. "We can maybe talk."

"Now?" she asks, and I should say no. I should tell her that tomorrow would be better.

"Yeah, now works. I just got home, and Ari has been fit to be tied, but I'm on the treadmill, and she's fine."

"Wait, you're on the treadmill right now?" she asks, and I smile.

"Yeah, she's in the Babybjorn," I say, looking into the mirror and seeing that she's sleeping now. Her head to the side.

"Take a picture," she says, and I wonder why. "Trust me."

"Okay," I say. "Does that mean you don't want to come over?"

"I guess we might as well talk about the next step," she says, and I want to ask her what next step. I want to tell her that I can't go there with her, that I don't want to go there with her, but that isn't true. I don't deserve to go there with her, is what I need to tell her.

"Send me your address, and I'll be over in thirty minutes," she says.

"Oh, and, Ralph," she says, "that was strike two." She doesn't wait for me to answer her before she hangs up. Looking down at my phone, I open the messages and send her my address.

I get off the treadmill and place Ari in her crib then rush to my bedroom and slip on jeans and a T-shirt. I look at myself in the mirror. "Don't fuck this up," I say to myself, but deep in the back of my head, I know there is no way not to fuck this up.

NINE

CANDACE

AS SOON AS I hang up my phone, I'm wondering if Ralph will call to rescind his invitation to go to his house. Not going to lie, I was pissed and taken aback when he said he didn't want any favors. I wasn't doing him any favors. I was being a decent human. I walked away from him before I made a scene, grabbing my bag and slipping out of the backyard. I tried not to think about him the whole time I drove home, but I was so mad I couldn't get him out of my mind. Then just when I took a nice deep breath and changed into my yoga pants, my phone rang. When I looked to see who was calling, I never expected to see Nico's name.

Getting off the stool, I close my agenda, getting ready to pack it to go. When the phone rings in my hand, I look down to see that it's Layla. "Hey, hooker," I say, answering the phone with her nickname.

"Hey, hooker yourself," she says, and I hear covers

rustling.

"Are you still in bed?" I ask and then look over and see that it's almost four in the afternoon. "I hope it's because you're napping and not because you've just woken up."

"Hey, this is a nonjudgmental phone call," she says, laughing out. "I got home this morning."

"Oh, good God," I say. "Do I want to know?" I ask. That is one of the things we are opposite about. I'm very conservative in the number of people I sleep with. I'm not saying that I'm a virgin or anything like that, but Layla is more of a "wham bam thank you for the Os" type of girl.

"His name was Chad," she says. "I think." She laughs. "Anyway, the man could eat."

"Oh my God." I shake my head. "Do I even want to be invested in this?"

"I mean, I gave him not my number." She laughs. "At first, I was going to give him my real number, but then I knew he would probably be a clinger, so I changed the last two numbers."

"You know one of these days that trick won't work, right?" I say, laughing as I pack my bag and grab a bottle of water.

"Listen, if he's going to go through all the numbers and actually find me," she says, and now I hear her walking. "Well, I'm going to have to marry the man." Now both of us laugh out loud. "I mean, maybe I'll just throw him a bone."

"Or you'll ride his bone," I say, and she laughs.

"Okay, enough of that," she says. "How are you do-ing?"

"I'm okay," I say. "It's always sad when Zoey leaves."

"God, I swear the minute you get off birth control, your eggs are going to be fighting to be penetrated," she says, and I hear her stir her coffee.

"That just made my uterus cringe," I say. "Anyway, I'm on my way to do Nico a favor."

"What?" she asks, shocked. I walk out of the house and get into the car, connecting the Bluetooth. "I mean if you are going to have a favor owed to you, Nico would be a good one."

"I know," I say, putting the address in the GPS and then buckling my seat belt. "But Nico called in a favor."

She whistles now and then takes a sip of her coffee. "Not a bad favor to have. Who is it for?"

"Ralph Weber." I don't know why I think she won't know his name, considering this is what she does.

"Shit, the one who lost his wife in childbirth," she says. "Dude, that was fucking heartbreaking. I still re-member they posted a picture of him at the gravesite with his daughter in his arms." I close my eyes and try not to think about the hurt he must have felt. I also don't want to look it up online and break his trust in me.

"What do you know about him?" I ask, and I want to kick myself, knowing she is going to know something is up.

"Wait," she says. "What do you want to know about him?"

"Ugh, okay, fine, I met him a couple of days ago when

Evan was down and threw a barbecue at my house," I say.

"Sick invite," she throws in, laughing. "Proceed."

"He came over, and there's something about him," I say, and then I shake my head. "And his daughter has to be the cutest kid I've seen after my Zoey."

"Jesus, you're already smitten with him," she points out. "If we were in high school, you would be doodling his name with hearts."

"I'm not smitten. He's a jerk," I say. "Well, he's a jerk and then not a jerk. I don't know. It's confusing."

"Well, raising a kid that looks exactly like your dead spouse would put you in the fucked-up category."

"Did you ever meet her?" I ask. I don't know why it's bothering me.

"Never," she says. "He usually came to things solo."

"What?" I ask, almost shocked. "Why?"

"No clue. I also know that he never really answered any personal questions. It was about the game. He did thank everyone all the time for everything. But he's Canadian, and they are always saying either sorry or thank you." She chuckles. "You know how it is, Canuck." She makes fun of me.

"Those Canadians." I shake my head. "Anyway, I'm on my way to his house to hash out details."

"Oooohhh, making a service call." She whistles.

"Why is it that everything you say sounds provocative?" I ask as I pull up to his house.

"I have no idea," she says. "But there has to be a reason that I have a mostly male audience."

"That's because you think you have a dick in your pants," I remind her, and she laughs.

"I'm the Alpha," she says, and I can see her with a huge smile on her face. "Anyway, I'm coming over one day this week after work. We can talk then."

"Sounds like a plan," I say. "Also, bring back my black heels."

"Oh," she says. "Um . . ."

"You owe me five hundred and eighty-five dollars," I say.

"Why would you buy such expensive shoes?" she shrieks.

"Why would you lose such expensive shoes?" I counter.

"I was making a getaway," she says. "I guess I could call and ask him."

"Do you even know his name?" I ask, and she doesn't answer. "Or where he lives?"

"Fine, I'll buy you another pair. God, next time tell me no," she says to me.

"Next time, stay out of my closet," I counter. "Okay, I'm here. Wish me luck."

"Don't fall for him," she says. After I hang up the phone, I get out of the car and grab my bag. I ignore the way my stomach flutters, and I ignore the way my palms are getting clammy. I ignore it all until I ring the doorbell, and he answers the door.

He's changed clothes. I don't know why I'm surprised since I did, too. He stands there, his white shirt pulling across his chest. "Hey," he says with a smile. "Thanks for coming." He moves away from the door to welcome me inside, and I smile and step in. "Welcome, keep your shoes on," he says. I see he's not even wearing socks.

Following him into his house, I pass the dining room on the way. "Where do you want to do this?" he asks me over his shoulder, and right before I'm about to answer him, we hear Ariella screaming. "And she's up." We stop in the middle of the family room that leads to a dining table. This one looks more used than the other one with Ariella's toys on it. "I'll be right back. Make yourself at home," he says, pointing at the three massive couches that all face each other and look at the fireplace and television in front of it. I put my bag on the big glass table in the middle of the family room and walk over to the windows overlooking his backyard. If I thought mine was an oasis, this one has me beat.

The massive pool in the middle of the yard has a rock wall to the side. A replica of the house is in the back and has Ariella's name written over the door, and I have no doubt it is filled with things for her to use when she is older. I turn and try not to invade the space, but my eyes fly to the picture hanging on the wall. My feet move on their own almost as if someone is pushing me to it. There is a picture of Ralph and a woman. He's standing behind her looking down at her stomach, and she is wearing a white top and a long white skirt with her belly sticking out. Her hair is dark exactly like Ariella, but she looks down at her belly so I can't see her eyes, but something about the picture isn't right. There is no smile on their face, nothing but a stern look. I am about to look at another picture when I hear his voice. "We have a visitor," he says as he walks into the room, and I see that Ari's eyes are still sleepy. My heart speeds up even faster, and the smiles just comes naturally.

"Well, hello there, little girl," I say softly. Walking to them, I rub her back as she lays her head on Ralph's shoulder, her pacifier in her mouth moving as she sucks on it. "Did you have a good nap?" I ask, and she just blinks.

"She's always slow to wake up," he says. "She definitely got that from me." He puts his cheek down on top of her head. "Do you want to sit on the couch or at the table?"

"Wherever is going to be most comfortable for her," I say and wait to follow his lead. He picks one of the long couches, and I see her bottle on the table next to a blanket. I grab my bag and take out a blank book that I have packed for notes and the calendar with it. "Okay, then," I say, sitting on the couch in front of him. "I think before we get this started there should be a couple of things said."

"You're right," he says. Sitting there with a baby on his chest, he taps her bum softly as she watches me from his chest. I try to not let it get to me. "I need your help. I'm not even going to lie. Every single time I ask someone about hiring someone, everyone brings up your name."

"Well, I think that's a good thing. But I am full. I can't possible take you on as a client and give you exactly the help that you need," I say and see his face fall. "But I will help you as much as I can. We can sit down and go over things, and I can help you plan things."

"At this point, I'll take it," he says, smiling at me. "I need all the help you can give me."

"If we are going to do this, two things have to happen," I say and wait for him to say something, but he doesn't, so I speak for him. "One, I'm over your hot and cold moods." I put up my finger. "If you're pissed or crabby, then I suggest getting a therapist or some of them squishy balls, but I am not going to be that person." I wait for any reaction from him. "Two, you have to be one hundred percent honest with me. I am not one to judge if you like to play bongos naked while a harem of women fan you or feed you grapes. That's a you problem." I see his lips roll. "But if this makes it a me problem, I need you to tell me about it." I take a deep breath in. "Now, if you can agree to those two things, we can continue. If you can't, then no harm, no foul, and I can recommend someone else." I set my hands on the two books on my lap as I wait for him to give me his answer. My heart beating just a touch faster than it should.

"Deal," he says and then looks down at Ari. "Just one more thing," he says. "I don't play bongos nor will I have a harem around. It's me and my girl," he says, admiring his daughter. "Just the two of us."

TEN

Ralph

I LOOK AT my daughter, thinking of the words she just said to me. Or better yet, her demands. I listened to her and held my breath at the same time. When I opened my door before I told myself it's just a girl, I already had her picture in my head, but it was nothing like seeing her. She had changed from her dress to a pair of black pants that molded her legs. A loose white T-shirt dips into a vee over her perfect tits. My cock started to rise, and I called him a traitor. It's a good thing my shirt was a bit loose and fell over to cover it. Now sitting with her facing me on the couch, I had to tell her I wasn't interested in her, just in case I sent the wrong message. Or was it the right message?

"Well, now that it's settled you don't have a harem." She smirks and then opens one of the notebooks she has sitting on her lap. "Why don't we start at the beginning?" she says, and it's Ari's turn to wake up and spit her pacifier out and squeal. "Well, then, princess, why don't I add that to the list." She looks at her and smiles, scrunching her nose. The way she is with Ari is honestly the hardest thing to watch. Seeing Ari smile at her and play with her just pushes the knife in my heart deeper, letting the blood slowly seep out. Candace reaches over and grabs a pen from her purse and then writes something in the book, and I suddenly want to sit beside her and see what she's writing. "So, what and who does Ralph Weber stand for?"

"What does that mean?" I ask her while Ari pitches herself forward. I catch her and stand her on my legs, looking at Candace. "That is a loaded question." I'm about to say something else when Ari squeals.

"What that means is pick five things that define Ralph," she says and then gets up and comes over to me. Even better, she sits next to me, and for one second, I forget that guard I have up and smile over at her.

If this were a different situation, and we were in a different time, I would sit back and take her in my arms along with Ari. The minute I think it, though, a picture of Cassie flashes in my head. I try not to break Candace's rule number one as she looks at me, waiting for it. Instead of saying anything, I get up and walk over to the corner where I keep all of Ari's stuff and sit on the floor with her. I set her between my legs and bring the toys close to us as she reaches out to grab the first thing she can and brings it straight to her mouth.

"Okay." She taps the pen on the book. "Let me ask you a couple of questions. What are your interests?"

"Hockey," I answer right away without thinking twice.

"Okay, so hockey." She writes it down. "Every account I run has a theme of five things so people know your branding. Like for Miller, it's fitness, hockey, his dog, golf, and fishing." I smile when she says that.

"Only Miller could do fitness and fishing at the same time," I joke. "Okay, so I'm hockey, fitness, Ari…"

"Yeah, I got those already. I had an idea on my way here to help grow your audience," she says. "I was actually looking through it after we got off the phone."

"You went to check me out?" I joke with her, and she rolls her eyes, making me laugh. It actually feels good.

"I always check out potential clients," she says, tapping her pen, and I can see she is a bit uncomfortable.

"But I'm not your client," I say. She shrugs, and I see that her face turns a bit pink.

"How comfortable are you with having Ari on your Instagram?"

"Not at all," I say right away. "I don't want her out there."

"But she's who you are," Candace tells me. "She is everything that you are. There is no Ralph without Ari," she says. "I don't know what happened." She avoids eye contact with me. "But you're a single dad."

"You don't know what happened?" I ask, shocked, and she shakes her head. "Cassie died giving birth to our child. Alone in a room without me. I stood there in the white hallway waiting for her to come back. They rushed her into surgery when her blood pressure fell." I swallow, thinking back to the day. I haven't been able or actually I haven't wanted to tell anyone anything. But with her, I want to tell her, and I'm ignoring the reason. "Told me they were going to get her situated and then come back out and get me. So I stood there looking up at the fucking ceiling while she died on the table." I say the words and see the pain on her face right away, and I don't want it. I don't want her to look at me with the same look everyone else gives me when I say the words out loud.

"Ralph," she says, blinking away the tears in her eyes and trying not to cry. "You don't have to—"

"When the nurse came out and told me that she died on the table, I collapsed onto my knees, and then I threw up. I must have passed out at some point because when I opened my eyes, I was on a bed and the doctor was examining me."

"I can't even imagine the horror of that," she says. She walks over to me now and puts her hand on my arm. "It must have been horrible."

"I don't even know if I understood what he was saying. It's almost as if I was having an out-of-body experience, and I kept thinking this has to be a nightmare. He has to be lying. I listened to the words that came out of his mouth, but I can't remember much from that time. What I do remember is when they brought Ari in and placed her in my arms. She was wrapped in this white blanket and a pink hat and the biggest eyes I have ever seen in my life and at that moment"—I smile now—"I knew then that I had to be strong for her. I live for her, and I'm not sure I'm okay with sharing her with the world."

"I get it," she says. "What if we have a Daddy and me segment?"

"What?" I ask. She leans over, her hand reaching out to rub Ari's cheek with her finger.

"It's Ari's and your world." She smiles at her and holds up her hands to grab Ari. I want to stop her from touching my girl, but Ari throws herself at her, and Candace catches her, kissing her cheek. "You can post things that you try with her. Little clips of what is working for you."

"Like how I get her to stop crying at three a.m. when she's been up for four hours, drank three bottles, and has a clean diaper, and all I want is for her to stop crying?" I mention. "How I put her in the car and took a drive for an hour just so she could sleep?"

She looks at me and then looks at Ari. "Yeah, like that," she says, and my eyebrows go together. "Are there any sponsored brands that you have to wear?"

"I'm working on that," I answer. "I just wear my Dallas stuff," I trail off, and she looks at me.

"Okay, so this is how we are going to start," she says. "We are going to close down your website."

I laugh at her. "I don't have a website." She looks at me smiling.

"Well, you actually will," she says. "I want to post a picture of last year's hockey thingy."

"Hockey thingy?" I joke with her, making Ari laugh. "You mean headshot?"

"Yeah, that," she says. "We are going to post it on your Instagram and Facebook and tell them that new content is coming and all that good stuff." I look at her. "What?" she asks.

"I don't really have a Facebook page," I say. "I mean, I did at the beginning, and then it slowly faded because I didn't keep up with it."

She looks at Ari. "Your dad is really making this hard for me." Ari turns to her, grabs her face, and sucks on her cheek. Instead of throwing her off or giving her to me, she just squeezes Ari closer to her. "Also, what do you think of doing charity?"

"What?" I ask, not sure my heart can focus on anything except the sight of my girl loving someone other than me.

"Is there a charity you promote or are associated with?" she asks. Ari lets go of her face, and Candace has drool running down her face and she just walks over to the table, not skipping a beat. "You used to help Justin with his, right?"

"Yeah, for underprivileged children," I say. "I never thought of starting my own. To be honest, it was on my bucket list. But with everything that's happened, it was put on the back burner."

"Do you have an assistant?" she asks, and Ari starts to whine in her arms.

"What do you think?" I laugh at her and just watch her with my daughter.

"Ariella." She looks at my daughter and wipes Ari's face before wiping her own cheek. "What are we going to do with your dad?" She looks at me. "Okay, I think we need more time to meet," she says.

"Well, my schedule is open most days. Miranda comes to watch Ari, but other than that . . ." I say.

"This is what you need to do. Step one is you need to set up a photo shoot," she says, and I put my hands on my hips. "It's going to be fine. We can use the pictures for a good six months."

"Great," I say and then see that Ari is getting really fussy now. I walk to the kitchen and prepare her bottle.

"What kind of charity do you want to work with?" she asks as she bounces Ari up and down to make her stop whining.

"Definitely underprivileged children," I say. And then without even thinking, I add, "I was bounced from foster home to foster home, and the only thing that saved me was hockey." She looks at me. "It's not something that I talk about," I say, avoiding looking at her. "My mother had me at seventeen. She couldn't handle a newborn with the need to party every single day, so my grandparents took me in. When I was seven, we were in a car accident, and I was the only one who survived." I make the bottle, trying not to think about the sound of metal clinking together as the firefighters fought to get me out from under the rubble. "They tried to find my mother, but she never did leave a forwarding address, so I was sent into foster care."

"That must have been hard for you," she says while she holds Ari lying down in her arms.

"It was tough not knowing where you were going to go next. All my clothes were in a brown paper bag." I have never told anyone this story—never shared this part with anyone—and I don't know why I'm doing it now. "Lucky for me, I was good at hockey, so I got a scholarship for high school and didn't really need anyone except for in the summertime." When I walk over to her with the bottle in my hand, I see her blink away tears, trying not to let me see. "It's why I'll never leave Ari or have someone do something for her. She is never going to feel unloved." I look at my baby girl as she looks at me but stays with Candace. I hold up the bottle. "She is never going to feel like that." I hand Candace the bottle, and she grabs it, but our hands touch, and I just hold it there. "It's also why I'll never give my heart to anyone." I don't say it's because I never gave Cassie my heart, which is why it hurts so much. "She owns my heart."

ELEVEN

CANDACE

IF MY HEART could shatter in my chest, it would be now as he looks at his daughter with all the love that he has. Telling me that she is the only one who will have his heart, I want to drop the bottle and hold his face in my hand and finally release the tears started when he told me about Cassie dying and then about his childhood. He avoided looking at me, and I was glad he did because he didn't see the tears rolling down my face that I had to quickly wipe away. The only one to see them was Ari as she looked at me with her big blue eyes, and at that moment, I fell more in love with her.

"Do you want to feed her?" I ask as we both hold the bottle. "She is pretty comfy." I look down, seeing her resting against my breast. "But I can hand her over."

"No," he says and drops his hand. I walk to the couch and look down at her. She opens her mouth the minute she sees the bottle. Her hand holds my finger as she drinks. "So do you think I'd be able to start a foundation?" I look at him as his eyes light up. "Not going to lie, it would be pretty cool if I could help people."

"I think you can," I say. "I think anyone who wants to help kids should be able to. I think that if you are comfortable with telling your side of the story, it might get even more notice," I say as I watch his eyes. "But you don't have to. You can just leave it at wanting to share."

"Justin had a great summer hockey one where all the underprivileged kids spend the whole summer. It's where he met Caroline."

"Yeah," I say, thinking of their fairy-tale love story. "I heard. I can also ask Allison how Max started his, and we can go from there."

"You would help me with this?" he asks, and I start to say no. My head tells me that it's not a good idea. My heart tells me to run away, but my mouth, it's not wired with the other parts of me.

"As much as I could," I say before I can actually tell him no. I look down at Ariella, and she smiles while she drinks, and some of the milk spills out at the same time she lets off the biggest fart. I just laugh as I hear the explosion happen. "Well, then," I say to her and then look up when I see Ralph shoot out of his chair and rush over to me. "What's wrong?"

"I'm going to say this as delicately as I can," he says, sitting on the glass table in the middle of the room. Looking around, I realize this room doesn't even feel like him. I look at him now as he sits down in front of me. His blue eyes look a little lighter. "When she blows, she blows."

"I'm going to say this as delicately as I can." I look at him. "I have no idea what you mean."

"I mean that fart"—he points at Ariella, who looks at me again with a huge smile as she lets another one rip—"can go from a fart to full blown everywhere." He uses his hands to mimic an explosion. I suddenly feel wetness soaking into my leg, and my mouth opens wide and so do my eyes.

"Oh, God." He gets up. "It's happening." I watch him as he runs to the kitchen, and I suddenly hear water running.

"Pretty girl," I say. "That is not polite." She kicks her feet and the hand that I have under her is now wet. "Um, Ralph!" I yell for him as he rushes out of the kitchen with a pair of scissors.

"What are you doing?" I ask him.

"I'm going to cut her out of her onesie," he says, and I laugh.

"What? Why?" I ask him, shocked, looking down to see the pink onesie with butterflies all over it.

"What do you mean why?" he asks. Getting up, I try not to move her as I walk over to the kitchen and put the bottle down on the table. "Trust me when I say this. We need to just cut it off her, or it will be everywhere."

"How many onesies have you cut off her?" I ask, trying not to laugh when he shrugs. "Can you get me two towels?" I say, and he just looks at me. "Trust me."

"Don't say I didn't warn you." He turns and runs down the hallway to the bathroom. "And her soap and shampoo," I say and look down at Ariella who is babbling away while chewing on her finger. He runs back in with what looks like four towels and then looks at me. I walk into his massive kitchen with stainless steel appliances. The light beige countertops make the dark wood cabinets pop more. Making my way over to the kitchen sink, I see that it's huge, and she could definitely be washed in there.

"Where do you give her a bath?" I ask, and he points down the hallway he just came from. "Is it a deep tub?" He just nods. "Okay, let's do it here. I want you to put a towel down on the counter right next to the sink." He walks over and puts one towel down and then another one over it.

"I don't want it to be too hard for her head in case," he says, and I swear if I could fall in love with a man, he would be it. I walk over and place her down on the towel, putting my hand on her chest to make sure she won't roll anywhere. I finally look down and see the brown stains seeping into my white silk blouse.

"I will pay to replace the shirt," he says, looking at me.

"You stay away from me and my shirt with those scissors. I refuse for you to cut me out of my clothes," I joke with him, and I suddenly picture his hands ripping open the buttons. Ariella's squealing cuts through my daydream.

"Is that water okay?" He walks over to the sink beside me and puts his elbow in and then nods his head.

"Okay, here we go," I say, seeing that she has poop all over her legs, and she is vigorously kicking. "I found out the trick once when I was watching Zoey," I start saying when I unbutton the clips. "It was everywhere." I look at him.

"That's why I just cut the shit off." He holds up the scissors, opening and closing them.

"The trick is to take it off downward and not over her head," I say and point at the flaps by her neck on her shoulders. "It's made like this so you can pull it down." He watches me as I pull her onesie down. "That way it's not in her hair." I roll it into a ball and then take off her diaper. "And just like that, all you have to do is wash her." I put her into the sink water, and she immediately starts splashing her hands in the water making it go everywhere. "I'm giving her a minute, and then I'm going to drain the water and wash her off," I say. He just looks at me, and I don't know what the look is for.

"I can take over if you want," he says quietly.

"It's okay. Can you get her a change of clothes?" He nods and walks out of the kitchen, but this time, not so frantic. Ariella screams with glee as she splashes water everywhere, and by the time Ralph comes back with clothes in one hand, my shirt is about soaked through. "She's almost done," I say, and I rinse off her body with water, and she laughs and tries to catch the water in her hand. "Do you want to open the towel and take her? Or you can lay a towel down so I can wrap her."

"I got her," he says, opening a towel as I hand her to him, his arms securing her in the towel. I watch him, and he looks at me. His eyes narrow almost to a slit, and he looks like he's glaring at me. I wonder if I did something wrong or if I overstepped somehow. The look he gives me makes my stomach sink, and I don't even know what to say.

"Are you okay?" I finally have the courage to ask him.

"Why don't you cover yourself up?" He avoids looking at me, and I look down and see that the shirt I'm wearing is completely see-through. The lace bra leaving nothing to the imagination. I turn quickly and put my hands in front of me.

"Oh my God," I say, ignoring the fact that he just saw me half naked, and from the look on his face, I grossed him out. "I'm going to get going," I say, keeping my back to him as I walk over to my purse.

"You can't leave like that," he says, and I look over my shoulder at him as he dresses Ariella. He rubs her cream on her as she now eats her toe. "Give me a second and I'll get you a change of clothes."

"No, you don't have to do that. It's fine; I'm going right home," I say, putting the books into my bag and then taking the keys. "I'm fine," I say and walk out of the room with my back to him. Once in the hallway, I run out of the house, slamming the door behind me. I ignore the smell of myself and ignore everything else until I walk into my house. I dump my bag at the door, not bothering to turn on the lights as I make my way upstairs to my bathroom. I peel the pants off me and put them in the sink with the shirt and my lace bra that didn't help at all. I step into the shower to wash off and then wash my hair at the same time. Once out of the shower, I slip on my big white plush robe and wrap my hair up.

I walk out of the bathroom and force myself not to think about Ralph. Heading to the door to grab my bag, I take out my books and put them on the island as I walk to the bedroom and grab my laptop. I set myself on the counter grabbing some leftovers and heating it up. I walk over to the counter to grab my phone but don't find it there. I walk back to get my bag and don't find it there either. I hear my computer ping, but I ignore it as I walk to my bedroom, looking on the bed and then in the sink where I have my pants, and it isn't there. I walk back out when I hear my computer start ringing, and I'm about to lose my shit going nuts for my phone. It stops ringing and then starts again, and I walk over, seeing that it's a FaceTime call from Ralph. I accept and wait as it says it's connecting, his face fills the screen with Ariella who is sitting on his lap looking into the phone.

"Hey," he says, and I have a sudden need to take my towel off and fix my wet hair.

"Hey," I say right back to him, not sure what to say.

"Ari wanted to thank you for washing her," he says with a smile, and for the first time since I've met him, he almost looks carefree. "And to tell you that you forgot your phone here." He picks up his hand and shows me said phone.

"I was just looking for it," I say. "Thank you for letting me know."

"I heard it ringing, and I think I saw that Miller called," he says, and I raise my eyebrows now. "Not that I was looking," he starts fumbling his words. "I thought it was my phone, and then when it stopped ringing, I saw that the screen saver was Zoey, and well, I put two and two together."

"You are just a regular Sherlock Holmes," I joke with him. He laughs, and I love, love, love the sound of it. I love how it's a hearty laugh. I love that his chest shakes, and I love the way his eyes go just a touch softer.

"I mean, I don't know about that since I just found out that a onesie can be taken off other ways, but I can definitely find the owner of a phone left in my house." He chuckles again. "Do you want to come get it now, or would you like to just get it tomorrow when you come over?"

"Um," I start to say. "I guess I can get it tomorrow."

"Great," he says. Ari whines now and arches her back. "I'm going to go and get this one to bed. I'll see you tomorrow."

"Great," I say, and then he hangs up the phone, leaving me just looking at myself.

"He's so out of your league," I say to myself. "His focus is on one thing, his daughter," I repeat again, closing the computer. "Not you." I push away from the counter. "His daughter and making a name for himself." I look up at the ceiling, telling myself all the reasons it's not okay. If only my heart was on the same page.

I fall asleep to the sound of him telling me his story again over and over. The night feels as though it is never going to end, and finally, when the sun starts to rise, I fall asleep until almost noon. I'm even shocked at myself when I grab my iPad and bring it to my face with one eye closed. I do my usual by checking emails, and then

I open Instagram. His posts come up right away, and I think I'm seeing something wrong because he's made seven posts today.

"What the hell have you done, Ralph?" I ask myself, sitting up in bed.

He posted a picture of his cereal with the word: Yum.

"Oh my God," I say out loud, my thumb clicking his name now and seeing that he also posted a picture of a running shoe on the treadmill, then a picture of his foot in a skate, and then after all of that, a picture of a protein shake. I see that the only person who has liked his stuff is his agent Becca.

My hand flies to my call list before I can even comprehend what it's doing, and he answers on the first ring. "Hey there," he says, his voice full and almost booming. "I took your advice," he says. "I posted on Instagram."

"I saw," I say, and I close my eyes. "And I've decided that I'm going to do you and the world of Instagram a huge favor." He laughs now. "I'm going to take you on as a client."

TWELVE

Ralph

I KNEW THAT I would be seeing her today since I had her phone, and I am going to pretend that wasn't the reason I was so excited when I woke up this morning. I did my normal routine, but something about today just made me smile. I worked out harder, I skated harder, and then when I walked out of the shower, my phone rang, and there she was. I told myself it was because she was going to help me, but I know deep down it was because she was going to be around. That isn't to say I didn't have guilt, fuck, but the guilt can bring you down the black hole faster than you know what to do with it.

When I hung up with her last night, I smiled, and my heart felt light, but then, the darkness came. The guilt crept in when I sat down and rocked Ari to bed. The guilt remained as strong as it was the first night I came home with Ari. Guilt for not being in the room with her when she delivered our daughter, guilt for not being the man she needed or deserved. Guilt weaves its way into your soul and never lets you go. And as soon as you think you'll be okay and that you can breathe just a touch lighter, it comes back in and sucks you back down.

She sounded sleepy when she called as though there was a frog in her throat, and then she said the words I've been hoping for. Well, moaning out my name wasn't an option, so this was second or maybe third best. "I'm going to take you on as a client."

I smile from ear to ear and sit down to slip on my shoes. "Is that so?" I chuckle. "Why is that?"

She laughs, and I hear the sheets rustling. "Are you still in bed?"

"I am. Actually, I'm out of bed now, but yes."

"It's noon," I say. "A little bit after noon."

"I know." I hear her starting the coffee machine. "I had a rough time sleeping last night, and then I saw the sun come up, and boom, I drifted off to sleep."

"Basically, you went to bed when I woke up?" I say, getting up and looking in the mirror at my blue jeans and a white crewneck shirt that fits me like a glove. First time I am wearing anything other than sweats or shorts. Grabbing my keys off the bench, I walk out of the arena and press the button to unlock my truck doors.

"Where are you?" she asks when I slam the truck door.

"I'm actually on my way to an event." I start the truck and put on the aviator sunglasses. "Becca set it up for a couple of her clients."

"Where?" she asks me right before she takes a sip of coffee, and I suddenly think back to yesterday. The whole diaper blowout, and how she placed Ari in the sink and was splashed on and didn't care. Then she turned around, and my heart stopped. I didn't think it was beating in those thirty seconds it took for me to get the words out of my mouth. She stayed there in front of me with her white shirt completely soaked, showing me her perfect pink pebbled nipples. I swear I think my mouth salivated, and if I would have stared any longer, drool would have come out of my mouth. I wonder if she's walking around the house naked. I close my eyes at the stupidness of that. Why the fuck would she be naked? I wonder what she wears to bed. I shake my head when I hear her call my name.

"Hello, are you still there? Ralph?"

"Yeah," I say. "Sorry, Bluetooth connected wrong."

"Can you text me the address?" she asks, and I look at the screen of the Bluetooth. "I can be there in about forty, depending on traffic."

"What?" I ask, surprised. "You're coming?"

"Yes," she says. "It'll be a good time to get some pictures and go over a couple of things. Will Becca be there?"

"She said she would," I say. "Do you want me to pick you up?" The words come out of my mouth before I can even think about them. "I'm at the arena now and can be at your house in about twenty minutes."

"I can make it work," she says. "If anything, I can take an Uber home later."

"Or I can drive you," I say. "I'll see you in twenty."

"See you then," she says, and then I press the end

button on the screen. I grab my phone again and call Miranda, who answers right away.

"Hey there," she says, and I hear Ari in the background saying da-da-da-da. "We were just talking about you."

"I can hear that," I say. "How is her day going?" I ask. This is going to be the longest I've been gone from home, and my stomach was in knots this morning when I kissed her goodbye.

"It's going amazing," she says. "She just had her lunch, and we are going to go take a nap soon."

"I don't know what time I'll be back," I say. "I should be finished at four, but it may go over."

"It's fine," she says. "I can get dinner started for you."

"No, that's fine," I say. "I'll pick myself up something. I'll try to call and check in when I can."

"Don't worry about anything here. We are fine," she says. "Have a good afternoon."

"Talk to you later," I say, hanging up as I pull up to Candace's house. I get out and walk to the front door. Ringing the doorbell, I turn to look at the houses while I wait. I really like this neighborhood. The houses are normal size, unlike the monster of a house I'm living in now. It's way too big for me. It was way too big in the beginning, but I bought it because Cassie liked it. I hear the locks and turn around, but I'm not ready for what I see. She stands there with a huge smile on her face, and I can't help but return the smile. "Hey," I say, and I'm not sure if I should kiss her cheek. Is it normal to want to do that?

"Hey," she says. "I was just slipping on my shoes." She motions to the shoes in her hands, and I watch as she slips her feet into the sexiest shoes I've seen in my life. Or maybe it's just the way she puts them on. She's wearing a long dress that's full of colorful flowers, goes well down to her knees, and isn't tight at all. A white silk shirt with little sleeves on it, tucking into the skirt. Nothing screams sexy about the outfit, yet my cock is dying to get out.

"I'm going to get my bag." She turns and walks away, and I see her hair tied back on the sides. She grabs her bag and comes back. "Are you sure you're okay with driving?" she asks, and all I can do is nod my head, my mouth dry. "Don't you look nice," she says with a smile as she puts on her sunglasses. I hate that I can't see her eyes anymore.

"You look summery," I say, and I want to close my eyes and groan when she laughs.

"I've never been called summery before." She walks beside me, and with her heels on, she reaches my chin. I walk to my side of the truck and then look over at her as she gets into the truck at the same time as me. I grab her phone from the cupholder and hand it to her. "Thank you," she says and starts going through things. Her fingers type away, and then my phone rings, telling me there is a text.

I open it and see it's from Candace. "Did you seriously just text me?"

She smiles. "Yes, in case I forget or you forget."

I read the text out loud. "Things to do: hire photographer, get info on the type of charity, schedule workout shots, talk about hiring an assistant." Shaking my head, I start the truck and pull away from her house. "One, I don't need an assistant."

"Maybe not now, but you never know," she says and then looks at me. "Can you stop at Starbucks?"

"Sure," I say, pulling into the upcoming Starbucks. I'm expecting her to give me her order, but instead, she leans over and shouts out her order. The smell of fresh apples fills me because she is so close. "Do you want anything?" she asks, and all I do is blink, trying to form words.

"Um," I start. "Iced coffee." She gives them the order, then goes back to her side. She slides me her phone. "What is this?"

"It's the app so I can pay for it," she says, and I pfft at her and roll my eyes.

"You aren't paying for this," I say, and she looks at me. At least I think she does. I can't really see with her glasses. When we pull up, I take out my card to pay for the drinks, and then I hand her the pink drink with berries in it. "I'm assuming this is yours."

"Yes, a berry refresher," she says and rips open the white paper off the green straw. "So good." I grab my coffee and place it in the cupholder. "So where is this event?"

"A sports store," I say. "One that does memorabilia and stuff."

"Oh," she says. "Those usually do really well."

"Yeah, it was advertised on the radio and shit," I say,

and when I pull up, I'm shocked to see that a line has already formed. "That's a lot of people."

"This is great," she says, smiling and starts snapping pictures as soon as she gets out. I hear some of the kids call my name when I climb out of the truck. Lifting my hand, I wave at them at the same time a sports car parks next to me. I walk beside Candace as the door opens and watch as the captain of the team steps out. "Well, well, well." She smiles at him. "If it isn't Mr. Manning Stevenson."

With a smile, he walks up to her and bends down to kiss her cheek. "Aren't you married?" I say the words before I can stop myself, and he laughs at me.

"Don't remind me," he mumbles, and I just look at him. "I didn't know you would be here," he says to Candace, and I have never wanted to throat punch someone more in my life.

"You should have brought your wife," I say. They both look at me, and he's about to say something to me when Becca shows up.

"There they are," she says, getting out of her Range Rover. She's in a pink pantsuit and looks likes she's wearing the same shoes as Candace, but hers just don't look sexy. "My two favorite people."

"Yeah, right," Manning says as she walks over to him, and he bends and kisses her cheek.

"What's with all the kissing?" I ask Candace, and she laughs. "Seriously." I point at him. "He's married. How do you think his wife would feel?"

"Well, I've met his wife," Candace says. "She's a

bitch."

I'm about to ask her if she's interested in him when Becca comes over to us. "Oh my gosh, Candace!" She kisses her now. "I'm so happy to see you here."

"Well, I thought it would be a good time to get a couple of shots for Ralph's Instagram," she says, and Becca laughs.

"Does this mean you're taking him on as a client?" she asks, clapping her hands together. "Please say yes."

"Did I have a choice?" Candace says, looking at me. I want to throw my arm around her shoulders and pull her to me. "Did you see his Instagram?"

"I almost reported him," Becca says, and now everyone laughs but me.

"It wasn't that bad," I say, rolling my eyes.

"It was pretty bad," Becca says and then walks to the door with Manning following her.

"Why don't we get something to eat after this?" Candace says. "We can go over things."

"I'd love that," I say, looking down and then up at her. "But I want to get home to Ari. I haven't been gone this long from her before."

"Oh, we can make plans when you're done," she says, putting her hand on my arm. "It's a fact that babies don't know the time. So even if you haven't seen her for seven hours, she will feel like it's five minutes."

"How do you know that?" I ask. The wind blows, and her hair flies in her face. My hands itch to push it behind her ear. Right before she answers me, I hear Becca call my name.

"Ralph!" she shouts, and I turn to look at her. "It's time."

THIRTEEN

CANDACE

I WATCH HIM turn and walk into the store, but I stop to say something to Becca before walking into the store. Becca motions with her head to follow her, and I walk behind her into the cool store. Two tables are set up in the back of the store, and Manning and Ralph are already sitting down signing things. "Is it just the two of them?" I ask Becca, looking around at all the memorabilia they have.

"No, I have two more clients coming in two hours, but they do football, so we thought it would be easier to break it up as hockey and then football," she says, looking around. I take out my phone and snap a candid picture of Ralph signing a jersey and then smiling at the owner.

"He should post that he is here on his Instagram," I suggest. "Excuse me."

I walk over to the table as he finishes with the owner,

and then he looks at me. "What's wrong?"

"Nothing," I say, getting close to him. "Where is your phone?"

"In my pocket," he says, taking it out and looking at Manning, who just shakes his head and looks away. "Why?"

"I want you to go on Instagram and do a story," I say. He just looks at me, and I hear Manning start to snicker next to him. "You don't make me take out my phone." Manning puts both of his hands up. I grab my phone and show Ralph the steps, and he looks at me like a deer in headlights.

"I don't know what to say," he says, looking around and then reaching for his bottle of water that they placed on the table next to the Sharpies.

"All you have to say is 'hey everyone, come down and see me today at blank, blank, blank,'" I suggest.

"That's weird, no?" he asks.

"You posted a selfie of your eyeball," I say.

"That wasn't a selfie. It was an I got my eye on you," he says, and I roll my lips and try not to laugh. "Okay, fine, it wasn't good."

I take his phone from him. "I'll record you. All I need you to do is tell them where you are."

Manning pushes away from the table, and I look at him. "I do not want to be on social media," he says, and I look up at the ceiling. It takes Ralph seven tries before I can post it, and when I finally do, the owner lets us know they are letting people in.

"I'm going to keep your phone and post pictures

during the event," I say.

"Miranda says she's going to call me if she needs me," he says, and I just smile at him.

"I'll come and get you if she calls," I say. The heat of his shoulder shoots through me when I place my hand on it. I wish him luck as I walk away to the side where I can take some pictures but still be out of the way.

"I have to tell you . . ." Becca comes to stand beside me, and I look at her. The woman screams business, she also screams don't fuck with me, or I'll tie your balls in a bowtie and make you wear them.

"This sounds serious." I try to make the situation lighter and to let my heart calm down. As I look from her to Ralph, who smiles with the fans and chats with them.

"It is," she says as fans walk into the store. "I was about to call in a favor." She starts to talk as we move to the side out of the way. "He needs your help. I have two amazing deals waiting for him, but the sponsors are afraid to take that step with him."

"Because he's practically an unknown," I say, and she nods her head. "His fan base is solid," I say. "I checked the fan boards last night."

"He got a shitload of press when Cassie died, but he refused to give any interviews." Her voice trails off.

"Which is normal," I say, my voice going just a touch louder. Becca looks at me and cocks her head to the side. Her eyes watch me. "I mean, come on, his wife just died, and he was a new dad."

"Girlfriend," Becca corrects me. "Regardless of her title. He refused to do anything with it." She looks at

Ralph, who is laughing with a couple of teenage boys as he signs pictures and then stands to pose for a picture. "He still refuses to do half the things I suggest." She crosses her arms over her chest.

"So why don't you stop suggesting things you know he won't do and bring him things that he will?" Her eyebrows raise. "I don't mean to sound like a bitch or step on your toes."

"No." She smirks. "But I like it. You like him?"

"As my client, I want him to succeed." I look at her point blank, and she raises her eyebrow at me. "He's my client, and I don't date my clients," I say.

"Then we are both on the same page," she says. "Why don't I give you a call next week, and we can go over a couple of things? Maybe come up with a plan." I don't want to tell her that I won't take the meeting unless Ralph is there, and he approves of things. At the end of the day, he is in charge.

"That sounds good," I say, and then I see the shield that she had up come down. Her gray eyes go a bit softer even.

"I'm glad he has you in his corner," she says and walks over to the store's owner.

I take a picture of Manning also, and when it's done, and there is no one else, I have them both pose for a picture together. "Okay, you two, let's do some cross-promo," I say, and Manning rolls his eyes.

"I told you I'm not going to be on social media," he says. "Especially not Instagram."

"What do you have against the 'gram?" I ask, putting

my hands on my hips.

"I am a private person," he says. "I don't want an Instagram account, I don't want Facebook, and I don't want a website."

"I want that," Ralph says, pointing at Manning. "Why can't I have that?"

"Because you gotta be the captain to have all the perks," he says, slapping Ralph on the shoulder. I shake my head. Out of all my clients, he has to be the most private man I've ever met. No social media ever, and he answers and gives interviews only during the season. He is never in drama; he is never in anything. He is the best defenseman, and he's also a monster on the ice with the hardest shot. He's the nicest man you will ever meet, and he's married to The Wicked Witch of The West. When I first started doing his social media, she poured a glass of champagne over my head, thinking I was trying to sleep with him. Needless to say, he's been apologizing for her during his whole career. "I have to run. I have to pick up the kids."

"I'll touch base with you next week," Becca says to him. He walks over to her and kisses her cheek. He's about to come to me when Ralph steps in front of him.

"Enough with the kisses, Romeo." He puts out his hand, and I see Becca's just watching the scene.

Manning laughs and looks over at me. "Keep me off social media," he says, walking out. His blue eyes glitter at me as he puts his glasses on.

"My job is to put you on social media," I call out, and he just holds up a hand. "I don't even know why I try."

"He pays you double," Becca says, laughing.

"That might be it." I laugh, then turn to Ralph. "Are you ready?"

"Yeah." Turning his head, he spots something. "What is that?" he says, walking to the hanging picture. Following him, I gasp when I see the picture of Evan when he was in Dallas. "Look at this."

"That was taken right before he got traded," I say of the picture. "It was his one-hundredth point in one season. He was at the top of his game." I hear Ralph laugh beside me. "I mean, he's still at the top of his game, he's just . . ."

"You look so young," Ralph says, his eyes on me in the picture.

"I was young, and I was such a bitch," I say, and he gasps. "I was horrible and selfish. I even tried to break up Zara and him."

"No way," he says, shocked, and I nod. Taking my phone out, I snap a picture of it and send it to Evan. "I can't picture you being anything but amazing," he says, his voice going low as he looks at me. The two of us don't break eye contact, and my heart beats so fast I hope he doesn't hear it. "I should call and see how Ari is doing." He finally looks away.

"Of course," I say, walking next to him while he calls. Suddenly, he stops.

"Why is she crying so hard?" he asks, and he looks around. "I'll be there in ten minutes." He puts the phone down and looks at me. "She's hysterical."

"Go," I say. "I'll catch an Uber." He looks at me, not

sure what to do. "I'm fine, go." I almost push him out of the store, and when he finally gets in his truck, that is when I finally blow out the breath I was holding.

"This is not going to end well," I say to myself. "It can only end with your heart being broken," I mumble.

FOURTEEN

RALPH

I HANG UP the phone, and all I can do is panic. I rush to my truck, leaving Candace there. The guilt almost makes it impossible to leave, but then I call Miranda again, and when she answers, Ari is still wailing in the background.

"I've tried everything," she says. "She isn't hungry."

"Did you try rocking her?" I ask, and the sound of her wailing makes my stomach turn. "I'll be there in ten minutes." I hang up the phone, and the ten minutes feel like an eternity. I barely turn off the truck before I'm running out of it and opening the door. I follow the sound of the wailing and see that Miranda is pacing back and forth as she tries to soothe Ari. "Hello, little girl," I say, and the minute she hears my voice, she stops crying. Her eyelashes are wet from all the tears she shed. She smiles when she sees me, and I guess I'm not fast enough to take her in my arms because she pouts and then yells at the top of her lungs. Big tears pour out of her eyes, and

I take her and bring her to my chest. "When was the last time she had a bottle?" I ask Miranda, who watches us.

"An hour ago," she says, walking over to the bottle that is on the table. "I tried to give her another two ounces, but she didn't want it."

"What is all the fuss about?" I ask Ari, and she just looks at me as she catches her breath from all the crying. Looking over at Miranda, I say, "I'll take over from here."

"I can stay and cook dinner for you if you like," she says, smiling at me.

"No, that's okay. It's been a long day." I look back at Ari, who lays her head on my chest and sucks her pacifier.

"I'll get going then," she says. Walking over to us, she leans forward and kisses Ari on the cheek. "I'll see you tomorrow."

I just smile and nod at her as she walks out. "What do you say, baby girl, want to sit and watch television?" I ask, walking over to the couch and sitting down. I want to call Candace to make sure she got home okay, but the phone is on the table, and Ari is finally settling down. I lean my head back, and we both drift off, and when she wakes again, I forget everything except Ari. After her bath, I walk over to the kitchen to grab a bottle and walk back to the bedroom to rock Ari. I turn on her night-light as I walk to the rocking chair and sit down. Grabbing the book, I begin reading it to her, and she falls asleep as soon as I get to the last page just like always. When I get up, I kiss her soft cheek. "I love you, baby girl," I say and place her down in the crib. Her arms are next to her head. I walk over to the night-light, looking up now at Cassie's picture. "Night, Cassie," I say and walk out of the room.

My phone beeps as soon as I enter the hallway, and I pick it up to see it's from Candace.

Candace: I hope everything is okay with Ari.

I want to text her back, but instead, I FaceTime her, and she answers right away. Her hair is loose and down, and her shoulders are bare. I have to wonder if she's naked.

I stop walking. "Are you naked?" I ask, and she laughs.

"No." She shows me her off-the-shoulder shirt, and I wonder if she has a bra on. My cock is suddenly very interested in this piece of information.

"It looks like you're naked," I say and don't add that if I was there, I would lean over and kiss her softly on the shoulder. I would trail soft kisses to her neck and then devour her mouth.

"Well, I'm not naked," she says. "How is Ariella? Is she okay?"

"Yeah," I say. "I have no idea what was wrong with her. Did you make it home okay?"

"I did," she says. "Lucky for me, Manning forgot something, so when he came back, he gave me a lift home." I try to ignore the burning in my stomach.

"Where are you?" I ask, trying to see where she is in her house. I've been there a couple of times now, but I have never seen that wall behind her.

"I'm in bed working on my lists," she says, showing

me the wall behind her that has three pictures hanging on it.

"What lists?" I ask, sitting down on the couch.

"Every Friday night, I email my clients a list of things I need from them in order to make my posts," she says. "And what big plans do you have on a Friday night?" She sits up now, and I see that she's sitting in her bed.

"I don't know. My Friday night isn't any different from my Wednesday night." I laugh. "Literally, the same thing."

"What would your Friday nights be like before Ariella?" she asks. Normally, I would cut people off at this point. I learned really early that no one could be trusted. I opened a bit to Cassie, but even with her, I stopped at a point, which is what many of our fights were about.

"Um, I was down with Netflix and chill before Netflix and chill became a good idea," I say, chuckling. "Making a nice dinner at home, turning on the television, and just watching a movie."

"What type of dinner?" she asks. Placing her computer down on the bed, she lies on her side as she talks to me. "I'm visual."

"I don't really have a favorite meal," I say, and she shrieks.

"Impossible! Everyone has a favorite meal." She laughs. "If you were given one meal to eat for the rest of your life, what would it be?"

"I have no idea." I shrug. "What about you?" I should thank her for the day and hang up the phone and just move on. The right side of my head tells me this is a bad idea at the same time the left side of my head tells me to shut up.

"Shrimp scampi," she says without missing a beat. "Or pizza."

"I don't think I've ever had shrimp scampi," I say, and she slaps the bed, making me laugh.

"Shut up." She gasps out.

"Is it good?" I ask her, now at ease with the way the conversation is going.

"It's only the best thing you will ever eat in your whole life," she says. "Like your whole life."

"Okay," I say. "I'll look up recipes and make it."

"How about I make it for lunch tomorrow?" she asks. "We can eat and then talk about the list I sent you."

"I don't want you to go out of your way," I say, the tightness in my chest slowly creeping back in. "It's fine."

"If I can have any excuse to eat it, I will. So technically." She smiles at the camera. "You're doing me a favor."

"Is that right?" I say.

"It is," she says. "I'm going to come over tomorrow at eleven. Is that okay?" she asks, and I nod. "I'll start preparing, and then we can eat right before we start the meeting. It should only be a couple of hours."

"Don't you have other things to do on a Saturday?" I ask, wanting to know if she is with someone, and if she isn't, why? How could someone as perfect as her not be with anyone?

"My Saturdays are spent going to the market, and then sometimes, I have brunch with Layla," she says, and I suddenly want to know who Layla is. But is it fair for her to be so open with me and I be who I am? "What about you, Sherlock?" She uses the nickname. "What do you do on Saturday?"

"Well," I say, smiling. "Saturday is a big day in the Weber house."

"Really?" she asks, rolling her lips.

"It is," I say. "It's nail cutting day and ear cleaning day."

"Whoa, all at the same time," she jokes. "Now that's what I call a party."

I laugh now at her jokes and silliness, and I'm about to say something else when I hear Ari crying. "Speak of the devil," I say.

"Give her a kiss for me, and I'll see you tomorrow," she says, and I just sit here one second watching her.

"Good night, Candace." I say her name softly.

"Good night, Ralph," she replies. She disconnects this time, and I don't know why I can't move off the couch.

I hear Ari fussy now, and when I finally roll off the couch and walk into the dark room, I look over and see her kicking her feet. "What's the matter with you?" Picking her up, I grab her pacifier and walk over to the chair. I sit down with her in my arms and rock her back and forth. I notice how much bigger she's gotten and wonder how it would be if Cassie was here. I wonder if we would argue about how to be with her. Would I still spoil her? Probably. Would Cassie spend more time with Ari than me? Probably. Would I feel the same way I did for Cassie? Probably.

I rock Ari for longer than she needs to be rocked, and

when I place her down in the bed, she stirs until I put the pacifier back in her mouth. She is up and down most of the night, and by the time the sun rises, there are bottles everywhere. She finally falls asleep somewhere around seven on my chest as I lie on the couch. The sound of the doorbell wakes us up, and I look over and see that it's eleven. I hold her to my chest and get up, walking to the door. I look down, seeing that she is closing her eyes. I open the door and spot Candace there, the bright sunlight making me close one eye.

"I'm so sorry," she whispers. "I would have knocked." She stands there in army color loose pants that cuff at the ankle. She is wearing a shirt that shows off way too much skin. It comes just above her belly button and has small spaghetti straps that are hidden by her hair. Her tan arms look soft. "You look rough." She closes the door behind her as quietly as she can.

"She was up half the night," I say, turning and walking into the house. "I don't know if it's a full moon or not, but she ate every second hour."

"She's going through a growth spurt, maybe?" She walks to the kitchen, putting the bags that she was holding on the counter. "I can come back later when you guys are both up." Ari starts to stretch, and I look down to see that she is opening her eyes.

"I think she's getting up," I say as I rub Ari's back. "We went back to bed at seven. I didn't know she'd be out this long." I walk over to the couch, then sit down.

"Do you want me to make her a bottle?" she asks from the kitchen. I look over at her, but I don't have the energy to do anything.

"Please," I say. "You just press the button." She walks toward the machine in the kitchen.

"I know. I have one for Zoey," she says, and I hear the machine working. Ari now does more stretching as her bum lifts up, and her small fists reach up above her head.

"Good morning," I say, and she smiles at me, and all the loss of sleep erases when I see her face.

"Do you want me to feed her so you can get dressed?" she asks, and I look down at myself.

"If I get dressed, will you get dressed?" I ask her, and she looks at me. "I have just as much skin showing as you do."

"What?" she asks, almost shocked. "This is fully covered." She looks down at her outfit.

"I see stomach, arms, shoulders." I start naming the body parts. "Top boobage."

"Boobage?" She repeats the word.

"It's the part that shows the top of the boob," I say.

"There is no top boobage." She pushes her hair behind her. "See."

"Oh, I see, and I still see it," I say, and Ari holds out her hand for the bottle. She bends down to grab Ari, and my cock goes on full command as I see down her shirt at the satin bra that is holding her together. Her eyes go from Ari to me. I move in, and my lips find hers for one second before I move back again. She looks at me, her eyes opening slowly now. Her finger goes to her lips, touching them.

"I . . ." I start to say.

Candace picks Ari up and kisses her neck, not saying anything about the kiss. "If I have to cover boobage, you have to cover the tentage," she says, turning and walking away from me. My eyes fly down to my shorts, and I see the tent definitely lifted. "I'm going to go change her diaper while you take down the tent."

FIFTEEN

CANDACE

MY HEART THUMPS in my chest so fast I can hear it echoing in my ears as I walk away from him. My lips still tingle from his kiss. It came out of the blue, and if I didn't see it, I would think it didn't happen.

When I showed up on his doorstep this morning, the last thing I expected to see was a sleepy Ralph, which is hotter than a fully awake Ralph. His hair all over the place, screaming for you to run your hands through it. Then holding Ariella with one hand to his naked chest. A chest that shows you how hard he works out in the gym, and fucking gym shorts. I always wondered why men would wear jogging pants or gym shorts with no boxers under them. He literally just showed me everything he had to offer, and all the warnings that I had in my head about not being with him just pushed it to the side.

I walk into Ariella's room and stop for a second before going in. The neutral cream nursery has plush cream carpet that my feet sink in as I walk over it to the cream-colored changing table with a memory foam pad on it. I place her down and look over at her crib, which is again cream with a lace coming from the ceiling draping over the sides of the crib. It's a princess-style crib, for sure. I look over at the matching rocking chair that has a book on it and the built-in wall units beside the crib that have little pieces of Ariella. Her footprint in clay, her birth picture, and right beside it a picture of Cassie.

I look back down at Ariella, who holds her hands together while she squeals at me. "Did you party all night long?" I ask her, ignoring the sudden feeling that I'm being watched. I look over my shoulder at the picture of Cassie as I feel her eyes on me. I look back at Ariella, who kicks her feet. "How much did you drink?" I ask her as I unsnap her buttons and her feet come free as she brings them straight to her mouth. "I wish I could bend like that," I say, grabbing a diaper from the side of the table and opening the wipes container seeing that it's heated.

"Hey." I hear Ralph say from the doorway. "Do you mind if I jump in the shower?" I look over at him as he stands there leaning against the doorframe. "It's fine if you don't feel comfortable."

I avoid his eyes. "I think she'll be okay," I say. "Do you change her pjs in the morning?" I ask him and finally look over my shoulder at him.

"I do," he says. "But you don't have to if you don't want. The stuff is in the first drawer." He points at the bureau. "If not, there is something in the walk-in closet."

He points at the door on the other side of the room. "But she hates being dressed up."

"For now," I say. "I'll give her the bottle when I'm done in here," I say, and he nods at me and turns to walk away, showing me that his ass is perfect.

"Your dad is too hot for his own good," I say to Ariella. "He is the whole package." Opening the drawer and grabbing a pair of white pants and the matching gray shirt with hearts all over them, I spot the headband folded with it. I picture him folding her small items. "He also has a big package." I bend down and kiss her stomach. "You are so pretty," I say, and she kicks her feet and tries to turn over. I stop her and dress her as fast as I can, and when I walk out of the room, I turn back and grab three diapers just in case I have to change her before Ralph gets out of the shower. I definitely don't want to come back into this room. I walk with her into the living room, grabbing the bottle. After putting the diapers on the table, I sit with her.

"There we go," I say to her as she drinks her bottle. I burp her as soon as she finishes and then get up with her, looking for a chair and spotting her bouncer. "Do you want to come cook with me?" I ask, and she just drools on my arm. Picking up the bouncer, I carry it into the kitchen area where I can put her in it but still see.

She smiles at me while I turn and walk into the kitchen and start searching for the things I need in order to cook. She starts babbling, and I look around, going to my phone and putting on the nursery rhymes playlist I made for when Zoey was with me in the car. "Do you want to sing, Ariella?" She looks at me as I start singing to her as I cut up the food. I wash my hands and then go and pick her up as we dance to Baa, Baa, Black Sheep. She laughs at me as I sing and make funny faces at her.

"What is going on in here?" Ralph asks, and I stop moving and then look over. He just got out of the shower because his hair is still wet. He wears another pair of black shorts, but he must be wearing boxers because I don't see anything, and I was totally looking, with a Dallas shirt with his number on it.

"We," I say, looking down at Ariella. "We are having a dance party," I say and then walk over to him, handing Ariella to him. "I started cooking, but I felt guilty that she was just sitting in the chair." I turn and walk back to the kitchen, where I start to prepare the food now.

"She loves that chair," he says and looks at her outfit. "Did Candace dress you up?"

"I found that outfit in the drawer," I say. "And it's cute."

Laughing, he comes into the kitchen, carrying her facing outward. "So this is going to be a bit awkward." He starts to talk, and I don't know if I even want to know what he is going to say. "There is a baby monitor in her room," he starts and my heart sinks and I'm sure my face turns beet red. My mouth opens as I try to say something. "I didn't want to hear, but I kinda did."

"Oh my God." That's the only thing I can say. "Oh my God." I wipe my hands.

"Listen, Candace." And the way he says my name makes my heart stop, and it also gives me chills. "You're amazing," he says, and I want to cringe. "And I totally crossed the line before with the kiss. I know this, and I am really, really sorry." He looks down and then back up again. "But I can't date you."

"Oh my God." my voice goes low and he doesn't give me a chance to say anything else.

"Even if I could, I don't have the time or the energy to add one more thing on to my overflowing plate," he says, looking down at Ariella. "She's my priority." I hold up my hand now.

"Okay, well, first off," I start to say, ignoring the burning on my neck and the fact that I feel like I'm going to throw up. I don't know if it's because he told me that he can't date me or if it's because he heard me discuss his size on a fucking baby monitor. "Thank you for thinking I'm amazing, because I am." I look down at the shrimp and add it to the pan. "And for apologizing about the kiss, it was out of line. I didn't want to say it before," I shrug and look at the pan, "but even if you wanted to date me I don't date my clients."

"Ever?" he asks, almost surprised. "Wow."

"Ever," I say. "It's a rule I made when I started, and well." I trail off, not wanting to talk about it.

"What happened?" he asks, and I haven't told anyone, not even Evan.

"It was stupid." I say and turn to cook so I don't have to see his eyes. "I got hired by my first client. I met him at one of the parties I went to with Evan. Let's just say he was using me to get closer to my brother. He thought because my brother was a big deal that I would make him big with social media." I close my eyes, blinking away the tears. "But he wasn't smart enough; he was sending dick pics on his Instagram that I managed. I should have known." I put the spoon down and turn to look at Ralph. "He was a ten, and I was a six."

"What the fuck?" he says, and I laugh at his expression.

"I was the DUFF in that relationship," I say, and he looks at me with his mouth hanging open.

"It's fine. He's now married to a model who hopefully cheats on him every single chance she gets," I say, and I have a sudden need to chase this whole conversation down with a shot of tequila. "Fuck, that was rough." I look up at him. "I haven't told anyone that story," I say. "Especially not Evan."

"Who is it?" he asks, and I shake my head. "Also, you know he's stupid, right?"

"It is what it is," I say the truth, ignoring the last part of what he said. "Anyway, that is why I won't date my clients." I turn back and, putting on a pot of water for the pasta.

"Will you tell me who it was?" he asks, and I shake my head.

"What about you?" I turn and ask him. "How did you know Cassie was the one?" He looks down, then at Ariella. "I'm sorry, I shouldn't have asked."

"It's not that," he says. "It's just something I have never spoken about to anyone."

"You don't have to now either," I say, trying to keep my hands busy. "It's probably too painful to talk about.

Let's talk about something else."

"I don't know if she was the one," he says in a whisper, and I turn around to see the horror on his face as he holds a now sleeping Ariella in his arms. "The more I think about it, the more I know she probably wasn't. But who the fuck knows." He looks down at Ari, his voice going into an almost whisper. "She will never know any of this. I will never admit it to her."

I walk over to him, putting my hand on his arm. "Do you love Ariella?" I ask, and he just looks at me. "Then you love Cassie," I say. "Just in your own way. People love in different ways."

"That is what I tell myself," he says, avoiding my eyes and stepping out of my touch. "It's what I have to tell myself." He walks out of the kitchen. "I'm going to go put her down. I'll be back." He doesn't wait for me to answer, and even if he did, I don't have anything else to say. His words have left me speechless, and the pain in his eyes, the anguish has left me heartbroken.

SIXTEEN

Ralph

I WALK AWAY from her as the tear slips down my face and onto my arm. I lay Ariella down in the crib and hold onto her railing as I watch her chest move up and down. I look over and see the baby monitor that made me laugh not long ago. I walked into my room, and I knew when I heard her voice that I should have turned it off. I knew I shouldn't eavesdrop, but then she mentioned my dick, and I couldn't not listen. I sat there laughing while she spoke to Ari. I also knew we had to discuss things. We were flirting, and it was already getting out of hand with the kiss, so I had to stop it. I thought talking about it was a good idea. I was wrong.

"I'm sorry, Cassie." I look at her picture and walk across the room. The weight of everything that we just discussed weighs heavily on my chest. Walking back into the kitchen, I see her cooking, and I want to turn everything off and sit her down. I want to force her to tell me who it was who made her feel like that. Who would take what she had to give and just toss it away.

Instead, I sit at the counter, watching her. I try not to notice that the back of her shirt is lace, and you see the white bra strap. "Is she sleeping?" she asks when she turns around and looks at me and I see that her eyes look like she was crying.

"Why are you crying?" I ask, knowing I shouldn't, but knowing that nothing is going to stop me from asking.

"It's nothing," she says, turning around.

"Candace." I call her name, and she turns around to look at me. "I told you things I haven't told anyone. Things that I try not to even speak for fear that Cassie can hear me and know how I really felt." I watch her. "So don't tell me it was nothing."

"Fine," she says, turning off the water and then turning to me. "One, this meal is going to suck because I fucked up the whole recipe, and two, I was crying for you and for Ari."

"What?" I ask, and she just looks at me.

"I know that one day she is going to ask about her mother, and I know that it's going to eat you up inside, but you have to know that deep down you love her," she says, leaning on the other side of the counter with her hands. "I know that it is going to eat you up inside, and I just want to kick you for you to see how amazing you've been."

I shake my head, her words hurting. "How am I amazing?" I ask her, and for the first time, I'm not fucking scared to let it all out. "I grew up lost and alone with no idea what love was." I start to give it to her, and my mouth goes dry. "Then I meet this girl in foster care, and I think this could be good. But we were like oil and water sometimes." I watch her face as she takes it in. "I don't know if I love her. I know that I like her a lot. I know that I want to be with her, but I don't know if it's love."

"Everyone loves differently," she says softly to me, and I shake my head.

"That is the thing. That's what I thought. Cassie would do things to get a rise out of me. I felt like I always had to prove to her that I loved her. And then it just got to be too much," I say. "I would sit down when I was on the road and wonder is this really love. I missed her, but if she wasn't in my life, I think I would be okay." I wait to see if disgust goes on her face, but her eyes are still soft with tears in them. "I would be okay, but I don't know if she would. I was all she had, and sadly, it weighed on me. When she told me she was pregnant, I was going to break up with her." I look up at the ceiling, the tears coming out of my eyes. "If I would have gone first in that conversation, it would have gone from being a happy moment to another moment I could kick myself over." She just listens as I pour out my heart to her.

"She loved this house the minute she saw it, and I fucking loathed it. I hate it even more now than I did before." I look around the room, seeing that it's not even a home. "I hope she didn't know that my heart wasn't as happy as hers." I put my hand to my chest. "I hope that she never knows that I thought she planned it. I hope that she never knows that I doubted her and her reasons the whole time. I hope she never knows that even though I looked happy, I was fucking petrified that I wouldn't know how to love my child. Petrified I would fuck her up, and for the rest of her life, she would doubt that her father loved her. I bought this monster of a house for Cassie, knowing that she never had a house. Fuck, she went into that room alone to give birth to our child and died for her. Died. She gave her life for our child, and I don't even know if I loved her."

"You can't be serious right now." She looks at me. "You would give your life for that little girl," she says with anger. "Would you trade places with Cassie?"

"What?" I ask, confused.

"If push comes to shove, would you have traded places with Cassie and leave her with Ari?" she asks the question I have asked myself.

"Without thinking twice," I answer honestly. "For both of them, I would do it."

"Then that, my friend, answers all the questions you have had. That is love. It might not seem big to you. It's no grand gesture, but to give your life for someone, that is love." She walks around the counter now. I turn and face her as she stands in front of me. "It might not seem like love to you, but it's love." She puts her hands on my shoulders, and I just feel her heat seep through my shirt. "Now would you have always stayed with her?" She shrugs. "No one knows the answer to that. Maybe she would have left you, did you ever think of that?"

"No," I answer. "I never actually thought of that. I

only thought of myself and the way I felt."

"You mean you only thought of ways to shit on yourself?" she says, walking away from me now, but my shoulders still feel her touch on them. "That is what you meant."

"I'm just sorry," I say as she walks to the sink and turns the water back on.

"What are you sorry for?" She leans back on the counter, folding her arms over her chest.

"I'm sorry that she died alone. I'm sorry that I didn't love her like she should have been loved, and I'm sorry she will never be able to see how fucking amazing our child is."

"So you're sorry for things that were out of your control?" She stares at me, and I just sit here, letting her words sink in. "You aren't the one who killed her." She points to me, and her words hit me in the chest. "You loved her the only way you knew how, and it sucks that she won't see how Ari is, but I have a feeling she is with her every single step of the way." She turns to grab the pasta and dumps it in the water. Neither of us says anything as she continues to cook.

"Thank you," I say softly, and she turns around and looks at me. "For." I put my hands up in the air and then shake my head. "I don't even know for what, but thank you for listening."

"You're welcome." She smiles at me. I want to walk over to her and hug her, and I do just that. I get off the stool and walk over to her.

"Are you allowed to hug clients?" I ask her and don't

really wait for her to answer when I bend down and wrap my arms around her tiny waist. She wraps her arms around my shoulders and leans her head against mine. "Thank you," I whisper and step away from her, but our eyes meet, and we stop moving. Our faces are at the same level with the way I'm bent down. I move her hair away from her face, and my hand finally cups her cheek. My thumb moves back and forth, and I see her chest rising and falling. I can hear my own heart in my chest, beating so fast. My mouth is so dry I don't even think I can lick my lips. Her lips part when my head moves just a touch closer, and I can taste her right now. I don't know what the fuck I'm doing, but I do know that I don't think I've ever wanted something more.

"Ralph." She says my name almost like she's asking me something or maybe she's telling me that this is not a good idea. Maybe she is telling me that I should not do this.

"Candace." I say her name back, and I don't know what I'm telling her, if anything. "You are always a ten," I say, smiling and bending just a touch more. "Definitely always a ten." I'm about to bend a bit more to close the distance between us when I hear Ariella cry. My hand drops from her face, and I step back. I look at her poke her tongue out of her mouth to lick her lips. "I'll be right back."

Turning, I walk out of the kitchen and stop when I know she can't see me. Leaning back against the wall, I wait as my heart slowly starts to calm down. I put my hands over my face, and I smell her now. I had my hand on her for less than a minute, and I smell her all around me. I don't have time to think of anything else because Ari yells even louder than before. I walk into her room, avoiding looking at the picture of Cassie.

"I'm coming," I say, and she stops the minute she hears my voice. I look over the crib at her, and she's kicking away, her hands moving up and down.

"Da, da, da, da," she says over and over again.

"Yeah," I say, picking her up, then bending my head to kiss her. "I'm here." I look at her, her bright blue eyes so full of happiness. "I'll always be here."

I walk back into the kitchen, and something about me is different, and I can't explain it. My shoulders feel lighter and my heart doesn't clench tight when I walk out of Ari's room. "It's almost ready," Candace says, and I see that she tied up her hair on top of her head as she takes the pot of pasta and drains it. "I'm also going to want to do this again if it doesn't taste good." She smiles, and just like that, the heaviness of what we talked about is gone. She acts like I didn't just dish out my whole world to her, and she didn't talk me off the ledge that I've been clinging to every single day. "You good?" she asks as the boiling water and steam fills the sink.

"Yeah," I say. "I'm actually really good." I smile at Ari, who just smiles at us.

SEVENTEEN

CANDACE

"I'LL BE THERE in ten minutes," Layla says as soon as I answer the phone, and she hangs up before I can tell her that I'm not home alone. I put the phone down and look over at Miller, who sits there typing something on his phone.

"Okay, so I think we have the rest of the summer up to speed," I say and he looks up at me, picking up his baseball cap and scratching his forehead. "What are your plans for the fall?"

"I have no fucking clue," he says, looking up and moving his neck side to side. "Hopefully, we start the season off good."

"Well, you are still getting on the ice, and from the looks at everyone else, training is going well," I say of all my clients who send me pictures weekly.

"Fucking Ralph." He mentions Ralph, and I try not to look at him in case he sees something that isn't there. Or maybe it is, who knows at this point. I haven't seen him in nine days, nine days, and every single day, he invaded my thoughts. The last conversation I had with him broke my heart, and it took me two days to get through the daze he left me in. If I close my eyes, I can still feel his hand on my face. I can still feel his breath on my face, and I can still feel the way my heart beat in my chest. I try to draw the line in the sand, and by not seeing him is what is working. I mean, I guess. I stalk his Instagram, and we text daily with ideas. Just today, he took a picture of himself wearing the Babybjorn with diapers, wipes, and bottles on the counter in front of him.

Is it hockey season yet?

His activity level is through the roof, and he's getting over two thousand followers a day now that he is more active. "What happened with Ralph?" I ask, suddenly wondering if he's sick or not. Maybe it's Ariella.

"He's been on the ice seven days a week for four hours," he tells me, and I wonder who is watching Ari? I wonder if he thinks about me, and I wonder if Ari misses me? I shake my head because of course she doesn't. The texts that we send are always professional, and I haven't asked him any personal questions. It is what I do with everyone else. "Then he works out three hours at night when his kid is sleeping."

"Well, he'll be ready to go next month then," I say, looking down at the computer. Then I hear the front door open and I look up at Miller to see his face when he sees who is coming in.

"I'm here," Layla says, walking in, and I see Miller's

face light up. It's not a secret that he's in love with her.

"Be still my heart," he says, putting his hands to his chest. He came here straight from training, so he's dressed in his gym attire.

"Oh, God, what is he doing here?" Layla says, and I look over at her. Even if she didn't want to dress up, she looks amazing. She's wearing blue jeans ripped at the knees, but it molds her with a white T-shirt that is tied at the side. Her sandy blond hair in beach waves. "Why didn't you tell me he was here?"

"Well, you hung up on me," I say, getting up and going over to the fridge to get a bottle of water as I watch the two of them fight.

"Why does me being here bother you so much?" Miller asks, stretching back in the chair.

"Is it because you want me?"

"Miller, the only thing I want from you," she says, crossing her arms over her chest, "is for you to stay in your corner." I watch them going back and forth.

"Did you get my Snapchat?" he asks her, and I about choke, thinking about when he accidentally sent out his penis picture to all of his contacts.

"I'm not on Snapchat," she says, and by the look he's giving her, I wonder what's up.

"You gave me your snap name." He gets up now, opening the app on his iPhone and turning it to show her and then coming to show me.

"Um." I look at him and then look at Layla. "She actually doesn't have Snapchat." I break the news for her, and I see the horror on his face.

"What?" he whispers and looks down at his phone like it might blow up. "I've been sending this person pictures of myself."

"Why the fuck are you sending pictures of yourself?" I ask, and he looks at Layla.

"Why would you send me pictures of yourself?" she asks him after me.

"To entice you." He winks at her, and I have to say he is very persistent.

"I'm not interested in you," Layla says. "Not before, not now, not tomorrow. It's just never going to happen."

"You know what they say." He puts his phone in his pocket. "Never say never." He smirks at her, gives her one more wink, and then looks at me. "Let me know if you need anything else."

He walks to Layla. "You call me if you change your mind." He tries to bend to kiss her, and she pushes him away.

"Gross, I don't even know where those lips have been or who you touched last." She runs away from him and hides behind me.

"If you give me a chance," he says to her, and she holds up her hand. "I'll see you later." He walks out of the kitchen and the front door slams shut.

"Jesus," Layla says, walking over to the sink. "I need a shower to wash all the cooties off after seeing him." She shivers and washes her hands. "You should have given me a warning or something." Looking over, she glares at me.

"You didn't give me a chance," I say, walking back to

my chair and closing the book that holds all of Miller's stuff. "You literally hung up."

"Ugh whatever," she says, walking over to my fruit bowl and grabbing the oranges and then going to the fridge to grab some strawberries. "He gets on my last nerve." Coming over, she sits down in the chair next to me and not in the chair that Miller just got out of.

"You say that every single time," I say, looking at her. "It's like all this pent-up se—"

"So, help me God, if you mention me and sex with Miller one more time, I am breaking up with you," she says, peeling her orange.

"You guys are like two cats." I bring the water bottle to my lips. "In heat." I wink at her when she fake vomits.

"Whatever," she says. "What are you doing now?"

"I was going to get my schedule for tomorrow going," I say, looking down at my to-do list that is slowly shrinking. The last thing I have on the list is to call Ralph. It's been on my list for the last nine days, yet I haven't called him once. Picked up the phone, yes. Dialed his number, yes. But actually, pressed the green button? Nope. I'm sticking to texting.

"You and your lists," she says, laughing at me. "Ohh, what is that last one?" She points at the pad with her perfectly manicured nails tapping the pad.

"I have to touch base with Ralph to ask him a couple of questions." I avoid her eyes, and I know she isn't going to let it go.

"You like him," she points out.

"I work for him." I tap my thumb on the table. "Which

means that he's a no-go zone."

"What if you didn't work for him?" she asks me, popping a strawberry in her mouth. "Would you go for him?"

"I don't think that matters," I say. "He's unavailable."

"How do you know?" She just watches me.

"We had a conversation," I say, and she raises her eyebrows. "Just stop, okay? I was at his house, and we had a conversation." Cutting the topic off. "Are we going to go shopping, or are we staying in?" I close my laptop. "If we go out, I have to change."

"Changing the topic." She winks at me now just like Miller did to her not too long ago. "Smart, we can go shopping," she says. "Or we can stay in and watch that new show on Netflix that people are talking about."

"Oh," I say, getting up. "And order Chinese food?" I smile and point at her.

"If I was not so into dick," she says, "I would make a play for you."

"Um." I laugh now. "Thanks, I guess."

"You know that getting involved with a single dad is not the smartest thing to do," she says and puts up her hand when I start saying something. "I know, I know." She gets up, cleaning up her mess. "I'm just saying if it goes sideways, you are not only going to lose him, you lose the baby also." My heart slowly speeds down, and it clenches tightly in my chest. "And you know how you get with kids." She pushes the chair in. "It's your kryptonite."

"If anything, I'm going to be his friend," I say. "I don't think he's ever had a friend."

"That's so sad," she says, walking to the kitchen and taking a bottle of water and a bag of chips out of the cupboard. "I don't know what I'd do without you."

"Aww," I say, putting my hand to my heart. "Be still my heart."

She groans as I repeat the words that Miller said. "Fuck, he's so annoying."

"But he's hot." I point at her, and she can't even deny it. He's like a walking talking sex ad. His black hair is just long enough to run your hand through it, and it comes out of his helmet in the back. His eyes are so black they pierce through you. His chiseled face is perfect and his lips are plump and full. There is a reason he's the most sought-after NHL player on and off the ice.

"Fine." She throws her hands up. "I admit he's hot, but he's probably got a tiny wiener and doesn't know how to use it." She looks away, and I know that is the end of the conversation.

"Now let's go see if love is really blind."

"What is that?" I ask, walking into the living room as she tells me about the show. I'm not really listening to her as I think about Ralph. I sit down, and she starts the show. I try to get into it, but all I can do is think about calling Ralph.

I get up in the middle of an episode when my phone beeps. Walking over to the table, I see it's from Ralph. My palms automatically get clammy, and my heart speeds up, and I can swear there is a flutter in my stomach. I open the message.

Ralph: Hey, I have a huge favor and was wondering

if you could help me out.

I sit down and type out.

Me: Sure, anything.

But I don't press send. No, I sit here at the table and erase it. That sounds too eager.

Me: That depends.

I also don't send it. Maybe he's going to think I'm a bitch. Before I can even answer, the phone rings in my hand, and I see it's Ralph. I get up and walk to my bedroom so I don't disturb Layla, who is yelling at someone on the show.

"Hello," I say, sitting on my bed.

"Hey," he says, and the minute I hear his voice, I immediately smile. "Sorry, I know it's a bit pushy to call you, but I'm running out of time." The urgency in his voice is apparent now, and I am already standing up and ready to get my keys and go over to his house.

"Oh my God," I say, suddenly stopping and the burning in my neck fills. "Is it Ari?" I put my hand to my stomach, feeling sick.

"No," he says, and his voice is soft now. "Oh, no, not like that," he says. "I mean, she's good. She turned six months, and she can sit up by herself, and well, yesterday, she pushed my hand away."

Sitting back down, I feel the fear that I had before go away. "Anyway, I've been craving your pasta," he says. "I think I fucked it up, but I was wondering if you could maybe give me the recipe."

"I don't really have a recipe," I say, and he groans out.

"I have the shrimp in butter and garlic," he says, and

I hear Ari yell in the background. I suddenly miss her more than I care to tell or say. "I started the pasta."

"I was actually going to call you about the things I found out about the foundation and about everything that I set up."

"Or why don't you come over and show me how to make this recipe, and we can do it over dinner?" he says.

I have to say no because there is no reason for me to go over there. It's going to be hard when we stop talking. It's not going to do anyone any good if I say yes. It's for the best that I stay away. "Sure, I can be there in twenty." I have lost my damn mind!

EIGHTEEN

RALPH

I KNOW I shouldn't have called her, and I should have just googled a recipe, but none of them looked easy. And when she was in the kitchen, I watched as she just added things here and there. It was the best meal I had in my whole life. I've craved it for the past nine days since she left me a fuck ton of leftovers that I destroyed the day after.

"Guess who's coming over?" I say to Ari, who sits with her toys around her, wearing a gummy smile. "Candace." I'm pretty sure she doesn't even understand me.

I just finished working out, and the only thing I did was shower because Ari started screaming bloody murder. Throwing on a pair of shorts and a T-shirt, I don't look like I was expecting anyone. I turn off the stove as I wait for Candace to arrive.

For the past ten days, I've buried myself in training. After I got over the guilt for leaving Ari too long, I finally let Miranda stay more than three hours. I pushed it to four, and I went hard on the ice. Every day, I'd push myself so hard that my lungs would burn when I got off the ice. I would go home, eat a fuck ton of carbs, and then do cardio and weight training when Ari would nap. Then I would set her up to play if I had more to do. I pushed myself hard all the time because all I wanted to do was call Candace and talk to her about nothing and everything. It was crazy how she pulled me in without even trying. I had to keep myself busy to keep from calling her. She texted me here and there, and with each text, it was professional. I always wanted to keep the conversation going, but I stopped myself.

I was shocked by just how easily and readily I opened up to her. The minute I did, I felt lighter but then I thought about how Cassie would fight with me about being more open with her, and I felt guilty about sharing shit with Candace. I tried to do it, I really did, but I just couldn't get there with her. Something would stop me, and I didn't even know what it was.

The doorbell rings, and a smile fills my face as I think about her standing there outside my door. I rush over to pick up Ariella, who hits my chest and says my name. "Let's go see who is at the door." Kissing her neck, I speed walk to the door, the whole time my heart pounds and my smile just gets bigger and bigger.

Clicking open the locks, I open the door to see her standing there. She is so much prettier than she has been in my thoughts and especially in my dreams. "Well, hello there." She smiles at me, and then when she looks at Ari, her smile gets even bigger. She's dressed in ripped blue jeans that are cuffed at her ankle and a black sleeveless shirt tucked in the front with flip-flops to show off her bubble gum pink toenails.

"You got bigger." She rubs Ari's cheek, and I don't know why, but I bend to kiss Candace on the cheek. "Hi," she says, leaning into me and then kissing my cheek back. Just the smell of her makes my cock rise. I thought it was stupid when I watched the other guys kiss her cheek and and doing it right then might have been stupid, but I couldn't help myself. Fuck, I even wanted to kiss her lips.

"Hi." Stepping back, I walk in and close the door behind her, watching her ass move perfectly in those jeans. She turns around and sets her purse on the floor, then reaches out her hands to grab Ari, and Ari reaches out for her. Candace smiles so big it makes her blue eyes get even lighter. Ari then grabs her face and goes in to suck her cheek.

"Oh my goodness." Candace puts her hand on Ari's back. "I think I'm in love," she says, hugging her close to her chest. Ari just squeals and giggles when Candace nuzzles her neck. "She smells so good." She finally looks at me, and I have to say seeing her just love on my daughter pushes something else inside me. I put my hands to my chest and walk down the hallway into the family room.

"Let's see what your daddy did." She turns Ari around in her arms so she faces out, and Ari kicks her feet. When she gets close to the stove, she turns Ari back on her hip, and I just don't know what to think of the way she is protecting her.

"I put butter in a pan with garlic, and then I cooked the shrimp," I say, gesturing to the pan. "I don't think I put enough oil or butter." The shrimp doesn't even have any coating on them.

"How much butter?" she asks, and I want to lean down and kiss her lips. I've kissed her for the past ten days in my dreams. Every single night, I kiss her like I want to kiss her. Right when I slip into bed, I close my eyes and fall asleep to the fact that I miss her and I want her. Every single day, I pick up the phone a dozen times to call her but then remember I told her that we can't go there. She was the one who agreed with me!

"One tablespoon," I say, picking it up, and she laughs.

"You don't think it tastes that good with a table-spoon of butter," she says and then shakes her head. "It's three-quarters of a cup of butter."

"Holy shit," I say. "That's like . . ."

"Heaven," she says, handing me Ari. "Let me see if I can save these poor sad shrimp."

"They aren't sad looking," I say, grabbing Ari. Ari is not keen on leaving Candace just yet because she whines to go back to her. All I want to say is me, too, princess. I'm about to say something when I hear the front door open and then close. Candace looks at me, and I look back at her and then hand her Ari while I put them behind me.

"Who is that?" Candace asks, and I don't think I've ever been more scared in my whole life. Did I leave the door open? I'm about to say something to her like run when Miranda walks into the room and she is holding two plastic bags filled with groceries.

"Hey," she says, smiling at me, and then her eyes go from me and then to Candace. "Oh, I didn't know you had company."

I stand here shocked that she is even here. "Candace, this is Miranda. She watches Ari." I look at Candace, who's holding Ari on her hip now. "Miranda, this is Candace." I don't give her a title because it would be silly. What would I say? This is my social girl who I dream of nightly?

"Hi," Candace says, and her eyes go to me and then back to Miranda. "I was just trying to save dinner, and then I'll be on my way," she says, handing me Ari and then turning around. I stand here, confused by what is going on. What *is* going on?

"You know I could write it down, and you two can do it together." She avoids looking at me.

"That would be great," Miranda says, and I just look over at her. She puts the bags on the counter and then smiles at me.

"What's going on?" I ask them, not expecting anyone to actually answer me.

"I thought we could have dinner," Miranda says, looking at me, and I'm just in shock.

"Actually," Candace says. "I'm going to text you the recipe." She starts to walk out of the room. "Have a great night," she says and avoids looking at me as she practically runs out of the kitchen. I stand here, not sure what to do or say. When Miranda comes closer, I see that she's wearing a shirt you can almost see through and a skirt that is a bit short.

"Hey, pretty girl," she says, touching Ari's cheek, and I move her away from the touch.

"Candace." Walking away from Miranda, I rush out as the sound of the front door slamming fills the silent hallway. "Candace!" I call her name again, and when she turns around, I can see that there was a tear on her face.

"Listen." She shakes her head. "I shouldn't have come or thought or did any of this," she says. "I'll send you the recipe in twenty minutes as soon as I get home." The sound of her car doors being unlocked makes my heart speed up faster at the thought of her leaving. Especially after I finally fucking got her here.

"Wait, why are you leaving?" I ask her.

"You are cooking for your date." She points at the house, and I look at her and then back at the front door again.

"She's the babysitter," I say. "That's the babysitter."

"Well, the babysitter wants to have sex with you," she says. I think of the way Miranda was asking me all sorts of questions this week and then staying later than she should have and brushing up against me.

"No," I say, shocked, and then I close my eyes. "I do not want to have sex with her," I say to Candace. "Oh my God, I don't want anything to do with her like that." I fumble the words, hoping she believes me and doesn't think I'm just messing around with her.

"I just want her to watch Ari, and now I think I'm

going to have to fire her." I look from Ari to Candace and then back at my house. "Can you take her and go to the backyard while I go in and fire her?" She looks at me, not sure. "Candace, I swear on Ari that I never, ever wanted anything to do with her. She never even crossed my mind." I speak the truth while leaving out that she's the only person who has crossed my mind.

She reluctantly takes Ari from my arms and hugs her close to her chest. "Do you think I should go for a drive with her?" she asks, looking at the door. "Like, is she crazy?"

"I don't know." I run my hands through my hair. "I didn't even know she felt this way."

"Okay, how about I just go and buy some food?" she suggests and then sees my face. "Or I can go buy some new ingredients to make the shrimp." She smiles for the first time since she walked out. "Don't take this the wrong way"—she rolls her lips—"but I don't think those shrimp are going to survive."

I laugh, the tightness in my chest that had crept in when I saw her walking out is now gone. "What do you say, baby girl? Do you want to go for a drive with me?" She walks to her car and then looks at me. "I don't have the right car seat."

I walk to the garage and press the code numbers, the door slowly opening and I pray that Miranda doesn't come to the door to see. I grab the set of spare keys and walk over to her. "Take my car," I say. "There is an emergency diaper bag in there, but there is no bottle."

"I'll get some if she gets hungry. I should only be

gone for thirty minutes." She walks over to the car and buckles her in with ease, then she climbs in the truck and lowers the window. "Will you text me a code?" I look at her, confused. "To tell me you're still alive and she didn't kill a rabbit or something."

Fuck, she's stunning and funny, and all I want to do is sit with her and talk. I want to know what she's done for the past ten days. Did she go out on a date? I mean, not that I have a say in it, but did she? "I'll call you the minute she leaves."

"We should have a code word," she says, and I think she's joking, but from her face, I know she isn't. "What color is the brown bear?" She looks at me. "The answer is."

"Brown," I answer her.

"No!" she shrieks out. "The color is purple. That will be a trick."

"Good God," I mumble.

"I saw it on a *Dateline* episode." I have so many questions now. "So when you call, if you don't say purple, I'm calling in the SWAT team."

"We are going to have so much to talk about when you come back," I say, shaking my head. "So much."

"Whatever." She rolls her eyes. "You'll thank me if you are being held against your will." She closes the window, and I watch her drive away and then brace myself for what I'm walking into.

Stepping inside the door, I smell cooking, and when I walk into the kitchen, I suddenly feel better about having a code word. With music playing, Miranda stands in the middle of the kitchen, cutting a red pepper, and a frying pan behind her on the stove is sizzling. "Oh, good, you're back. I was making a stir-fry," she says, looking at me with a huge smile on her face.

"Um, Miranda," I say to her. "I think we need to talk." She looks up at me. "I don't know what is going on." I stay on my side of the counter. "But if I somehow said something or did something for you to think that . . ." I use my fingers, and she puts down the knife, shock on her face.

"But you told me you like having me around," she says almost in a whisper.

"Well, I like having you around to take care of Ariella. I'm happy you take good care of her," I start to say. "I am happy that she doesn't cry with you, and that she's okay."

"But you smile at me all the time," she says, walking around to my side of the counter. "And you said you'd like to have me around more."

"I said that I might spend more time training so you can be around more." I repeat the exact words I told her three days ago. "Only because Ari was coping well, not because—"

"Is it because of her?" she asks, pointing at the hallway where Candace walked out of. "She's young, and well, she doesn't look like she's your type. She looks like one of those puck bunnies that you see all over these hockey players."

"Okay," I say, putting up my hand. "I think you need to stop right there. Number one, you don't know me or what my type is." My anger starts to get a hold of me, not because of what she said but because of how she just described Candace. "And number two, you're fired."

"What?" she asks, shocked. "How can you fire me?"

"Well, considering that you came into my house un-invited and threw yourself at me, I'm going to say that it's better for us to part ways now," I say. "Plus, just for clarification, it didn't matter who else I was interested in. This"—I point at her and then to me—"would never happen. I wanted you to take care of my daughter, and that's it."

"I have never ever been fired before." She glares at me, walking closer to me. "Ever," she hisses. "And it's all your fault." She yanks her bag from the table and then looks back at me angrily. "Don't even think about calling me and begging me to come back because the answer is going to be no." Her voice rises now. "It'll be a fucking NO!" she yells and storms out of the house, the front door slamming after her.

I stand here in shock and then look around. The pot on the stove is starting to sizzle, and the smell of burning food fills the air. Walking over, I see that she was frying stuff, but it's now sizzling and black, so I take it to the sink and turn on the water. The sound of hissing fills the room along with a huge cloud of smoke. I dump the pan in the sink and then go to my phone and dial Candace, who answers right away.

"Hey." I sit on the couch.

"I just paid for the food, and I'm walking out. What color is the brown bear?" she asks, and I can tell that she is rushing to the car.

I want to laugh, but I know that if it were me, I'd be worried, too. "Purple."

"I'm not going to lie," she says, now quietly. "I almost called 911 anyway."

"Are you on your way?" I ask, my voice serious. I'm not sure that sounded good or not, but I know I want to say things, and I've learned that time is something you can't control. "We need to talk."

NINETEEN

CANDACE

THE WAY HE says we need to talk, I don't question him. I'm actually too afraid to question him. The whole thing with Miranda threw me for a loop, especially when she showed up in some skank clothes. And trust me, she was all skank.

"Are you ready, baby girl?" I ask her when I buckle her into her car seat as she smiles at me. Kicking her feet, she's babbling about I don't know what. "Is that so?" I kiss her before I close the door and get into the truck to make my way back over to Ralph's house.

The minute I park the truck, I look around to make sure Miranda isn't lurking in the trees anywhere or hiding in some bushes. I don't have to wait long before the garage door opens, and Ralph comes out. He walks toward the truck, opening my door first and then opening the back door and grabbing Ariella.

"Did you have a good time?" he asks Ari, kissing her

neck. "You smell like Candace," he says. She's babbling, and I try to control the way my heart is beating. This whole thing is uncharted territory, and I don't know how to navigate.

"Are you okay?" I ask him, getting out of the truck and closing the door. Walking to the back, I take out the bags as he waits for me.

"What did you buy?" he asks, looking at the bags in my hands.

"Well, I bought the stuff for tonight, plus I bought some things for Ariella," I say, picking up the bag full of stuff for her. "I had to waste time." I shrug and walk with him inside the house.

He opens the door for me, and I notice the burnt smell right away. "What happened?"

He puts Ariella in the high chair that he must have just got because I didn't see it before. "When I came in, she was cooking stir-fry." I stand here with my mouth open in shock, and he chuckles. "I know. She had a knife in her hand."

"Ralph," I say his name, and put my hands down on the counter. "I'm going to say this the best way I can." He looks at me, waiting. "Bitches be crazy." He throws his head back and laughs, then Ari copies him while putting her hands together. "I'm not kidding, Ralph."

He walks over to me and puts his hands on my arms, and my eyes drop to where his hands are on me. "I promise you I kept a safe distance." I look up at him, and I get lost in his eyes. "Needless to say, we got some wires crossed, and I fired her," he says softly, and I wonder what it would be like to hug him, to put my arms around his waist and lay my head on his chest.

His hands drop from my arms, but the tingling he left from his touch remains.

"Now, what did you buy?" he asks, walking over to the two bags that I brought in. "What the hell is this?"

"It's a jolly jumper," I say, walking over to him and grabbing the thing from his hand. "Zoey loved hers." I put it together in no time, and then he just looks at it. I walk over to Ari and take her out. "Are you ready to bounce?" I ask her. She just looks at me as I put her in it, and then she bounces. Sitting on my knees in front of her, I clap my hands as she bounces and then look over at Ralph as he just stares at us. "Is everything okay?"

He looks at me and then looks at Ari and then back to me. "I'm going to order pizza."

"I thought you said you wanted shrimp scampi," I say. Getting up, I look at him and then the other bags. "I can have it done in twenty minutes," I say. "Go give her a bath, and by the time you come back, I'll be all done."

He stands there for a minute more, looking at me and then at Ari, who starts to whine. "Fine," he says, taking Ari out. "Then we can talk."

"Sounds good," I say. He nods and walks out of the room. I start to clean the room after I put the pasta on. By the time he comes back some twenty minutes later, the water is ready for the pasta, and I have just placed everything in the dishwasher. "Holy shit," he says, looking around. "When I left, this was like an explosion."

With a laugh, I look at Ari, who is freshly washed and

her hair is combed over to the side. She smiles when she sees me as he walks over and gets her bottle ready. "She has to be the best looking baby," I say when I walk next to her, and she throws herself at me. I take her in my arms, and she lays her head on my shoulder. "She smells so good."

"It's lavender," he says, getting the bottle prepared. "It's supposed to help her sleep, so I put it in the bath with her, and then I rub it all over her." I kiss her cheek, and when he finishes the bottle, he holds it up to show her. Ari looks up, and she goes back to her father.

"Good night, baby girl," I say, rubbing her back. "How long does it take her to fall asleep?"

"I usually read her a book while she has her bottle," he says, and my heart just bursts open. "Maybe twenty minutes."

"Okay." I smile at him. "I'll keep the water low and then put it on when you come out."

"I didn't get to see how you prepare it," he says, and I laugh.

"I wrote it down for you." I walk over to the paper that I had started.

"Or you can just come over and cook it for me," he says with a smirk, turning and walking out of the room.

Was he flirting with me? I look at his retreating back. "Don't go there," I say to myself. "Don't think too much into it." I grab my phone and make a couple of notes about things to do once I get home, and when I hear him walking into the room, I look up at him. "Is she out?"

"She is," he says, putting the bottle in the sink. "It

smells amazing."

"I know." I smirk as I walk to the stove and put the pasta in the boiling water. It's been boiling for the past four minutes. "How long is she out for?"

"It's Russian roulette." He laughs, leaning back on the counter as he watches me stir the pasta. "It could be a ten-minute catnap, or it could be a seven-hour stretch."

"If she gets up, I can get her," I say, "so you can eat."

"I have so much shit to do," he says, and I look over my shoulder at him.

"Can I help?" The words are out of my mouth before I realize it.

"I mean, unless you know a babysitter." He rubs his hands over his face.

"I could help out for a bit if you want." *What are you doing?* The left side of my brain asks the right side.

"I couldn't do that to you," he says, taking a deep breath. "We need to discuss something," he says. My heart skips a beat, and my hands suddenly start to shake, and I don't know why. "Jesus," he says. Putting his hand on the counter, he flexes his arm, and his T-shirt stretches so tight across his chest that I can see the definition of his pecs. "I don't even know how to start this."

"Well," I say softly, looking back at the pasta. "I have been told that you should just say it like you're ripping off a Band-Aid."

"Really?" he says, folding his arms over his chest. I can tell he's nervous about something.

"Really," I say to him, suddenly afraid of what he is going to say.

"Fine," he finally says. I hold my breath, waiting for him to say the worst thing I can think of—that he doesn't want me to come over anymore. "I want to fire you." My mouth flies open. "But I know I need you."

"Okay," I say, not sure what to say. "Can I know why you want to fire me?"

"I need you to help me with social media. I need you to help me set up the foundation, and when I read the email you sent me two days ago, I was in awe. You just, you're amazing," he says, and the struggle on his face is real.

"So why would you want to fire me?" I ask him, my mouth suddenly dry, and the lump in my throat is forming. Tears sting my eyes, but I blink them away.

"Because," he says softly, "I want to date you."

The words hit me straight in the heart, and my mouth opens. "I know it's stupid," he says, pushing off the counter. "And you don't have to say anything." I try to say something, anything, but the words are all stuck in my throat. "And it'll probably be super awkward now, so you can ignore what I just said."

"Why?" I ask him, and he just looks at me.

"Why?" he asks me, confused. "Like why do I want to date you, or why do I want you to ignore it?"

"You said that you can't date anyone," I remind him of his words.

"Yeah." He nods, and the stove beeps, telling me that the pasta is ready. I drain the pasta and then put the pot down because my hands are shaking. I'm so confused right now. "Well, for the past ten days, all I did was think of you," he says. He then comes over to me and grabs me by my hand to pull me to the couch. I walk with him to the couch, his hand sending lightning bolts up my arm. "Sit." He points at the couch, and I sit just because I don't think my legs can hold me up much longer. He sits on the table in front of me, and we are face-to-face now. "I tried to tell myself that I couldn't do it. I tried to tell myself that I couldn't do it to you. That you deserved much better than a single father who literally feels like he is failing every single day. But . . ." He laughs now. "But then all I could do was think about kissing you."

My heart speeds up to an unhealthy rate, and I would normally assume I'm having a heart attack, but I know that this is all because of the man sitting in front of me. "You thought about kissing me?" I point at him and then myself.

"More times than is humanly possible," he says with a sly smile. "I might have also thought of other things, but . . ."

I laugh now, throwing my head back. "Which is why I'm so torn. I don't want to take advantage of you." His voice goes low, and he looks down, then up again. "I never want you to think I'm using you." The fear returns to his eyes. "That is not my intention."

My hand flies up to his face. Whereas before, I would never cross the line, something in me just won't stop it, and the words come out in almost a whisper. "I want to date you, too."

TWENTY

Ralph

I DON'T KNOW if it's the words or the way her hand feels on my face, but the minute she lifted her hand to my face, all I wanted to do was turn my face and kiss the palm of her hand. Instead, I just watched her blue eyes light up. "But you said you don't date your clients," I repeat the words to her.

"You didn't let me finish," she says and then looks down. I know that she is going to let me down, and I brace myself for it. I also think I shouldn't have said it, but I tried to stop it. I tried not to let it get to me, and I tried to sweep it under the rug, but the way she is with me and then the way she was with Ari, I knew that I couldn't not say anything. "I can't date you, but that doesn't me I don't want to."

"Yeah," I say, almost holding my breath. *This is it*, I think to myself. This is going to be the letdown.

"But," she says softly. "There is something about

you." She shrugs, and now I see the tears in her eyes. "I'm petrified." She swallows back the tears. "I'm petrified of getting hurt in all of this, and I'm petrified that if I don't take this chance, I'll regret it for the rest of my life."

"Candace," I say her name as I hear my heartbeat going louder and louder in my ears. She rubs her thumb on my cheek, and my hand comes up to push her hair away from her face, putting it over her shoulder.

"I'm going to kiss you now." I lean in, and she doesn't move. I don't know if she's okay with it or not, so I stop, not sure what to do.

"Ralph," she says my name softly. "I don't know if I'm going to be able to stop you." Her voice trails off as I lean in and rub my nose under her jaw. "This is not a good idea," she says as she moves her hands to my chest. "This is a very bad idea."

I smile now. "Or a very good idea." My hand comes up on its own, and I cup her face.

"We shouldn't be doing this. I shouldn't want you this much," she says softly. I don't wait for the rest before leaning in and kissing her lips softly. I move back a bit, seeing her eyes go dark, and then she moves her hands up my chest and grabs my face to pull me back to her. Her lips find mine, and she tilts her head to the side. When I open my mouth, and her tongue slides into my mouth, I swear the world stops. Her hand goes from my face to the back of my head, and if I thought it would be okay, I would push her back and make out with her on the couch like I was in high school. The way her tongue slides with mine or my stomach literally flips just a bit, it feels like we've been kissing like this forever. I'm about to pull her against me when I hear crying. She lets go of my lips softly. "You go get her, and I'll try to salvage dinner."

"Or," I say, getting up with her at the same time. "I can put her back to sleep, we can order pizza, and then make out on the couch."

"Go take care of Ari," she says. "Then we can talk."

"Fine, we can do fifteen, then ten," I say. She just looks at me, and I swear her lips are just a touch plump from my kisses. "Okay, twenty-five, then five." Ariella cries again, and I look over at her. "Twenty-five minutes making out, then five minutes talking."

She laughs now, throwing her head back. "I'll get her. You clean up and order pizza," she says, walking back to the bedroom and then stopping. "Do I just give her the pacifier?"

"Yeah," I say, and then I see her eyes flying down to my cock that is at full height.

"I see tentage." She points at my pants. "Should I show boobage?"

"If you show me boobage, there might be an explosion. And that is not something I really want to admit to the girl I'm crushing on," I say, and then she looks at me.

"You're crushing on me?" she asks, and right before I'm about to answer, Ari lets out the biggest cry of her life. We both rush to her room and see that she is none too pleased as she sits up in her crib.

"What is all the fuss about?" Leaning down, Candace picks her up and holds her close as she cries, yet Ari lays her head on her shoulder and shudders from her crying. "There we go," she says softly, rubbing Ari's back, and this right here is one more reason she has worked her way into my heart. "Now, now." She kisses her cheek. "No more tears." She looks at me. "Will she go back down?"

"I don't know. She's never cried that loud before," I say. "I can take her."

"I have her." She walks over to the rocking chair. "Why don't you go clean the kitchen?"

"Okay," I say, not sure I want to leave her but knowing that she couldn't be in better hands. I walk out and go to the kitchen, cleaning up and putting the shrimp away while I order us food. After fifteen minutes when she doesn't come back, I walk back to the bedroom and see that she is still rocking her, but Ari is not even close to going to bed. "She is not going to go to sleep," I say from the doorway, and Ari turns her head to look at me and calls my name.

"I figured that out when she looked at me and babbled for a good three minutes," she says and then looks down at my daughter in her arms. "I was telling her that she interrupted a very important moment."

I laugh now. "Really, and what did she say?"

"Well, she said that you're hers, so I have to back up a bit." Ari turns now, squirming to get out of Candace's arms.

"See, she wants her daddy," she says, getting up and carrying her over to me. I take her into my arms, and she looks at Candace and says my name with a huge smile on her face. "See." She points at Ari, and then we walk out into the living room.

I sit on the couch with Ari on my chest as she dims the lights. "This is romantic," I say to her, laughing.

She sits on the couch next to us. "I haven't seen anything sexier in my life." She curls her feet under her and leans down on one hand on the couch. "So, what time do you leave in the morning?"

I look at her. "You can't really be serious?" I lean back into the couch with Ari on my chest. She's sucking on her pacifier as I tap her bum. I wish she would sit closer to me. "I can't let you do that."

She sits up now straight. "Well, one"—she puts up her finger—"you aren't letting me do anything." And then she brings up another finger. "And two, I'm offering to help, so let me help."

"But you work." I reach over and grab the hand she is holding up, linking our fingers. "Plus, we have to talk about how this is going to work."

"Well, I was talking to Ariella about that when you interrupted me," she says, leaning over. I think she's going to kiss me, but instead, she rubs her nose on Ari's cheek, then she looks up at me. "How about we take it day by day?" she says, and I move just a touch closer to her. "Let's start with tomorrow, and we can work it as we go along."

"I just don't want you to think . . . " I start to say, and she puts her fingers on my lips. "That I'm taking advantage of you," I say with her finger across my lips.

"Jesus," she huffs out. "What's it going to take for

you to shut up?"

"I can think of a couple of things," I say when her hand falls from my lips. I want to lean over and kiss her, and she must see it all over my face.

She gets up and starts to pace in front of me. "I don't think this is a good idea," she starts to say. "Actually, the more I think about it, the more I know it's a bad, very bad idea." Ari and I both watch her walking back and forth.

"Why?" I say, and she looks at me. "Explain to me why."

"Well, we work together." She holds her hand up with one finger. "And two, I don't date my clients."

"I told you I wanted to fire you," I remind her. "Right before I told you."

"I know, Ralph." She crosses her arms over her chest. "I was there."

"Yes, you were." I smile at her. "Right before you kissed me."

She opens her mouth. "I didn't kiss you; you kissed me."

"Potato, potahto," I say. "Either way, it ended with my lips on you, so I don't even care at this point."

"That's the whole point," she says. "I don't do that. I have never even wanted to." She rubs her hands over her face.

"Good," I say, and I'm already over this conversation. "Do you know what I want?" I ask, and she shakes her head. "I want to put my daughter to bed." I look down at Ari whose eyes are getting heavier and heavier as she listens to this conversation. "Then I want to come and sit down with you and talk to you. For nine days, I wanted nothing more than to call you and talk to you. I wanted nothing more than to ask you to come over or to make an excuse to see you."

"Ralph," she says my name softly.

"I get you're scared to date me, and I'm scared to date you. Heck, I don't even know if I'm good at dating. If maybe I'll just fuck it all up, but I know that I want to try it with you."

"That's just the point," she says. "It's making the lines all blurry."

"What if we don't label it then?" I counter. I'm willing to do and say whatever I need to right now to make sure that when she leaves here, she knows that she and I are going to happen.

"What do you mean?" she asks.

"I mean, what if we just do what we are doing and not say it's dating?" She laughs and rubs her eyes. "What if it's just two friends getting to know each other?"

"Would we be kissing?" she asks.

"Fuck yeah," I answer, and I see she wants to say something. "What were you afraid of right there?"

"I wasn't afraid to say anything." She rolls her eyes at me. "I just didn't know how to word it."

"Well, someone once told me that the best way is to just say it, like ripping off a Band-Aid." I wink at her, and she pushes my shoulder.

"That sounds like a smart person." She winks at me. "What I wanted to say was we have to think about how Ariella would feel in all this."

"What?" I ask, almost shocked.

"I don't know if she's ready for this. I mean, she hardly knows me, and I'll be kissing her man all the time, and well, I don't know how she's going to feel about it."

I sit up, holding Ari's back as she sleeps on me. "She's six months. The only thing she feels strongly about is having her milk when she wants it and not sitting in her poop for longer than two minutes."

"Yeah, but it might be weird for her," she says, and I stand now.

"You know that she likes you, right?" I say. "She smiles at you and goes to you. It took her four days to get used to Miranda."

"Well, that's because she had a sense that she was batshit crazy." She folds her arms over her chest. "You need to change the locks on the house."

"Fuck," I say. "I didn't even think of that. Do you really think that she'll come back?" I look around as Ari softly snores on me.

"Oh my God." She smacks her head. "The woman came here unannounced," she starts, putting up her fingers, and I noticed that she does this often. "Dressed in her sluttiest clothes." She puts up another finger. "And then she tried to make you stir-fry." She holds up the fourth finger. "Batshit crazy."

"You know what?" I say, walking over to her and bending down while I hold Ari. "You're cute when you get all flustered and start using your fingers." I kiss her lips, and she kisses me back. I shake my head and walk toward Ari's room, leaving her lips lingering with my kiss.

TWENTY-ONE

CANDACE

I PARK MY car right next to his and get out, grabbing my bag with my laptop and my agenda. I look around, seeing that some of his neighbors are already up and getting the lawn work done before the heat of the day sets in. I feel like I just left here, but it's been over ten hours. The only thing that keeps replaying in my head is that this is a bad idea. "Don't go there."

Between admitting to him that I actually wanted to date him and then having him kiss me, yesterday was a mix of emotions for me. But what a fucking kiss it was. They say some kisses rock your world. They say some kisses you'll always remember. They say there is always that one kiss you'll tell your grandkids about. Last night was that kiss. It's a kiss I know I'll never forget, and it's a kiss I silently begged for. But just as fast as I told him I wanted to date him, I told him why I couldn't. I repeated it over and over again, but each time, his lips would touch me, and I would be pulled to him. It was a force I've never felt before, and I have no idea what to do with it.

But the most shocking thing was that every single time he kissed me last night, it was like the first time. My heart would speed up just a touch, and I would give my last breath for just a taste of him. Last night when I finally got up to leave, he cornered me against the front door. His hands on either side of my head and my hands on his waist, he just kissed me, and I left there in a daze. My lips were swollen from his kisses, yet I wanted to go back for more.

I knock on the door in case Ariella is sleeping, and I hear the locks click right away. The door opens, and he stands there in black gym shorts with the team logo on the bottom cuff, a matching T-shirt, and a black baseball cap on his head backward. A smile fills his face, and his eyes turn a crystal blue.

"Good morning," I say, walking into the house. In two moves, he has the door closed behind me and pressed me against it with his body flush with mine.

"Good morning," he whispers right before his mouth claims mine. My hand drops my bag by my feet, and they both go to his waist, then work their way up his hard chest as I feel him. He buries his hand in my hair, making us both moan. His tongue slips into my mouth, and I realize that I was wrong before. This, this right here is the kiss I'm going to remember. Even when his lips leave mine, it takes me a second to open my eyes, and then all I see are his lips. I lean back in to take some more. I forget where I am, and I forget who I am. He kisses me softly, then lets go of my lips, and I just can't get enough. "God, you are going to make leaving really fucking hard."

My eyes flutter open, and I just look at him. "Is she up?" I look over his shoulder.

"She is," he says, "which is why I kissed you at the door." He winks at me, laughing, and I push him away.

"Shut up." I walk past him, picking up my bag, and as he walks next to me, our hands graze each other. I walk into the living room and see Ari sitting there in the middle of the room with toys all around her. "Good morning, princess," I say. She smiles at me, and I grab her, bringing her up and kissing her neck. "Did you sleep well?"

She babbles at me. "She did. She slept a full six hours," Ralph says, and I look at him. "Are you sure about this?"

"Ralph." When I say his name, he walks over and kisses me on the lips right in front of Ariella. "Why did you do that?"

"Because I can." He winks at me. "And because I love when you say my name. Now, she's just had a bottle," he says to me. "She usually goes down for a nap or two."

"We got this," I say and then look at Ariella. "Don't we?" She closes her eyes and scrunches up her nose. "Is there anything else you feel the need to tell me?"

"Well, she likes to have cereal, but I should be back for that," he says and then looks around. "Make yourself at home."

"I will," I say. "Don't you have to go?"

"I do," he says, kissing Ari on the cheek and then looking at me. "I'm going to kiss you so I hope Ari is looking the other way."

I don't even try to argue with him. I just kiss him back, and when he steps away from me, I look at Ari, who is too busy trying to get her hands to go into each other. "Be safe," I say, and he just smiles.

"I'll call you, and if there is anything . . ." he says nervously.

"Go." Shaking my head, we walk him to the door and wave as he drives away. "Your father, I tell you, Ari. He's too much."

Walking back inside, I start setting up my day. I clean up the kitchen a bit, and when she starts to get a bit cranky, I grab a bottle and sit with her on the couch while I go over my emails on my phone. When she falls asleep, I put her down in her crib and then look around. *This room is so bland*, I think to myself. There is no color; it's just cream and cream. I close the shades a touch, and my eyes avoid the picture of Cassie. When I walk back out, I grab my laptop and get ahead of my schedule, and when she wakes up from her nap, my work for the day is done.

"Do you want to go for a walk?" I ask as I carry her out, preparing her a bottle and then looking in the garage for a stroller. Cardboard boxes fill half the garage, and I'm shocked when I see his name on all of them. I'm still searching for the stroller when my phone rings. I don't even check to see who it is before I answer. "Hello?" I say and then hear my brother's voice, and then I realize that I'm on FaceTime. "Hello," I say to the phone when I see Zoey sitting on top of Evan.

"Auntie CanCan, can I come over?" she asks me. I

smile at her, my heart hurting a bit more as I think about how much I miss her.

"You can come over anytime you want to, sweetheart," I say. Ari babbles next to me, and my brother comes into view now.

"Where are you?" he asks, and then I see Zara come into the picture as she holds her coffee cup in front of her mouth while her eyes widen.

"I'm actually helping Ralph out," I say, hoping that I sound like it's a normal thing and not that I'm actually falling for him. Or that I've decided to throw the only rule I had out the window for him. "He had to fire his babysitter and was stuck."

"What?" my brother asks. "Why would he fire her?"

"She showed up at his house, and well, she thought that he wanted her to do a lot more than just watch his daughter," I say, giving them the PG version instead of the drawn-out one. Walking out to the garage and back into the house.

"Wow," Zara says. "This is why we are never going to hire babysitters." She glares at Evan, who holds his hands up. "Bitches be crazy, Evan."

"Yeah, Dad," Zoey says. "Bitches be crazy." It's my turn to laugh.

"Don't say that," Zara tells her. "It's a bad word."

"Okay, Mama," she says and then looks at the phone. "Auntie CanCan, can you come here?"

"Oh, I wish, baby girl," I say. "But I can't come just now."

"It's not fair," she says, then looks at Evan. "Can we

go there?"

"Soon," he says, and she gets off his lap. I walk over to the couch placing Ari in my lap as she looks at the phone. "So why are you helping him?"

"Leave your sister alone," Zara says. I want to thank her, but Evan just looks over at her.

"Why do I have to leave my sister alone?" he asks her, and then he must get to something because he turns and looks back at the screen. "Do you work for him?"

"I do," I say, hoping he remembers my rule never to get involved with anyone I work for.

"See, she works for him, so she won't get involved with him," he says almost like a kid when they stick their tongue out at their sibling.

"Sure," Zara says. "Either way, it doesn't matter. She's a grown-ass woman, and she doesn't need anyone's permission to date anyone."

"Can I know why you guys called me?" I ask them when Ari is over their conversation and arches her back and tries to turn around.

"Zoey wanted to chat," Zara says, looking at the camera, and when she's about to say something else, the front door opens, and I look at Zara, widening my eyes.

"Okay, got to go, bye," she says, disconnecting, and I breathe a sigh of relief. I am not ready for the questions that my brother is going to ask me. Fuck, I'm not ready for the questions Zara is going to have for me when she calls me back. This is followed up by a text that comes to my phone as soon as I hear Ralph speak.

Zara: *You owe me a fuck ton of answers.*

"There you are," he says. I look over at him and see he's dressed almost the same way as when he left, and when he comes closer, I can smell the hockey on him, and it's not a pleasant smell.

"Eww," I say when he gets close enough, but Ari lights up and reaches for him. "Don't you dare. You need a shower. Why would you come home without showering?"

He kisses Ari, who taps his chest and doesn't care that he smells like an old bag of cheesy chips. "I missed you guys." He avoids my eyes and looks down.

"You're lying." I laugh, pointing at him. "You didn't think I would be okay." I get up, shaking my head.

"It's not that," he says quickly. "It's just I didn't want you to have an extra burden."

"Oh, for heaven's sake," I say, throwing my hand up in the air. "I was fine. We were going to go for a walk," I say. "But I couldn't find her stroller."

"It's in my car," he says, and I look at him almost like he has two heads. "I didn't think you would need it."

"Well, I was going to go for a walk with her," I say, not wanting to overstay my welcome. I mean, I've never been in this position before. "But now that you're home, I guess I'll head out."

"Why?" he asks, and I shrug.

"I'm sure she is more comfortable here, but . . ." I say the truth, shrugging. "It's . . ."

"Why don't I go hop in the shower, and then we can go and get a stroller," he says, not bothered by what he just said. "Then we can get some lunch and take her for a walk.”

"Are you sure?" I ask. He just looks at me, and the look in his eyes is something different.

There is a lightness that wasn't there before. "Never been more sure of anything." He comes to me and bends down to kiss my lips. Forgetting about the way he smells, I just put one hand on his head, and I let him kiss me.

TWENTY-TWO

Ralph

I RUN TOWARD the shower, and then I turn back around. "You know," I say, and she looks at me. "If she was sleeping—"

She shakes her head. "I'm not even going to let you finish that sentence," she says, turning around and walking to the kitchen. "You better go and shower, or I'm going to take Ari, and we are going to go out for lunch without you."

"I was just going to say that you could have washed my back." I hold up my hands now. "But whatever."

"I'm giving you three minutes," she says, and I look at her. "And that tentage is not okay."

I look down, and my cock is ready to come out and play. "I'm going to need more than three minutes," I say. "I mean, unless you want to—"

"If you say another word, Ralph." She shakes her head, and I can see she is just as affected by me as I am by her. "So help me God."

"Fine, I'll rub it out fast, and then I'll be ready." I don't wait for her to reply before I run into my room and take the fastest shower of my life. I grab my black Calvin boxers and then a pair of black shorts with a white polo shirt. I brush my hair back with my hand, and when I go in search of them, they aren't in the living room. "Candace," I call her name, looking around.

"In the bedroom!" she yells, and I walk back down to Ari's bedroom and see that she is changing her outfit.

"Is everything okay?" I ask. Walking in, I stand next to her, wrapping my hand around her shoulder. Candace looks up at me.

"You smell so much better," she says and then looks at Ari. "You smell that, baby girl? It's called soap." She picks her up and I see she has dressed her up in a pink rose romper that I've never seen before. "You are so pretty."

"Where is that from?" I ask while she puts on a pink headband, and the only thing that Ari does is squeal and drool.

"I bought it yesterday," she says, "but I washed it this morning." She kisses Ari and then hands her to me. "Do you want to grab something to eat now or after the walk?"

"I'm good. I had a protein shake in the car on the way home, but I can also eat."

"Good," she says and smiles at me. "I had food delivered."

"How?" I ask, and she shrugs.

"I made the order online this morning when you left." I watch how she gets kind of shy, and I can't help but smile. "I didn't know how long you would be gone."

"But you ordered for me also?" I ask, and she glares at me.

"Well, I didn't want to be rude in case you came home and saw me eating," she says, avoiding my eyes still.

"Look at me," I say, and she rolls her eyes before looking up at me. "You ordered me food?"

"No." She shakes her head in defiance. "I ordered myself food. I just ordered too much."

I throw my head back and laugh. "Whatever," she says.

She tries to walk past me, but I catch her around the waist. "Not so fast there." My voice comes out soft, and she doesn't put up a fight. "Thank you," I say. "For watching Ari and for getting me food."

"You're welcome," she says. "But this doesn't change anything."

I shake my head and lean down to peck her lips. "Everything changed the minute I put my lips on you."

"It was curiosity," she says softly. "We were both curious about things." I walk with her to the kitchen, and only then do I notice the brown takeout bags on the counter that I missed before when I was looking for them.

"Okay," I say, putting Ariella in her high chair and giving her a couple of toys to keep her busy. "Let's say we were both curious. But now that I've kissed you and tasted you, I'm a whole lot more curious."

I walk over to the bags and take out the two meals she

got. The first one is a huge bowl of salad with chicken on top. "That's mine," she says, and then I grab the one at the bottom, and it feels heavier.

"I got you steak and some steamed veggies with rice." I put my container down next to hers and walk over to her. She looks like she is going to run, but she doesn't. She stands there, and when I get to her, my hand goes to her waist. I pick her up and place her on the counter in front of me in one swift move.

"Ralph," she says my name as her hands go to my chest, and I hope she can feel how fast my heart is beating. She puts her head down, and her hair falls around her face.

"Candace," I say softly. She looks up at me, and I tuck the hair behind her ears. "I've been in one relationship my whole life," I say. I don't know why I'm bringing this up, but I want her to know everything when it comes to me. And I selfishly want to know everything about her.

"It was with Cassie. We broke up quarterly because I just couldn't get there with her. There was a step that I just couldn't take, and she knew it. But then we would spend two weeks apart, and she would call, and it would start the routine all over again." My heart hurts, not for Cassie, but knowing I did that to her. "She wanted an all-in sort of relationship, and even though I said I would be all in"—I shake my head and swallow the lump—"I was never all in." I take a deep breath. "I want to be all in, and I want to do it with you."

"But—" she starts to say, and I put my finger on her lips.

"But let's just have lunch, and then we can go for a walk. I don't want to hear your buts, and I don't want you to tell me we shouldn't be doing this. Let's just—"

"Have lunch." She smiles shyly at me. "But." I groan now when she says the word but and she chuckles. "How about . . .?" She opens her legs, and I step closer to her. "You thank me properly." Her hands pull me even closer, and she tilts her head back. "I mean, I did buy you lunch."

Smiling at her, I tilt my head to the side, leaning in and taking her lips. I slide my tongue into her hot mouth at the same time as she puts her hands around my neck and pulls me in closer. Our tongues wrestle with each other. My cock presses against her as she wraps her ankles around my waist. "If we don't stop . . ." I pull back, and the sound of us panting fills the air. "You're going to be my meal." I watch her eyes widen as she blinks. Her legs fall from around my waist, and she just looks at me.

"I think it would be a good time for me to go," she says, and I look at her. "I have things that I didn't do this morning." She pushes away from me, and I watch her hop off the counter. She walks around and kisses Ari.

"Maybe tomorrow we can do the whole walk thing." She grabs the salad. "I have to go." She puts the salad in the bag, and before I know it, she's out of the door.

Instead of going after her, I sit at the counter and eat the meal that she ordered. I send her a text that goes unanswered. I feed Ari and play with her, the whole time thinking about Candace. I replay the scene over and over in my head, making a plan.

"What do you think, baby girl?" I ask her as I change her diaper and prepare a bag with more bottles than I need. "Do you want to come with Daddy?" She just smiles at me, and I snap a picture of her. "Want to go for a walk?" I ask, and she bounces a bit. She whines when I put her in the car seat, but I put the pacifier in her mouth, and she settles down. We make a quick stop, and when I get to her house, I pop open the trunk and get the stroller out and set Ari in it. She looks around, not too sure of what and where she is.

"Okay, here we go," I say as I move the stroller to the passenger side and grab the big pink bouquet that I'd stopped to pick up on the way. I asked them for every single pink flower they had. I walk up the driveway, and I hold my breath before I press the doorbell.

"This, baby girl, is the first step to wooing her." I look at the flowers now. "Or at least I hope it's step one," I mumble.

I hear her footsteps approach the door, and then she unlocks it before she opens the door. Her eyes go wide when she sees me. "Hey," I say, looking at how beautiful she is. She's still dressed in the jeans from before, but I see her hair has been put up in a bun on top of her head. "We were wondering," I start to say, suddenly feeling nervous. Shit, maybe I should have thought this through before showing up at her door. "I was wondering, and well, Ari," I say and then stop. I look down at my girl smiling at Ari and moving her hands as she looks at her. "If you would like to go for a walk with us."

"Ralph," she says softly, and I have the sickening

feeling that she is going to end things. From the tone of her voice and the way she hasn't come out and got Ari or even spoke to her. My heart sinks. Oh my God, I did this. I pushed her too hard, too fast. I should have gone in slow, but I just couldn't.

She's about to say something else when I hear a man's voice behind her, and my heart sinks. "Who is at the door?"

TWENTY-THREE

Candace

WHEN I PULLED open the door, I expected it to be my pizza that I ordered. The last person I expected it to be was Ralph. He was standing there in the exact outfit he wore before, and he was pushing a stroller with one hand while the other hand held one of the biggest bouquets that I have ever seen. Ari was dressed as she was before, and she smiled at me, her hands moving a million miles a minute, and it took everything I had not to step into her and him.

I have to admit that when he kissed me on the counter, I forgot everything, including all my rules. That is what he did to me. With just one touch, I let go of my sanity. I took off fast so I could think, knowing that if I stayed close to him, I wouldn't be able to.

"Who is at the door?" I see the look on Ralph's face, and now it really does take everything for me not to go to him. "Jesus, I've been waiting," Miller says from behind me and steps beside me, putting his hand around my shoulder like he always does. "Hey, man," he says, smiling at Ralph. "What are you doing here?"

"What am I doing here?" he asks, but his tone is just a touch pissed off, and I hear the crinkling of brown paper as he squeezes the flowers in his hand. "What are you doing here?" He puts his hands on his hips, and I tilt my head and side-eye Miller, who looks a bit shocked and surprised at his tone.

"Well, I had a meeting with Candace," he says, now taking his hand off my shoulder. I look over at him as Miller looks at me and then at Ralph as he tries to figure out what is going on. And I guess he's not the only one. "Wait a second," Miller says. Putting his hand up, he points at the flowers in Ralph's hand. "Hold on." Then he points at me and then he takes his hand and pushes my head. "Eww, no, no, no." His face grimaces. "Gross."

"I'm right here." I push his head back. "And you are the gross one." Then I look over at Ralph. "Now that this is out of the way."

He just looks at me, not saying anything, and then looks at Miller. "Aren't you leaving?"

He laughs now. "I think that is my cue to get the fuck out of here, or he's going to kick my ass." He looks down at Ari. "Sorry for swearing, pretty girl." He looks at me. "If you need anything, call me." Then he looks at Ralph. "And I mean about work, not a booty call." He puts his hands up. "You can be rest assured that there is nothing that Candace has that I want."

I roll my eyes now and huff out. "Again, I'm still

standing right here."

Miller walks past Ralph and slaps his shoulder. "Good luck, dude." He then looks at me. "She looks angry."

"Miller, so help me God," I say with my teeth clenched together as he now jogs to his truck and takes off.

"Candace," he says, and I make the mistake of looking at him. "I got these for you," he says, handing me the flowers. "*We* got them for you." I bring the flowers to my nose and smell the roses.

"Come in. It's hot outside, and Ari is going to get fussy," I say, moving aside, but he doesn't move.

"Are you sure that you want me to come inside?" he asks, and I just stand here. "I don't want to interrupt."

"You are not interrupting, and even if you were, he left." I point at the empty spot in my driveway that Miller just vacated. Bending down and grabbing Ari out of the stroller and bringing her in the cool house, "I'm sorry," I say, "for just running out before."

"I want this," he says. "This thing with us, whatever it is, whatever it's going to be? I want it." He looks at me. "Whatever happens in all of this, all I want is for you to be happy." He steps closer. "Whatever happens, I want you to find love."

"You can't do that," I say, blinking away my own tears. "You can't just come in here and say all the perfect things when I've been sitting and staring into space all day long, thinking about you and this and us. And everything that will go with it, if we actually do whatever." I don't want to say the word dating, but he closes the distance between us and puts his hands on my face. I don't think my heart could beat any faster. I don't think I could fall for a more complicated man. I also don't think I stood a chance.

"Also," he says, bringing his head closer to mine, "I was about to throat punch Miller." He laughs, and I look down, smiling and then look back up. "Imagine how that would have been." His thumbs rub my cheeks. "I don't think I would be able to explain that to Nico."

"Does that mean that this thing"—I feel Ari playing with my hair, so I turn and kiss her cheek—"is exclusive between the two of us?"

He glares now. "Pretty much saying we are exclusive," he says. "Now, before you say anything else." He licks his lips and puts his forehead on mine. "Can I kiss you?"

I think about dragging it out. I think about just ending it and trying to be his friend. I think about how my head tells me it's the smartest thing to do, and then my heart answers for me. "Yes, please," I say, and he moves just a touch until his lips are on mine. The kiss is soft, and if I wasn't watching him with my own eyes, I would think it was my imagination. He moves his head to the side and slowly slips his tongue into my mouth. I lean in just a touch, and it must startle Ari, who now moves from her head on my shoulder and calls for Ralph the same time my pizza delivery gets there. Ralph lets go of my lips and stands next to me with his hands over my shoulder. "I have to get my purse."

"I got it," Ralph says, taking money out of his pocket. He hands the driver money in exchange for the medium pizza I ordered.

"I'm sorry I didn't know you were coming," I say and turn to walk into the house. His arm never moving off me. "Is she sleeping?" He nods his head.

"I'm going to put her down in the crib," I say, and he stops and kisses my lips before letting me go. I walk into the room and close the shades and then place her in the middle of the crib and cover her up. She doesn't move, and I quietly walk out of room to the kitchen. I look for him, and I don't spot him anywhere. I hear the front door close and look over to see him walking back in with the diaper bag.

"Is she down?" he asks, and I nod my head. "I have to put the milk in the fridge." He lifts the bag so I can see. "But after that, I was wondering how really really hungry you are?" He places it on the counter right next to the pizza. He walks over to me and puts his hands on my hips. My eyes go down, and I look at his hands on me. A shiver runs through me as he comes closer toward me, putting us chest to chest. "Because I'd like to show you how much I've missed you."

He smirks at me, and then my hand goes to his chest, and I feel his heart beating as fast as mine. "I am okay with this plan," I whisper to him, my hands feeling every single muscle he has as they move up his chest, then wrap around his neck. "I want this," I say. "I'm scared and petrified that in the end, I will be the one who gets hurt."

"Candace," he says, and I swear I could ask him to say it over and over again. I wonder how he will say my name when I take him down my throat. I wonder if he'll close his eyes. I wonder if I can make him forget everything. "I can say this honestly." His thumb rubs my chin so soft, and then his index finger rubs around my lips. "That if this goes south, you might not be the only one who isn't left standing." His lips meet mine, and the both of us sigh. Literally, sigh out as his tongue slides into my mouth, and I try to get even closer to him than I could. Any closer and I would be inside him.

The kiss is frantic, unlike the other ones before, and my hands go from his neck to his back. His hands leave my face and grab my hips again, this time pulling me closer to him. His hands squeeze my hips harder, and I arch into him, feeling his cock, and we both groan out. In one swoop, he's got me up. I wrap my legs around his waist, and he walks us over to the couch. He sits on the couch, and I straddle him, his hands going now to my ass as I grind on him. I let go of his mouth to moan out his name, "Ralph." He buries his head in my neck, and I move my head to the side to give him more access. His tongue comes out to lick, and then he bites me softly, then sucks in. "Ralph." I wrap my hands around his head, and he grabs my hair, pulling it back to give him more access to my throat. I've never been so out of control in my life. My life is filled with control; it's the only thing I can count on not to let me down. But here, this with him, I'm throwing it all to the wind, and I'm hoping like fuck it doesn't backfire.

TWENTY-FOUR

Ralph

"RALPH," SHE SAYS, and my cock gets so hard I feel like it's going to break through the zipper of my shorts. I attack her neck as the smell of her all around me and making me lose my mind. Everything about her pushes me. When I showed up and heard a man's voice, I got a burning sensation in the pit of my stomach, and then when I saw Miller put his arm around her. Well, let's just say I wanted to take his hand and pour acid on it after I throat punched him. It got to the point I couldn't even think. All I could do is stare at the hand draped around her, and I saw red. It had to take me a couple of minutes to process what I was feeling because I have never had this reaction. I never got jealous because I was confident with myself, but seeing her with someone else, I just . . . I couldn't even think about it without getting angry.

"Ralph," she says breathlessly as I pull her closer to me. My hands claw at her back, bunching up her shirt as her hips grind into me. Her hands now claw at me as much as I am clawing at her.

"Candace," I say. Moving my hands up to her hair, I grab a handful and pull it back and seeing her eyes flutter open. "You're so beautiful," I whisper to her, and she now puts her hands on my face. "Thank you." I kiss under her jaw. "For giving me a chance."

"You mean, like I really had a choice." She smiles at me, rubbing my cheeks with her thumbs. I lean in and kiss her.

"I mean, not really, but I thought it would be nice to say," I say right before I go back for another kiss, her mouth opening for my tongue. Her hands fall from my face to my chest as she bunches up my shirt in her hands. I want her to rip the shirt off. I want to rip her shirt off, and I want to bury myself in her as she calls out my name over and over again. My tongue slides with hers, and just when I'm about to flip her on her back, the sound of crying fills the air. Both of us look toward the hallway, our chests rising and falling. We both wait to see if it's actual crying or if maybe she is going back to sleep, but then I hear Ari scream again.

"I'll go get her," Candace says, kissing my lips before climbing off me, and I swear I hear my cock cry out and beg her to come back. I put my head back on the cushion and rub my face, taking a couple of minutes before I get up and make a bottle for Ari knowing that she is going to want to drink something. I look over at Candace walking back into the room with Ari lying on her chest, sucking her pacifier. "She was not a happy person," she says, smiling at me and coming closer.

"What is the big fuss about?" I say, and Ari gets up now and cries for me. "I'm right here," I say, taking her and turning her to the side so she can drink her bottle.

"You go sit down," she says. "I'll warm up the pizza."

I bend down, kissing her lips, tasting her again if only for a little bit. I walk over to her couch and sit down, and I look around her place. This place is neutral, but there are touches of color and pictures that show you it's a home. There are about five pictures of Zoey on one table, and I spot a picture of Candace looking all dressed up with Zoey in her arms also dressed up.

"You look really good in that picture." I point at the picture when Candace comes to sit next to me.

"Thank you, it was taken last summer at the Max Horton foundation." She smiles. "I painted her nails that day a light glittery pink, and she thought I was the shit." The way she talks about Zoey you feel the love right through her.

"You are the best aunt ever," I say, and she smiles. Something tugs at my heart, and I ignore it, not ready to face it. "So, tell me." I smirk at her. "What did you get on the pizza?"

She curls her feet under her next to me, and I want to reach out and pull her to me. "Um." She looks down.

"Oh, God, you're one of those," I say, sitting up now as she looks at me and is trying not to laugh. "You know." I point at her.

"What are you talking about?" She throws her head back, and I can see little red dots on her neck from my beard, and I want to lean over and mark her more.

"I'm talking about pineapple," I say the word, and I make a disgusted face. "Is there pineapple on that pizza?"

She laughs now a fully belly laugh. "Do you not like pineapple on pizza?"

"It's fruit," I say, and Ari arches her back, trying to roll out of my arm. I stop her and sit her up in my lap. "You can't put fruit on a pizza."

"It's not that bad," she says, and I groan out.

"You did," I say to her, standing Ari up in my lap. "Didn't you? You put pineapple on a pizza." I look down and I know that I'm going to have to eat the pizza with pineapple because that is what Candace would do for me.

"You can relax." She leans in and takes Ari, who smiles and then drools all over her. "I ordered meat lovers."

I put my hand on my heart. "I'm not going to lie," I say. "You just raised the bar from here." I motion my right hand above my head and then move it higher. "To here."

"Good to know that a way to your meter level is through meat." She laughs as she kisses Ari's neck, making her giggle. "What if I was vegan?" she asks, and I look at her.

"Then that's a you problem," I say, getting up and then bending to kiss her, and then I kiss Ari. "Now let's eat so we can take missy over here for her first walk." As I hold out my hand for her, she slips her hand in mine and gets up, putting Ari on her hip. I watch her walk over to the corner and open the door, bringing out a high chair. "You are the first woman I know who is equipped for a baby without having a baby."

"I'm an over-the-top aunt who didn't want her niece to get hurt. Besides, and also . . ." She puts Ari in the high chair and takes out a Ziplock bag. She opens it, taking toys out and putting them in front of Ari, who looks fascinated by them as she focuses to get one of the cushion blocks. "I figured if I had everything here that when Evan and Zara came to town, they would crash here, and I can get to spend time with Zoey."

"So it's a win-win." I smile and sit down in the chair next to Ari and her chair. I watch her carry the pizza box over and place it in the middle of the table, and then she hands me a white plate. "Thank you." I smile. She opens the box, and I gasp out loud. "What is on this pizza?"

"Pepperoni, sausage, bacon, ham, salami, onions, black olives, and cheese," she says, smiling as she grabs a piece of pizza and doesn't even use the plate before she just bites into it. "It's so good."

"You know what I said before?" I say, grabbing my own piece and taking a bite. "That you were sexy?"

"Um, yeah." She takes another bite.

"I lied," I say as I chew and take another bite. "You are the sexiest right now."

She throws her head back and laughs. "Good to know that all I need to be sexy is meat."

"Want to play a game?" I ask, and she looks at me.

"Like strip poker?" She winks at me, and I choke on the piece of pizza in my mouth. I put my hand in front of my mouth and cough. She snickers while I almost choke to death. My cock suddenly goes hard as I think of her naked in front of me. I get up and get a bottle of water from the fridge and take a long pull. "I almost choked to death," I say, still coughing.

"You were the one who mentioned playing a game." She points at me and takes another bite.

"And you assumed it would be strip poker?" I ask, and she shrugs.

"I figured it would be a good way to get you naked." She winks at me again, and this time, my cock gets so hard it hurts.

"I meant like speed round questions," I say, standing in the kitchen away from her. If I get close to her, I am going to throw her on the table and sink into her. Forget that my daughter is in the room.

"Oh, that sounds like fun," she says, taking another bite of her pizza, not even affected by the fact that I'm standing here with my hard-on. "I can go first since you seem to be . . ." She looks down at my cock and then smirks. "Having a hard situation."

"Funny," I say, laughing, and I walk back to the table. "Go."

"Favorite color," she asks me.

"Blue," I say off the top of my head, and I didn't even know it was my favorite. I laugh. "That is brand-new information to me." She looks at me with her head cocked to the side. "I never thought about it before, but now I had to answer, and blue was the first thing to come to my mind." I take a bite of the pizza. "What about you?"

"Pink." She smiles. "But not like pink bubble gum. Like a soft pink."

"Dogs or cats?" I watch her as she thinks about it.

"I think I'm more of a cat person. I had dogs, and Evan has two, who I used to watch when he went on the road." She shrugs. "I guess I like cats because they are so independent and don't really need you. What about you?"

"I always wanted a dog," I say. "But Cassie hated pets."

"So get one now," she says.

"I would, but I don't know if Ari is allergic or not," I say. "Favorite pastime?"

"Reading." She smiles. "All the romance books."

"Like *Fifty Shades*?" I ask, winking at her.

"There is more to that book than just the sex," she says, and I just cock my head to the side. "What is your favorite music?"

"Everything," I answer her. "In the locker room, either country or hip hop is playing. When it's my turn, I just hand it to the rookie, and he puts on whatever. What about you?"

"Same," she says, grabbing another slice. "But I got to love me some Drake."

I laugh now. "Favorite snack?"

"I'm a potato whore," she says. "Chips, fries, baked, scalloped, you name it, I'll eat it." She closes her eyes. "You?"

"When I'm training, I stick to no sugar and a clean diet," I say, and she nods. "I guess with Evan, you are used to it."

"Yeah, I remember he would come over to my house just so he can have Pop-Tarts and pretend that I didn't see it."

I laugh, thinking about my next question. "Beach or pool?"

"I'm a beach bum." She lights up. "I love the beach; the sand between my toes is heaven."

"Yet you live in Dallas." I shake my head.

"What about you?" she asks. I look at her to see her face when I say the next words.

"I've never been on a beach," I say, and her eyes widen. "I mean, I've seen the beach when we've played in LA and Florida, but I've never ever been on the beach."

"What about summer vacation or winter break?" she asks, and I shrug.

"It was never a must," I say. "Favorite drink?"

"Hmm, I mean, I will never say no to wine." She smiles and looks down. "But I'm a huge vodka cranberry girl."

"Beer?" I ask her.

"Allergic," she says, and now it's my turn to stare wide-eyed.

"But you have a whole fridge full," I say.

"Well, I can't drink it, but Evan was here, and there was a party," she says and then tosses down the crust of her second piece. "You?"

"I don't drink," I say. "I got drunk once and then figured it wasn't worth the four days of hell after."

"Wow," she says. "I say that every single time, but I

still drink the wine that is poured into my glass."

"What type of drunk are you?" I ask and then look at Ari, who calls my name.

"What do you mean?" Getting up, she walks over to get the bottle Ari didn't finish, then comes back and holds it to Ari's mouth. "I mean, do you get angry, or are you a giggle laughing kind?"

"Oh, that." She laughs. "I'm the giggle type. Unless I'm angry, then I think I'm Mike Tyson. But mostly, I think I can dance like JLo, but then I see the videos, and I look like Tina Fey." She sets the empty bottle on the table and looks at me, and I see the glitter in her eyes. I bring the bottle of water to my lips and take a sip right when she says the last part, and I spit out all over the place. "But mostly it makes me horny."

TWENTY-FIVE

CANDACE

"THE PHOTOGRAPHER IS going to be here at one," I say as he nibbles on my neck, and I have to close my eyes and ignore the tingling going on through my body. It's the second day that I am over to watch Ariella while he goes to the rink. "And I have someone coming today to apply for the nanny job."

"You." He kisses my neck and sucks in a bit. "Are." He moves up to nip at my jaw. "All that," he says. He slowly kisses his way toward my mouth, and then he claims my mouth, not giving me a chance to say another word. His tongue slips into my mouth, and my hands drop the pad I was holding to trail up his chest. Bringing him closer to me, I get on my tippy toes, turning my head to the side so I can get the kiss deeper. He groans into my mouth and picks me up. My hands wrap around his neck, and my legs wrap around his waist. I feel us moving, but I'm so into the kiss that I only notice when my ass is placed on a hard surface.

"Baby," he says, and I swear my toes curl and my whole body goes on alert. I always thought it was a stupid nickname, but now when he says it, his voice low and breathless, it's the hottest nickname I've ever heard.

"You need to go," I say as he pushes the hair away from my face. "Or else you'll get back late and then." I smile when he smiles at me.

"Fine," he says. "But tonight, we have to seriously make out." I shake my head.

"We did that last night," I remind him.

"Fine, we need to do it a lot then." He kisses me one more time.

"We did it a lot yesterday, bud," I say as he walks away from me, and I get off the counter. "That's the second time my ass has been on this counter." His laughter fills the room.

"Shit, I need something in the garage," he says, walking to the door, and I follow him. "I need to give them a shirt," he says as he moves boxes around.

"Why are your boxes in the garage?" I ask him as I lean against the doorjamb and watch him walk around the twenty or so cardboard boxes that he has in there.

"I didn't know if I wanted to unpack," he says, tossing one box to the side while he opens another one.

"You didn't know if you wanted to unpack?" I laugh now. "What does that mean?"

"It means I hate this house," he says to me, and then he just looks at me. "It's a monster of a house with seven bedrooms and ten bathrooms. Who needs all this space?"

I don't answer him as he just continues talking while he opens boxes. "It's so cold."

"Well, maybe if you unpack, it will feel more like home," I try to tell him, and he shakes his head.

"I never liked the house," he says when he opens the fifth box and looks through it. "I just got it because Cassie wanted it." He closes the box and then opens the next one. "I figured she'd spend most of the time in it, so I got it for her."

"So why don't you move?" He looks up at me at the same time that I hear Ari start to talk from her bedroom. "If you don't want to live in this house, move."

"But," he says, and I don't want to push it.

"I'm going to go get Ari," I say, turning to walk into the house, and I finally take a second to look around and see that nothing is personal here, nothing on the walls, nothing on a table. There are baby toys scattered around, and baby stuff in the kitchen. You know that a baby lives here, but that is all. I walk down the hallway, looking at the white walls, and finally see that it's bleak. Even Ari's bedroom is decorated and filled up, but there aren't little touches that say I live here. There are just things that say a child lives here. Their only pictures are the ones that are professionally taken, and it's only of Cassie. Ari sits up in the middle of her bed. "Good morning, sweet girl." I pick her up and kiss her neck. "Are we ready to slay the day, pretty girl?"

Walking over to the changing table, I put her down and unsnap her out of her pajamas, then change her diaper while pretending to eat her toes. "Okay, I'm out." I look over my shoulder at Ralph as he walks in and kisses my cheek and then bends to kiss Ari. "I'll be back soon. Be a good girl for Candace."

"Drive safe," I say, and he just waits there, looking at me.

"What?" I ask him.

"Give me a kiss," he orders. I laugh, but he comes forward and kisses my lips. "Tonight, we have to go over the rules."

"The rules?" I ask him, confused.

"Yeah, rule one, always kiss before one of us leaves," he says, and I lean forward and kiss his neck, smelling his soap.

"Is that so?" I ask him, shaking my head. "I can't wait to hear rule two."

"Oh, that is for another time," he says. "I'm going to be late."

"Get out of here," I say and dress Ariella in another pajama and start the day with her. "Do you want to take a walk?" I ask her while I sit down with her and her bottle. I take her on a two-hour walk, and get back at the same time as Ralph pulls up in the driveway. I can tell just with the way his hair curls around the front of his head that he didn't shower.

He smiles at the both of us, coming closer, and I hold up my hand. "Shower, then kisses."

"Rule number two." He laughs at me, stopping beside me. "Always kiss when arrives regardless." He bends, and I kiss him even though he smells.

"I would like to counter on rule two," I say, and he

laughs.

"Got to go shower. The photographer will be here soon," he says, and I just shake my head.

I walk in the house with Ari still in the stroller, grabbing some water and then sitting on the stool to go through my emails. I'm answering an email when the doorbell rings, and I look over to see if Ari wakes up. She doesn't, so I slip off the stool and walk over to the door. Opening it, I see Monroe, the photographer.

"Well, there she is." He walks in with two bags, and air kisses my cheeks. "I came a bit early to set up," he says, and I just smile at him.

"I don't know what you were thinking," I say as we walk into the house. "I was thinking of some shots of him working out. A couple of shots of him doing dad things."

"Yes," Monroe says, putting down his bag, and Ariella wakes up screaming.

Walking over to her, I pick her up, and she lays her head on my shoulder as I rub her back. "It's okay, baby girl," I say. "Are you going to say hello to Monroe?" I ask her, and she turns her head but still leaves her head buried in the nook of my neck.

"She is a beautiful girl," he says. "And those eyes. Those eyes are like a beautiful blue sky." I smile at him and then look over his shoulder at Ralph who comes out wearing a shirt and shorts, his hair wet from the shower.

"Hey," he says, smiling at Monroe and then walks toward me. "There is my girl," he says. Ari lifts her head as soon as she hears his voice, and she smiles around her pacifier. "I missed you." He grabs her out of my arms, and I smile at them.

"He is much better looking than I thought," Monroe says and winks at Ralph, making me roll my lips. "Definitely want some shirtless shots. Maybe of him running on the treadmill."

"I can get you some baby oil," I say, trying not to laugh as Monroe's eyes widen, and Ralph side-eyes me. "We should rent a wind machine."

"That would be amazing," Monroe says, and I can't help but laugh now. Ralph shakes his head, and I throw my head back and laugh. "Okay, I'm going to get set up. I have a list of things that Becca sent me and also a couple of things that Candace suggested."

"Do I have time to eat before we start?" Ralph asks, and Monroe shakes his head no. "If you want, we can start in the gym. You can go set up; it's down that hallway." Monroe nods his head, grabs his bags, and walks down the hallway.

"I have your lunch in the fridge," I say, walking over and taking it out of the fridge.

"I can do that," he says, and I shake my head at him.

"Spend some quality time with Ari," I say, heating his food and then bringing it to him as he talks to Ari about his day. "Here you go," I say, placing the food at the side of him. "I was wondering," I start to ask him, and he looks up at me. "If it would be okay to bring Ari to my house while you do the whole photo shoot thing."

"You don't want to stay here?" he asks, taking a piece of chicken and chewing.

"I was thinking I could take her in the pool, and we can be out of the way," I say, and he smiles at me.

"Rule number three," he starts, and I groan and roll my eyes. "You are only allowed to wear a bikini in your backyard when there is no one else but me there."

"You're kidding, right?" I lean on the counter. "I don't own anything other than bikinis," I say, laughing. "I have cheeky or thong." I wink at him, and now it's his turn to groan.

"Parka," he says to me. "Okay, why don't you go, and then I can come over and cook you dinner."

"You're going to cook me dinner?" I look over at him and then walk to his side just to be next to him. "You don't have to do that."

"I know," he says, grabbing another piece of chicken. "I know that I don't have to." He smiles at me, leaning forward to kiss my lips. "I want to."

"Then that sounds like an amazing plan," I say. "Maybe, well, if you stay late enough, and Miss Ariella is sleeping, we could, I don't know." I wrap my arms around his shoulders and lean in to whisper in his ear. "We could go skinny-dipping." His fork falls onto the plate, and he puts his head back.

"If you don't step away from me, I'm going to go meet Monroe with tentage, and it's going to be awkward for both of us."

"What do you say, baby girl?" I look at Ari. "Want to go in the water?" She hits Ralph in the chest and calls his name. "Yeah, I get it. He's yours." I smile at her and then look back at Ralph, who just looks at me. He leans in and kisses me softly. "She's going to have to share," I whisper in his ear, making him laugh.

TWENTY-SIX

Ralph

"I JUST NEED one more shot," Monroe says of me holding the coffee cup while sitting on the couch with a pair of skates on the floor beside me and a diaper bag beside me. "Look here," he says, and I look over at him. "That is going to get all the women." He smirks at me, looking through the shots that he got.

He's been here for two hours, and I'm over this whole thing. I swear he must have taken a million pictures. We started with me on the treadmill and then moved over to the bike. He got me to pose with my hockey equipment and then shirtless for a couple of them. I felt so uncomfortable, but I did it because he knew what he was doing. I also did it because Becca was now here telling me I had no choice.

"That was the best one," Becca says, standing behind Monroe. "That shot is going to get you onto billboards."

"Whatever," I say, leaning forward and picking up my

skates and bringing them to the garage. I clean up the mess that I made while shooting as Monroe starts to pack up his stuff. He shakes my hand when he leaves, then turns to mention to Becca that he will be sending her the proofs in the next couple of days.

"Thank you so much, Monroe," he says. When he leaves, I'm itching to leave with him. "I have a feeling a couple of those shots are going to be the signing point," she says to me, sitting on the couch when she hears the front door slam shut. "Where is your sitter?"

"I fired her." I walk to the fridge and grab a water bottle. "A couple of days ago."

"I'm sorry, what?" Becca says, leaning forward in her chair and looking at me. "Where the hell is Ari?"

"Candace took her over to her house," I say, sitting on the couch, and I watch the way Becca is processing all of this.

"Why the fuck did you fire your babysitter? It took forever to find her," Becca asks, ignoring the beeping phone in her hand.

"I know," I say. "But she showed up here out of the blue ready to cook me dinner while dressed like a hooker."

"Oh my God." Becca puts her hand to her mouth. "Did you have the locks changed?"

"Yesterday," I say. "Candace did that, and she has a meeting with a new babysitter today. So I have to get over there."

"So you fire your babysitter and call in Candace?" She just eyes me as she asks me the questions.

"She was here when it happened." I am not hiding it from her. "I'm dating her."

"I'm sorry." She shakes her head. "What?"

I watch her as I say the words. "We are dating."

"I don't think that is a good idea," Becca says softly.

"I don't care," I say. "It's a great idea to me. She's amazing, and she's smart, and she's beautiful."

"Yes to all of those things along with other things, but you dating her."

"I'm not going to lie. It took me by surprise also." I lean forward. "I mean, it's not like I was on Grinder looking for chicks."

"You'll have a hard time finding chicks on Grinder, Ralph, since that's for gay men," she says, and my eyes open wide while she laughs. "Jesus, can you imagine?"

"I can't." I shake my head. "I want to sell the house," I say, and she stops laughing.

"But . . . ." She looks around.

"You know I hate this house," I say. "You know I've hated this house from the beginning."

"Yeah, but I figured with Cassie gone and with her being here," she starts to say, and I shake my head.

"I want a house, a home. I want a smaller house with three bedrooms and normal amount of bathrooms. I don't need a cinema room or a fucking rock wall swimming pool that I haven't ever been in."

"If you're sure, I actually know someone who is looking for this exact style house," she says.

"I don't even want to make money from the sale."

"Well, now, I'm going to stop you right there." She

holds up her hands. "I know you might not want it, but I want it, so I'm going to have someone come and appraise the house, and then I'll talk to my client."

"Is he an NHL player?" I ask, and she shakes her head.

"New up-and-coming golfer," she says. "Wife is a debutante who loves big and bigger."

"Gross," I say, getting up. "And grosser."

"Meanwhile, I'll get you with a realtor, and you and she can chat," she says. "I'm still in a little bit of shock over you and Candace." She smiles now. "You know that she doesn't date her clients, right?" I nod my head. "The rookie," she says. "Vincent, he chased her hard last year at the NHL awards, like hard. Like roses to her room, waiting in the lobby for her."

"Really?" I ask, shocked but not surprised.

"Yeah, it was funny watching Evan glare at him." She laughs. "Then the whole Stone family followed suit."

"Oh, Jesus, he never stood a chance." I shake my head happy that he didn't and suddenly wanting to slash his stick for even thinking about her like that.

"Are you sure about this?" she asks, standing. "I mean, you know I love you, and I will be behind you whatever you decide, but—"

"It's fucking nuts." I run my hand through my hair. "But I tell her things." I look at her. "Things that I don't tell anyone, and with her, all I want to do is tell her more things, tell her everything."

"I'm happy for you." She smiles and comes over, giving me a hug. "If anyone deserves even a little happy, it's you."

"Thank you." I hug her back, and the minute she leaves, I'm jumping into my truck, and I'm on my way over to Candace. I pull up, seeing that there is a car there, and I wonder if it's the nanny. I knock on the door, and two seconds later, the door swings open, and I stand here with my mouth open.

Candace is in front of me with a white bikini top and a bottom that looks like it's too small with pineapples all over it. She wears a long white button-down shirt over her, but it's open, so you see all her skin. "What the hell are you doing?" I say, pushing her into the house and then looking around now to see if anyone saw her. "You can't answer the door naked."

"Oh, for the love." She rolls her eyes, and I see that her hair is tied up on top of her head, and she has a little bit of a tan. "I was with Bernadette," she says, turning to walk into her house, and I see her ass cheeks through the white shirt.

"Baby," I call her name, and she looks over her shoulder at me. "You need to go get dressed."

"I'll button the front if it makes you feel better," she says, not stopping to walk and not walking to her bedroom as she walks into the living room and I see an older lady sitting on the floor with Ari as she sings to her and claps her hands together as Ari gives her the biggest smile. "Bernadette," Candace says. "This is Ralph, Ari's dad."

I walk over, and Ari sees me. She whines a bit until I pick her up, and then she smiles. "Hello there, pretty girl," I say and see that she is in a one-piece blue swimsuit with white polka dots. "Did you go in the pool?"

"No, we didn't," Candace says. "We took a nap, and then we watched some *Baby Einstein.*" I look over at her. "I wanted the sun to go down a bit." I don't think my heart can get anymore full at the moment.

I look at Bernadette. "So Candace tells me that you've been watching kids for a while."

She fills me in about all the work that she's done, and who she's worked for, and I'm shocked to find out she worked with Manning's children. We make a plan for her to try it tomorrow during the day with Candace there. I smile at her and walk her to the front door and close the door behind her, then turn to Candace. "Rule number four."

"Rule number four, don't bug me about my swim-suits." She walks up to me and gets up on her tippy toes and kisses my lips. "Let's go into the pool, baby girl." She grabs Ari from me and then turns to walk away from me. "You need to get the pole down before you come outside."

I look down, seeing my cock hard. "You showed boobage. What did you expect?" She throws her head back and laughs, and I watch her walk away. I follow her outside where she has everything set up for Ari. She puts a hat on her head and then grabs the green and yellow blow-up pool chair for Ari, with its own umbrella to stop the sun. She unbuttons the shirt and shrugs it off, and all I can do is look at her. Her tits are pressed together with her bikini top, and it looks like it's tied in the middle of them. Her stomach flat with her long tanned legs, she turns around and walks to the pool, and I see the thong bottom piece where it shows her perfect fucking ass. An ass that I want to put my hands all over. "You coming in with us?"

"Oh, I want to come all right," I mumble, and she laughs at me as she walks in the pool. I pull off my shirt and walk into the pool with her. "This water is like a bath."

"I know." She looks at me as she puts Ari's toes in the water. "I turned up the heater when I got home." She takes her hand and pours water on Ari to make sure she likes the water, but Ari's feet are already going a mile a minute as she splashes. She puts Ari in the chair, and she splashes the water all over herself.

I walk over to them, getting into the water on my knees in front of Ari. "Are you having fun?" I ask and then look over at Candace, who also sinks down in the water. "I missed you," I say to her as I pull her closer to me. I put her in front of me, boxing her in with my arms while holding on to Ari's chair while she splashes her hand in the water.

"Did you now?" Candace says, turning in my arms. I feel her hands go to my waist. I stand now, holding onto Ari with one hand. Candace stands, too, and I swear I see her nipples through that white bikini top that I'm going to fucking burn tonight. Her hands don't leave my waist. "I missed you, too," she whispers, and I swear if it were up to my cock, he would be joining this party. "I kept thinking . . ." She stands right in front of me now, pressing herself into me. "About tonight."

"Did you?" I ask, one hand holding onto Ari while the other grabs her ass, squeezing it. "Rule number five," I say, leaning down close to her ear. "You are to never wear this out of the bedroom." I nip her earlobe. "Or I'm going to make this ass sting."

TWENTY-SEVEN

CANDACE

"WHERE THE HELL is my phone?" I search and walk toward where the ringing is coming from. "I'm coming," I say to the person who has called me twice in a row now, yet I still haven't found it. I toss the clothes that are all over my bed and finally find it right when it stops ringing.

Looking down, I see I missed a call from Layla, so I call her back right away, and she answers on the first ring. "Well, well, well," she sings. "Look who is alive."

I laugh at her. "What are you talking about?" I fold the clothes on my bed now.

"I haven't heard from you in forever." I roll my eyes at the exaggeration.

"I spoke to you two days ago," I remind her.

"You spoke to me six days ago when you had shit all over you and a screaming child," she reminds me, and I stop folding midway.

"No," I say, thinking back. "I'm sure that was two days ago."

"Do you even know what day it is?" She laughs.

I start to count the days in my head. "It's Friday." My hand falls in my lap. "Shit, sorry it's been a crazy week."

"You don't say." I hear the tapping of a pen.

"Yeah, we finally got the babysitter down." I smile when I think about how amazing Bernadette is. I'm not going to lie; I was on the fence even though I know she came highly recommended, and she was amazing with Ari. She took care of her, but I was so scared that Ari wouldn't feel comfortable, but thirty minutes in, I knew she was the best thing for her. She had a way to hold her when she got whiny, and she made her smile all the time, and she sang to her all the time. I'm not even going to deny that I put a baby cam into the house so I can watch her.

"We?" She chuckles. "So we are a we now?"

"I mean, we are spending time together," I start to say, and she groans. "Okay, fine, I like him."

"What are we, in middle school?" Layla says. "Did you bang him yet?"

"No," I answer, shocked, and it's her who gasps out.

"You've been with him for two weeks now," she says.

"I have not been with him for that long," I say, thinking. "I mean, we've been—"

"Listen, it's been longer than a week." She points out, making me think about how long it's actually been. "Regardless, have you done anything?"

"I mean we've made out," I say, and I smile. We've

spent night after night making out on my couch or his couch. Actually, yesterday he spent the night after we fell asleep on the couch and only woke at five a.m. when Ari cried. At that point, it was silly for him to leave.

"Oh my God, you are in middle school." I can see her now with a disgusted face on her. "You need to get in there and ride the D."

"Oh my God, why are we even having this conversation?" I ask, and I don't wait for her to answer. "Is that what you were calling for?"

"Well, it was for that and also to pick a date to go shopping for the gala." I close my eyes, inwardly swearing to myself. How could I have forgotten about the gala next week? It's a gala that brings in money for kids to get lunch at school. Something that I didn't even think about until Manning joined forces with it.

"I think Zara sent me a couple of choices," I say. "I can send you the pictures, and you can choose."

"That would be even better," she says. "Are you bringing a plus one now that you are a we?"

"I don't know," I answer her, and then I hear the doorbell. "I wonder if he even wants to go."

"Well, either way, I'll be your wingman," she says, and the doorbell rings again.

"You mean, I'll be your wingman until you get your prey and then leave." I laugh and open the door and stand here open-mouthed. "Um, can I call you back?" I don't even wait for her to answer before my hand comes down. "What are you doing here?" I ask Ralph as he stands there dressed in jeans and a white polo, holding a bouquet of pink peonies in his hand.

"I'm here to take you out on a date." He smiles at me, walking in and stopping in front of me. My hand is still holding on to the door as he bends and kisses my lips. "Hi," he whispers, and I wait for his kiss. His kiss that I always think I'm going to be used to, yet makes me giddy every single time. It could be him simply pecking my neck or kissing my forehead, but I could spend days and days lost in his touch.

"Hi," I whisper back to him as he snakes a hand around my waist, pulling me close to him, and I immediately go to my tippy toes. "I thought," I start to say, and I have to stop when his lips fall on mine. His tongue enters my mouth, and I suddenly want to get him naked. He closes the door behind him.

"These are for you." He hands me the flowers. I grab them and bring them to my nose. "Thank you. Where is Ari?"

"She's with Bernadette," he says. "I wanted to take you on a date." I smile now at him as he stands there with his hands in his back pockets. "Fuck, I didn't think I would be nervous."

"What are you nervous about, silly?" I kiss his jaw. "It's me." I turn and walk into the house with him following me.

"What are you wearing?" he asks, and I look back at him, confused.

"Jeans." I stop walking when I see his eyes roam up and down.

"But why are they so tight?" he asks, coming close to

me and putting his hands on my hips. "Did you go out wearing this today?"

"I went to Target," I say. "And the post office."

"Wearing these?" His voice goes low as he looks at my ass.

"It's jeans." My voice comes out soft, and I don't move as he moves his hand down and cups my ass. We've been really good with our hands, and both of us have not gone further than groping each other's ass. I am not going to lie; a couple of times, I want to feel his cock through his pants, but I refrained myself.

"It's jeans that leave little to the imagination," he says, and I turn around now.

"I can take them off if you want." I watch his eyes turn a light blue to a crystl blue, and his mouth opens and then closes. I put the flowers on the counter, and in one motion, I take my shirt off, leaving me in just my white lace push-up demi bra, making my b cup boobs look like full C cups.

"Candace." He doesn't just say my name; he growls it out.

"What would you do," I say when I unbuckle the button to my jeans. "If I said." I pull the zipper down, and I can see his fingertips on his hips turning white. "I didn't want to go out." I shimmy the jeans over my hips, pushing them down. "And I just wanted to." I step out of my jeans, and I stand here in the matching lace thong, leaving nothing to the imagination. "To stay here with you tonight." I walk to him and it takes all the courage in the world. "On the couch." I pick up his shirt and feel his skin under it, I get up on my tippy toes and I see his restraint tethering on going over the cliff. "Or even in my bed," I say right before I kiss under his jaw softly.

"Candace," he says my name through clenched teeth. "I'm trying really hard right now to be good." His hands still grip his hips as I move my hands up on his chest. My fingers tracing each defined muscle that he has. "Respectful," he says out in almost a whisper and my body tingles.

"I want you to pick me up and carry me over to whatever surface you want and I want you to have your way with me." I picture all the ways I want him to touch me, my hand slides off his chest and I finally get the courage to feel his dick through his pants. I palm him through his pants, and I swear he stops breathing. "I want you to."

I don't finish because he, picks me up by my waist, and my ass hits the cold counter, putting my whole body on high alert. "You know what I want to do?" he asks, and I open my legs for him to stand in the middle of them and I'm hoping to God he touches me soon, or I'm going to look like a hussy while I finish myself off. "I want to rip your bra off." His hands cup up and push down the bra under my tits. "And I want to bite." He leans forward and takes a nipple into his mouth, and my head falls back. "This nipple," he says of the nipple that he is now biting down, and my hips thrust up as he moves to the other nipple, giving it the same attention. I groan out and I swear I can come just from him playing with my nipples. "After that I want to eat your pussy like it's my last meal." I watch him bend down and push the lace to the side, and he doesn't mess around. His tongue comes out, and he licks me up. My hands lean back, and I hold the counter or I'm going to fall back.

"I want you to watch me make you come." He looks up before he buries his face between my legs. He's tongue fucking me while his thumb plays with my clit. I want to spread my legs as wide as they can go. "Heaven," he says between lapping me and sucking my clit into his mouth. My arms feel like jelly as they tremble. He leaves my pussy and stands up, his mouth landing on mine as I taste myself on him. He wraps his arm around my waist, and I feel his other hand rub up and down. I stop kissing him when the moan rips through me. "Wet," he says right before his two fingers slide into me. My ass flies off the counter, and he grabs me, holding it in place as he finger fucks me with his face buried into my neck. "I'm going to make you come so hard," he says and just breathes on my neck. I wrap one hand around his neck and open my mouth to moan, and he devours my mouth, his hand moving in and out so fast. I'm getting so wet I can feel it running down my thighs. "All fucking night," he says. "I'm going to make you call out my name." I can feel myself about to come.

"I'm so close," I say, biting his lower lip as he looks down at his hand.

"Watch my hand," he orders me, and I look down to see his hand. But I can't control my body this time. I start to fuck his fingers back, I start to move with him to make sure that I come. "Fuck," he says, knowing I'm close. "So fucking tight around my fingers." I have never had this overwhelming sensation before. I've never been this out of control before. I can't stop my body.

"That's it, baby," he says. "Come on, that's it, baby, squeeze my fingers, come for me, baby." His tongue licks my lower lip. I want to watch, I really do, but I close my eyes as I jump off the ledge, and in the middle of my kitchen, I come harder than I've ever come before in my life, with his name on my lips.

TWENTY-EIGHT

Ralph

HOLY SHIT I think to myself as I finger fuck Candace
on her counter. I've never lost control like this. I'm the
calm and collected one. But she undressed in front of
me, and I snapped and lost control. On her counter, I de-
voured her. I'm about to tell her I'm sorry for not bringing her to her bedroom and laying her on her bed, when
she turns her head and her tongue slides into my mouth.
Her hands go from my neck down to my chest and then I
feel them at the button of my jeans. I want to stop her, but
her hands move at record speed, almost as if she's afraid
something is going to stop it. "Candace," I whisper her
name as she pulls my pants down over my hips.

"I need you to move." She pushes me, and my fingers
slip out of her. I pick up my fingers and clean them off in
my mouth. "Jesus, I think I just came again." She moves
one of her hands between her legs and moves it side to
side. "Move," she says to me, and I just look at her as she

gets down off the counter and gets on her knees in front of me. She grips my cock in her hands, and I swear I'm going to come in her hands from just touching me.

"Baby." I look down at her. "You don't have to," I say and she covers my cock with her mouth and I stop talking. "Why don't we . . ."

"I'm going to suck your cock. I don't care if I'm in the middle of my kitchen or in the bathroom," she says, licking up the shaft. "Bottom line, your cock is going to fuck my mouth." I don't say another word since she swallows as much of my cock as she can. She closes her eyes as she takes my cock deeper and deeper into her mouth. Her small hand moving along with her mouth, I move her hair and hold the back of her head, and I slowly fuck her mouth.

"Baby," I say, reaching down and rolling a nipple between my fingers, and she moans. I see that her other hand is between her legs, and it's the hottest thing I've ever seen. "You playing with your clit?" I ask her as I go deeper into her mouth, and she rolls her tongue around the head of my cock.

"Slip a finger inside yourself," I say, watching her finger disappear inside her. "That's my pussy," I say as she squeezes my cock tighter, and I can feel myself getting ready to come. My balls start to get tight. "Fuck, I'm there," I say, and she just moves her hand faster and faster. I want to pull away from her when I come, but she won't release my cock, and I come down her throat. She swallows all of it and then she moves her mouth away from my cock, and I see that she is still playing with herself. I touch her face, and she looks at me. "You want to come?" I ask, and she nods her head. "Want to come on my cock?" She just shudders. "I'm not fucking you in the middle of your kitchen," I say, pulling her up and then bending to take a nipple into my mouth. "The first time I fuck you, I want it to be with you lying down." I suck the other nipple. "Spread eagle." I pick up her hand and lick the finger that was in her pussy. "Pussy glistening and ready for me."

"If that isn't in the next four seconds," she says, "I'm going to push you down and take that cock in me." She holds my cock that is not even ready to go down. "So we better get my back on a bed." She turns and leads me to her room, and I stop for a second, and she turns back to look over her shoulder. "I'm losing my patience."

I laugh and get down on my knees and bite her ass cheek. "That looks much better," I say. "My mark on you." I squeeze her ass now and then slap it. "Get your ass on the bed," I order her, and she almost runs to the bed. I follow her, taking off my shirt in the process and tossing it to the side, kicking off my shoes. "Naked," I say as she rips off her thong, tossing it aside and then she slips off her bra. "Now, spread eagle," I say, and she walks to her bed and gets in the middle of it, and she does exactly like I told her. "Fuck," I say as I kick off my pants and lean over to get a condom.

"You better hurry up." She lifts her hips. "Or I'll start without you."

"Yeah?" I say, getting on the bed and grabbing my cock in my hand. "And how would you do that?"

"I'd make you watch me fuck my vibrator." She moves one hand to her pussy. "So you better get to—" She stops talking when I push her hand away from her pussy, and my mouth covers it. "Oh, yeah," she says, and my cock is done waiting.

"Next time," I say, ripping open the condom. "It'll be slower." I take the condom out and sheath myself.

"If you don't get that cock in me, there might not be a next time." I take my cock and rub it through her slit. "Put it in," she moans and pleads.

I slide into her as slowly as I can, the both of us hissing and groaning. "Fuck." I stop once I'm balls deep in her. "How do you want it?" I ask her as she pulls her legs back, and I slowly pull out of her and then enter her again.

"Hard," she says. "Hard and dirty."

"You are going to be the death of me," I say, slamming into her.

"Harder," she says after I slam into her. She takes her hand and slips a finger into her mouth and then moves it to her clit. "Faster." I go in slow. "Would you fucking move!" she almost cries out.

"I am moving," I say. "As fast as I want to move." I pinch her nipples. "You are going to get my cock how I want to give you my cock." I slam into her, and I pull right back out and slam into her again.

"Ralph, I'm not going to break," she says, moving her legs back, and I sink in deeper. I lose it then and thrust into her over and over again, my balls slapping her ass. "Yes," she says, pinching one nipple while she plays with her clit. "I'm going to come."

I fall onto her, my hands going to the side of her body as I fuck her as hard as I can. She arches her back and tries to fuck me back, but I'm going so fast she can't keep up with it. Finally, I feel her pussy squeeze my cock, and my thrusts get shorter and shorter until her head falls back, and she comes all over my cock. I don't stop the pace as I follow her over, and I groan out as I fill the condom.

I fall to the side, taking her with me, the both of us panting, our body slick with sweat. "That was . . ." she starts. "I want to do it again." She kisses my neck. "This time, I want to be on top."

"I'll do it as many times as you want to do it," I say and then kiss her lips. I slip out of her and walk to her bathroom and dispose of the condom. When I walk back into the room, I grab my phone and dial Bernadette, who answers right away.

"Hey, I'll be over in about thirty minutes," I say. "Can you make sure that you pack the diaper bag for the night with bottles and diapers?" I hang up and look at Candace who just lies on the bed on her side.

"I have to go get Ari," I say, and she gets up on her elbows. "Then I was thinking we can put her to bed."

"And then I can do all the dirty things that I want to do to you?" She gets up. "I'll come get her with you." She stands next to me. "Also, I would like to pour water down your chest and see if it flows all the way down." She uses her finger to trace my abs. "I can do this while my mouth is on your cock." My cock suddenly decides that it wants to play again. "We can do the logistics then."

She walks over and bends down to grab her thong, and I pounce on her, grabbing another condom. I slap her ass, my print now on one side while my teeth mark the other. "Don't move," I say as I put the condom on. She holds the bed as my hands grab her hips and pull her up just a bit so I can sink my cock into her.

"Not fair," she says, looking over her shoulder. "I was supposed to ride you next." I slap her ass again, and her eyes close. "Again," she says, and I pull out and slam into her, slapping her ass again then rubbing it. I feel her hands grab my balls from under me, and I know she is ready to play with herself. I grab both her tits in my hands and squeeze them as I fuck her, the both of us panting and not saying anything as she plays with herself.

"I'm coming," she finally says. "Don't stop." I couldn't even if I wanted to, and for the second time in twenty minutes, I'm coming in her. I slow my pace and let go of her tits, and she falls on the bed. "You have to promise me," she says, looking over her shoulder, "that you will do that to me every time I'm naked and bent over." I throw my head back and laugh. "I'm not kidding. I don't care if I'm in the middle of whatever. If I bend over, you have to fuck me just like that." I slip out of her.

"What if I don't?" I ask. She stands up straight and walks over to her side table and pulls out her vibrator. I glare at her.

"Then you are going to sit in that chair." She points at the chair in the corner. "And watch me fuck myself."

"You're playing with fire," I say, walking to her and

grabbing the vibrator in my hand. "This can give you pleasure for a couple of minutes. But my mouth, my fingers, and my cock can make you come for hours." Her eyes light up. "Rule number six, the next time this is in you, it's me that is fucking you with it."

TWENTY-NINE

CANDACE

"I'LL GET HER," I say from beside Ralph as he slips out of me. We have just finished another marathon of sex. I slip out of the bed, and I swear I can still feel him in me.

"What's the matter?" he asks, getting up on his elbow.

"I still feel you in me," I say, and he laughs.

"Next time, don't tell me harder and then mock me that you can't feel it," he says, getting up and going to the bathroom. I slip his T-shirt on and walk to the bedroom, hearing Ari scream. "Good morning." She sits in the middle of the crib waving her hands up and down. I pick her up and kiss her neck, then walk back out to my bedroom. "Where's your daddy?"

"I'm here," he says, coming out of the bathroom dressed in his boxers. "Good morning," he says, reaching for her.

"I'm going to go make coffee," I say. Walking into the

kitchen, I see that the stool he leaned me over last night after we finished snacking is still on the floor. I smile as I make coffee and open the shades. Taking a bottle out of the fridge for Ari, I prepare it so it's ready when he comes into the kitchen a couple of minutes later.

"Thank you, baby," he says, kissing my lips. I clean up the mess we left in the kitchen. I spot an open condom wrapper in the middle of the kitchen and then look over at him as he picks another one off the couch.

"The condom wrappers are around the house like it's confetti." I walk around, picking up six.

"I need to get another box." He winks at me. "Maybe even two."

I don't tell him that I'm on the pill. "I can order them in bulk if you want," I say, pinning my hair on top of my head. "Do you want coffee?"

"Yes, and then I want you to come sit with us on the couch," he says. I make two cups of coffee, then walk over to the couch, seeing Ari lying on the couch on her own with Ralph holding her bottle. "Here you go." I hand him his coffee, and I laugh when I see my teeth marks near his nipple.

"What are your plans for the day?" he asks when I sit down and look down at my legs.

"I swear you would think I went to war," I say, counting five bite marks that I have on my legs.

"That's what you get when you sit on my face and don't listen to orders." He winks at me, and I am not even going to lie—I loved every fucking second of it.

"I have to try on dresses," I say, "for the gala next

week. Are you going?"

"You think you're going without me?" he asks, leaning back on the couch.

"Well, I was going before you came into the picture," I say. "And I didn't really know what the rule was."

"The rule is I'm by your side," he says without thinking twice. "Unless you don't want me to be."

"Of course not," I say. "I'm more worried about you. You have to keep some of your life private."

"I'm not saying that I'm going to go and bang you in the coatroom," he says, and I smirk.

"Fuck." He looks at me. "You would let me bang you in the coatroom?"

"I mean, if it's quick, and we are hidden." I shrug. I don't tell him that I have never even thought about doing it. But with his hands on me, I know that I would not say no. "So I will get a loose dress just in case."

He shakes his head. "I already told Bernadette about it, so she knows it will be a late night."

"I usually go with Layla," I say, taking a sip of coffee. "Are you okay with that?"

"I don't think I have ever met her," he says. "I used to attend these things to show my face, take a couple of pictures, and then I'd duck out."

"Did Cassie not like them?" I ask, and it hurts my heart to think about it.

"She never came to one." He takes his cup of coffee. "She never thought she fit in, so I would go without her."

"That's too bad," I say and then look at him. "Are you going to skate today?"

"No," he says. "I planned to take the day off, thinking we could spend the day together."

Smiling, I put my cup of coffee on the table and then cuddle up to him. "I like that," I say. "Do you have enough milk for her?" I ask.

"We can take a drive and go get some," he says.

"Or," I say. "I can watch her, and you can go and pack a bag and spend the weekend here." I look up at him. "With me."

"Why do I feel like a piece of meat?" He bends down, kissing me.

"Because I plan to be using your meat." I cup his thick cock. "A lot." Ari sits up now and looks at us with a gummy smile. "Do you want to get changed and go for a walk?" I ask her, getting up and picking her up. "Go get dressed and get your things. Hopefully when you get back, she'll be napping, and I can use your meat." I walk away from him and change her going into my bedroom and placing her on the floor while I get dressed. Ralph kisses me and Ari right before he leaves, then he comes back and gives me a really good kiss, squeezing my ass right before finally walking out.

The number of bite marks and love bites I have is close to twenty-five. My breasts look like I was attacked by bees. I slip on jean shorts but have to change them out for pants when I look at myself in the mirror and can see all the marks. Slipping on loose brown linen pants and a white tank top, I walk back to the kitchen to get my phone. When we finally start to take a walk, she sits in the stroller and babbles. The three of us spend the whole day in my house. She naps twice, and while she naps, we get lost in each other. I think my moaning woke her up at least once. We visit the pool again, and when she finally goes down for the night, we head back to the pool this time naked.

The whole week we get into the routine of him getting up and taking Ari back to his house. He goes on the ice and then comes back to my house where we shower together, and then he leaves to pick up Ari after we both get our fill. The nights are usually spent watching television, and it usually escalates with me riding his face or riding him. "What's going to happen tomorrow?" he asks when we crawl into bed.

"What do you mean?" I cuddle up to him, and my body just becomes alive when he's around.

"I mean after the event. I don't want to wake Ari up and drag her here," he says, kissing my lips.

"I can come to your place if you want." I try not to think that it's Cassie bed that I'm going to be sleeping in. "Apparently, the glam squad is going to be here at three, and the car is going to be here at six."

"Is Layla coming over?" he asks, and I nod. "Did you decide what you are wearing?"

"Yes." Kissing him, I roll him over on his back and straddle him. I lean over him and grab a condom from the side table. "Now can you do me a favor?" I say, rolling the condom over his cock.

As I slide onto him, his hands come up and roll my nipples. "What is it?"

"Do you think you can fuck me hard enough that I'm

going to feel you in me tomorrow night?" I ask as I rise and fall.

"Only one way to find out." He flips me onto my back and fucks me with everything he has, and it's wonderful.

"I need to soak in the tub when you leave," I say when we have coffee the next morning, sitting down and wincing.

"Still have another round to go when she takes her nap," he says and winks at me. I think he's joking, but when he bends me over, grabs the hair from my neck, and pulls me back while he slams into me over and over, I know he came to play. "That should keep you until later," he says when he pulls out of me. I want to say that it will, but ten minutes before Ari wakes up, I straddle him one last time. I kiss them goodbye, and when they leave, it hurts my heart to be away from them. I swallow it down, though, because it's silly.

When Layla gets here, she brings a bottle of champagne, and I literally wince when I sit down. "Looks like someone finally got it in."

"Oh, I got it in alright," I say. "The man is a beast."

She sits on the stool and then looks at me. "Did you fuck on this stool?" I nod as I take a sip of champagne, and she gets up and walks to the one next to me.

"That one, too," I say, and her eyes travel to the other one with a question. "Yup."

"Jesus Christ," she says, taking a sip of her champagne.

"I wouldn't sit on the couch either or the counter." I point at the counter. "That wall." I point at the one he picked me up and had his way with me. "He didn't even take my clothes off." I smile. "The table also."

"Okay, how about this." She goes to the kitchen and grabs some Lysol wipes. "Where haven't you had sex?"

"The crib," I say, and we both laugh.

THIRTY

RALPH

"I SHOULDN'T BE home that late," I say to Bernadette when I hand over Ari. Ari smiles at her and then looks at me. "She had a bottle at three," I say, and she smiles at me.

"We are going to be fine," Bernadette says. "Why don't you go out and have some fun? Enjoy your night." I lean forward and kiss Ari on the cheek, telling her to be good before walking outside to the waiting car. The driver opens the door for me, and I get in, the tie tight around my neck. I haven't worn a suit in forever, and even when I tried it on last week, I knew it was going to be tighter than before. I've gotten a touch bigger with all the training I'm doing. We make our way over to Candace's house, and I can't wait to see her. I hated saying goodbye to her when I left. It just felt wrong. I wanted to get ready with her. I wanted to sit with Ari on the bed while she got her shit done, and then I wanted to mess her hair up.

When we pull up to the house, I get out of the car, and I'm almost running. Should I ring, should I knock? I don't even know what to do. *Fuck, should I have gotten her flowers?* Before I can answer myself, the front door opens, and I stop in my tracks. She looks . . . I can't even explain how she looks because there are no words that would do it justice.

"Well, hello there, handsome." She smiles, and her eyes light up as she walks toward me, her long leg peeking out from a slit in the front. I put my hands on her arms, and I look down at her. She is wearing a one-shoulder light blue dress that makes her eyes pop. Her one sleeve is cut open so you can see her arm, and it's cuffed at her wrist.

"You look . . ." I start to say, rubbing my thumbs up and down her arms. "You look."

"Yeah, we get it, Romeo." I hear a female voice say from behind her. "She looks good."

Candace puts her head on my chest and laughs. "Layla's cranky." She leans back, and I kiss her lips and feel gloss on my lips.

Layla walks past us and looks over her shoulder as she says, "You would be cranky, too, if you were standing all day."

"Why was she standing all day?" I slip my hand into hers and bring it to my lips.

"I was standing all day," Layla says once she gets to the car and looks back at us, "because you've defiled every surface in the house." She bends to get in the car, and Candace laughs, getting in after her.

"We didn't defile the whole house," I say, getting in. "I'm Ralph, by the way."

"Layla." She leans forward. "Nice to meet the man who made this one sit on ice packs all day."

Candace gasps, and I put my head back and let out the biggest laugh. We make idle talk on the way to the event, and when we get there, there is a line of cars waiting to let people out. There is a red carpet with photographers taking pictures as they walk the red carpet. "How are we doing this?" Layla asks. "Should we do a group shot, or do you guys want to do a couples thing?" I look over, not sure of the answer.

"Why don't we do a group one?" Candace says. "Just so there are no questions about anything."

Layla laughs. "Did you see his puppy dog eyes?" she asks Candace. "The man is smitten; everyone is going to see."

"No, he's not," Candace says the same time I say, "Puppy dog eyes?"

We don't have time to say anything else because the car stops, and the door opens on both sides. "You look good," Candace says to me, leaning in. "I think I want you to do me against the wall wearing the suit." She kisses my cheek and then gets out, leaving me looking down at my cock that is ready to do what she wants. I get out, and the three of us walk down the carpet, smiling. I stand between them, and then as soon as I walk into the event, I slip my hand in hers.

The first person we see is Manning, who is dressed in a suit and holding a glass of what looks like whiskey. "Hey, thanks for coming." He leans down and kisses Candace on her cheek and then takes a sip of his drink. I see Layla head to the side to talk to a couple of people who she knows.

"This looks like an amazing event," Candace says, looking around. Manning finally sees our hands together, and I see he has questions but doesn't say anything.

"Manning." I see his wife, Murielle, coming over dressed in the tightest dress I've ever seen, and she looks so fake, and I look down and then up. "There you are. They want to take our pictures," she says and then looks at us and then side-eyes Candace. "Oh, hello." She then looks at Manning. "I'm going to go freshen up my lipstick." She turns and walks away.

"God, I hate her," Manning says, taking a sip of his drink again. "Caught her fucking her trainer in the basement today." He laughs, and my mouth hangs open. "The man is doing me a favor. If only she will sign the divorce papers." He shakes his head. "I'll see you later." He walks away.

"She is such a bitch," Candace says of her, and I shake my head, not knowing the story. We walk hand in hand pretty much the whole time, saying hello to a couple of people. We mingle and laugh when Miller comes in and tries to get Layla to take a picture with him. Candace pulls me onto the dance floor when a song she likes comes on, and I stand with my hands around her waist.

She lets me go, and I walk over to the bar to grab a water and stand here for over an hour laughing with the boys, and it feels good to let loose.

I look around for Candace and find her talking with five other women and make my way over to her. It's time to take my woman home and find out what she's wearing under that dress. I smile, thinking of all the ways I'm going to make her scream tonight when I hear words that stop me in my tracks. "I can't wait to have my own kids." Her voice comes out energetic and full, and I don't move. I can't move even if I wanted to.

"Hey there." I'm slapped on the arm by Nico. "I'm heading out."

"Yeah," I say, blinking and trying to find words.

"Are you okay?" he asks, and I look at him. "You look a little pale."

"Yeah." I shake my head. "I'm fine. Just hungry."

He laughs. "You never eat at places like this." He looks around the ballroom. "That's why you hit up a drive-thru as soon as you leave." He smiles. "Have fun, and I'm happy for you, man."

"Thank you," I say, nodding as he walks away. Then I feel an arm slip into mine, and I look over, seeing Candace.

"Hey there," she says to me softly. "How about we blow this popsicle stand and head on home?" She leans her head back, expecting me to give her a kiss like I always do, but instead, I nod my head. Her words replaying over and over in my head.

"Do you need to tell Layla you are leaving?" I ask, and she looks around.

"I don't even see her." She looks at me. "She must have already left."

We walk down the stairs, and I wave to a couple of people before we walk over and get into a waiting car. I open the door for her, and she steps in while I give the driver my address. I put my head back on the seat and close my eyes. "Someone isn't used to staying out late," she says jokingly, and I grab her hand, bringing it to my lips.

"I just have a headache," I say and keep my eyes closed until the car stops. I wonder if she knows something is bothering me. I wonder if she feels me pull away from her. We walk up the walkway to the house beside each other, the only sound is the clicking of her heels. I don't hold her hand, and I wonder if she noticed.

"You are quiet. Why are you so quiet?" she asks. I try to act as natural as possible, but my heart and my head have been spinning and reeling. I unlock the door and walk into the living room, seeing Bernadette watching television.

She looks over at us, getting up. "You look so beautiful, Candace," she says to her, smiling, and I have to agree with her. She is the most beautiful woman I've ever met.

"How was tonight?" I ask, putting my hands in my pockets and ignoring the look that Candace is giving me.

"It was fine. She was fussy a bit at bedtime. I had to read the story to her five times, but then she went straight to bed." She smiles at me.

"I'm going to go check on her," I say, walking out of the room and getting away from them. I step into the dark room and walk straight to the crib. Ari is lying on her side, and her soft snores fill the room. "It's you and me, baby girl," I say softly, putting my hands on the railing of the crib. I take a deep breath, and I ignore the pain I have in the middle of my chest. A pain that I've never ever felt before. I watch her hanging my head. "I'm so sorry," I say, turning and walking out of the room.

When I walk back into the kitchen, I see Candace standing by the counter. "Bernadette just left," she says, and I force a smile at her. "What's wrong with you?" she finally asks me, and I shake my head.

"I'm fine." I walk to the fridge, avoiding looking at her. "I'm just tired."

"You're lying to me," she says the words softly, and I make the mistake of looking at her. Her face is like a fucking angel. She is perfect in every meaning of the word.

"I'm not lying." I brush it off, and I want to finish and avoid this conversation so hard. "I'm tired."

"Rule number six or I don't know seven." She puts her hands on the counter in front of her. Her hair falls over her bare shoulder when she looks down at her hands and then looks up. The worry is written all over her face, and I want nothing more than to go to her, take her in my arms, and hold her. Kiss her lips and tuck her hair away from her face. But my feet are stuck to the floor like there is glue under them. "Whatever number we are up to. You don't lie to me. If something is bothering one of us, we talk about it." Her voice goes low.

"Nothing is bothering me; I'm just . . ." I start to say, and I look at her. If anything, she deserves the truth from me. "I heard you talking to the other women, and I don't know, it . . ."

"What did you hear?" she asks with a confused look on her face.

"You want children." I say three words that stab me in the heart.

"Of course I want children," she says to me, and I look at her, and at that moment, I know that I have to let her go. "I'm not saying that I want them now." She throws up her hands. "But eventually, I want to have children."

"I didn't . . ." I start to say as my heart starts to pound, and my neck starts to tingle. I feel the room spinning, and I can hear her words over and over in my head. I loosen the tie around my neck.

"I did not keep this a secret from you," she says, and I shake my head. How is this happening right now? Tonight was amazing laughing, dancing, holding her hand; it was fucking perfect and then hearing her gush to the other women about kids. My heart sank, my stomach sank, and I knew I should have just made an excuse and left her there. "Ralph." She calls my name. "You're an amazing father. Why would you not have more children?"

I snap and slam my hand down on the counter, the rage ripping through me, and I roar out, "Dammit, Cassie, I'm not having anymore kids!"

THIRTY-ONE

CANDACE

I KNEW THE minute we sat in the car that something was off, and now here it is. "Dammit, Cassie, I'm not having anymore kids!" he roars. I take a step back, and it feels like he just slapped me in the face. But nothing could hurt more than my heart being shattered in my chest.

"Candace," I say my name. "My name is Candace, not Cassie." He looks at me, and I shake my head. I don't say anything to him. I just turn and walk out of the room.

"Candace," he says. I feel his hand wrap around my arm and yank it away from him.

"Don't touch me," I hiss. "Don't ever fucking touch me." I can't stop the tears even if I wanted to. This night was so perfect with us as a couple. No one really said anything, but we got looks. I held his hand softly and danced with him, and I could not be happier.

"I . . ." he starts to say. "I—"

"You nothing," I say. "I don't want to know, and I definitely don't want to hear it." I look around one last time, knowing I will never come back here. "I think it's fitting," I say, taking all the courage and strength that I have in me, and there isn't much. "I fell in love with you in this room while you cooked," I say finally. I have wanted to tell him I love him every single day, but I stopped myself. Thinking we had time. "It's only fitting that I fall out of love with you in the same room." I look down at my hands that are shaking, and I try to stop them from shaking. "Goodbye, Ralph."

"Candace." His voice is broken, but I don't turn back. Instead, I grab his car keys from the table and walk out of the house. "Candace, please listen to me," he says, following me.

"I'll have your car returned to you tomorrow," I say, getting in and turning on the car. I close the door and lock it just in case he swings it open.

"No," he says. "Please listen. I made—" I pull out of the driveway, and the tears fall down one after another. I don't know how I make it home, but when I do, I pull out my phone, seeing that I have forty-five missed calls from Ralph. I walk into the house, not turning on the lights, and I pick up the phone, not even sure what time it is.

He answers after one ring, and just the sound of his voice makes me sob. "I need help," I say, and I can hear the rustling of covers.

"Where are you?"

"Home," I say. "I'm home."

"Zara, call Matthew." I hear Evan say. "Cand."

"It hurts, Evan," I say, rubbing the pain in my chest. "It hurts so much."

"Are you hurt?" he asks, frantic, and I hear Zara in the background telling him that it's going to be okay.

"I can't be here. I have to leave," I say, looking around the bedroom.

"I'm coming to get you," he says, and then Zara gets on the phone.

"Candace," she says my name softly, and I shake. My body is shaking.

"I'm . . ." I start to say. "I love him." My teeth clatter. "He called me Cassie."

"Oh my God," she says. "Listen, Matthew is getting the plane, and we are taking off in thirty minutes."

"I can't stay here." I look around. "I don't want to see him."

"Okay, listen, you need to go pack a bag and meet us at the small airport," she says, and I want to answer her, but I can't.

"I can't stop shaking," I say. "I'm . . ."

"I'm going to fucking kill him." I hear Evan in the background. "Listen to me," he says, grabbing the phone from Zara. "We are going to be there in four hours," he says to me. "I'm sending you a car that is going to pick you up in an hour."

"Okay," I say, lying on the bed. I'm looking out, replaying the whole scene in the kitchen. His eyes were so guarded, and then he was so angry. I've never seen him that way, and never has he raised his voice to me. The phone falls from my hand as I lie here shaking, the tears soaking through my pillow. I force myself to get off the bed and slip out of the dress. I take off the special bra and panties that I wore, thinking this night would end up so much more different. I throw them in the trash and pack my bags. I ignore the buzzing from my phone, and I ignore the pain in my whole body. It's almost like I'm on autopilot except everywhere I look, I see him in my space. I go to get my laptop, and there on top is the blanket that Ari likes to be wrapped in when she lays on the couch. I walk to it and pick it up, bringing it to my nose and smelling her.

In my whole life, I have never ever felt this pain. I cry into the blanket and fold it. Gently putting it down, I ignore the fact that I didn't even get to kiss her goodbye. I didn't even get a chance to hug her one more time. The doorbell rings, and I stand here in the middle of my kitchen, scared that it's Ralph. I walk quietly to the door and peek out of the hole, seeing a man dressed in a black suit. I open the door, and he smiles. "I'm here to pick up Candace Richards."

"Yeah," I say, wiping my eyes. "I'll be out in a couple of minutes."

"Actually, there is a message for you from Evan. He said to call him right away," he says, turning and walking back to the car. I walk to my room and see the missed calls and ignore the way my heart feels when I see Ralph's name.

I click Evan's name, and he picks up right away. "Candace," he says my name. "Change of plans, there is a plane waiting to bring you here."

"What?" I ask him, and I hear voices in the background.

"Matthew called Nico, and he has a plane for you," Evan says, and I sit on the bed. "He promised Matthew he would not say a word."

"Okay," I say. "I'm walking out the door in two minutes," I say, getting up and grabbing my small carry-on bag. "Thank you." I sniffle and wipe away the tears.

"We are going to be there to pick you up," he says, and I can't talk anymore, so I just nod. "I'll see you soon." I hang up the phone and walk out of my house without looking back.

The plane is waiting for me, and when I look at the time, I see that it's after one a.m. I walk over to the bed that is set up for me and slide on it, though I never fall asleep. I play the whole thing over and over in my head, and when the wheels touch down in New York, it hurts to get up. My body feels like it got run over by a truck, front and back.

The door opens, and I step out, seeing Evan with his black truck standing there with Zara by his side. His face is filled with worry and fear, and when I see him, I start to shake. He runs to me right before I can fall to the ground. "I have you," he says to me. "I got you." The sob rips through me as I feel myself being carried. "It's okay, Cand," he says over and over as he puts me in the truck, and I want to tell him I'm okay. I want to tell him that I have it, but I don't.

"He broke my heart," I say and see the tears in his eyes. "I lost them." It comes out in a whisper. "Both of them. I lost them, and I didn't even know," I say. "I just."

"It's okay," he says, grabbing my face. "It's going to be okay." I just nod at him. He gets out of the truck, and Zara slides in next to me.

"I love him," I say. "I didn't even tell him I loved him before all this. I didn't even know until I knew I would never see him again."

She puts her arm around me and brings me to her. "I'm so sorry, Candace."

"He was everything." I close my eyes, and all I can see is his smiling face. "He . . ." I close my eyes. "He's my everything." That's the last thing I say before I let the darkness suck me away where the pain doesn't hurt. Where I'm happy again, where he hugs me and kisses me, and I'm whole once more.

THIRTY-TWO

Ralph

"ALL THE TESTS came back normal," the doctor says. I get up from the examination table, putting my shirt back on. "If your symptoms change." He starts to talk, and I zone him out as I fold my tie and put it in my jacket. I've been at the hospital for the past three hours, thinking I was having a heart attack. Now I'm just itching to leave and to go find Candace.

"Thank you," I say, opening up the door and walking out. Grabbing my phone, I dial Candace, and it goes straight to voice mail. "Baby," I say, rushing out. "Please call me." I wipe the tear away. "Baby, please."

I hang up and call Becca. She answers right away. "Ralph," she whispers, "are you okay?"

"Yeah, I just left. I'm fine," I say, getting into the waiting car that Becca arranged. "I'm on my way."

"Okay, Ari woke up twice already, and she's not in the best mood," she says, and I hang up.

The second I said Cassie, I knew I had fucked up beyond anything that I could ever do. I saw Candace's face, and I wanted to take it all back. I wanted to erase it, but I couldn't, so when I reached out and she shoved my hand off, I was in shock. It was all happening so fast, and then she said the words I was planning on saying that night.

I loved her; I loved everything about her. I loved her smile, I loved her laugh, and I loved the way she made everything okay. I loved the way she loved with her whole heart. I loved the way she hugged me and the way she held my hand. The way she would slide into bed with me at night and roll into me, kissing my neck. I fucking loved her, and I hurt her. Who does that?

When she drove away from me, I dropped to my knees. The pain in my chest shot through me, and I thought I was having a heart attack. I tried to call her back, but nothing and then the pain got worse. So much worse I couldn't breathe, so I called 911.

Then I called the only other person I could. I called Becca and told her that I was waiting for the ambulance. She got there the same time that the ambulance did.

"Excuse me," I say to the driver. "Can you make a pit stop?" I ask him, giving him Candace's address. He stops, and I see that my car is not even there. I get out, running to the door and ringing the doorbell. "Baby," I say softly, touching the door and then going to the garage and putting in her code. The door opens slowly, and I walk in, calling her name. "Candace?" I call her name, and I'm expecting her to be there. I walk in, and the house is eerily quiet. All the lights are off. I walk into her room, and the pain fills my chest again. Her dress is in the middle of the room, but her bed is still made. I smell her all around, and there in the middle of the bed lies Ari's blanket. I pick it up and feel the wetness to it.

I get up and walk out of the garage, closing the door and getting back in the car, watching the outside while I'm driven back to my house. My car is parked in the driveway, and my heart speeds up. She came back; I don't even wait for the car to come to a complete stop before I jump out of the car and run inside. "Candace," I say, running to the living room and see Becca jump up from the couch. "Is she here?" I ask her, looking around, and she just shakes her head.

"No one is here. Someone dropped off your car keys an hour ago." The stinging of tears fight to come out. "Oh my God." She gasps. "You look like shit."

"Good," I say, taking off my jacket and tossing it aside. "I feel worse than I look."

"What the fuck happened?" she asks, sitting down now.

I rub my face with my hand. My whole body hurts, and then when I say the words, my chest hurts again. "I fucked up." I look over at her. "Like really fucked up."

"Oh, dear, how did you really fuck up?" She waits for it.

"I called her Cassie," I say, and her mouth opens hanging open. "Yeah, that's about the extent of it."

"There will be no turning back from that," she says. "Like lying about an orgasm is one thing. Pretending to like her cooking is another." She points at me. "But calling a woman by another woman's name? A dead one who you have a child with is . . ." She puts her hand on top of her head. "Is all the way fucked up." I rub my chest. "Wait a second," she says. "When did this pain in your chest start?"

"It started the minute we started having the conversation about her having children," I say, and she just listens. "Then I called her Cassie." I don't tell her about her admitting that she loved me and hated me all in one sentence. "I followed her out, and when she drove away is when my heart started to hurt."

She gets up now and chuckles. "You weren't having a heart attack, you jackass. It's called a broken heart."

I look at her. "What?"

"The pain in your chest." She grabs her jacket and puts it on. "It's your heart breaking."

"Please." I shake my head. "Thank you," I say, and she bends and kisses my cheek.

"You're welcome," she says, and then she turns to walk out, stopping. "Do you love her?"

I nod my head. "Can you live without her?" I roll my eyes, the pain in my chest starting up again. "Think about it," she says. "Don't answer me, but think about it. Cassie isn't here, and you moved on. If Candace wasn't here, how would you be?" I don't answer her. I also try not to think of it. I don't want to ever think of that. I take my phone and dial her number again, and it goes straight to voice mail.

"You've reached Candace. I'm away from my phone right now but leave a message, and I'll get back to you as soon as I can." Her voice makes me smile. I wait for the beep, but instead, it tells me that voice mail is full. I bring up her text and text her.

Me: Please call me. Please. I just want to make sure you're okay.

I put the phone down and stare at it, hoping the bubble comes up. I just need to speak to her. I just need to make sure she's okay. I just need her. The tears come now, not one but a whole fucking ocean comes as I think of the hurt I made her feel. The hurt that I'm putting her through. Who does that?

I sit here on the couch as the night becomes day. Ari gets up, and I prepare her bottle and play with her. My mind is never there as I call Candace over and over again. The voice mail is always full; my chest starts to hurt more and more as the minutes turn into hours, and then at ten, I put Ari in the truck and go back to Candace's house. I ring the doorbell, but she never opens the door. I go back home, and the day drags on.

I finally cave and call Miller, who answers right away. "Yo."

"Hey," I say. "It's me."

"I know. I have caller ID. What's wrong?" he asks me right away.

"I was wondering if you had Layla's number?" I ask him, and he laughs.

"Of course I have her number. It's even in my favorites." He laughs. "But why do you need it?"

"I'm trying to get in touch with Candace, and I can't." I don't go into the whole story. "I thought she might be with Layla."

"I'll text you her number," he says, hanging up, and then a text comes in with her number. I don't even think twice before calling it, and she answers after three rings.

"Hello," she says.

"Layla," I say her name. "It's Ralph," I say, getting up and pacing,

"What do you want?" she says, and from her tone, I'm going to guess that she knows what happened.

"Listen—" I start to say, and she snaps.

"No, you listen," she says angrily. "You fucked up."

"I know that," I say softly. "I just want to make sure she's okay."

She laughs bitterly this time. "If she's okay. Oh, she is *not* okay. What is the opposite of okay?"

"Is she with you?" I ask, getting ready to go over there to talk to her.

"Even if she were, I wouldn't tell you," she says.

"I just want to make sure—" I start to say, and she hangs up on me.

"Fuck," I say, wanting to throw the phone out the fucking window. I get Ari in the car and drive to her house again but still nothing. The whole night, I stay away, looking outside and wondering where she is. The whole night, I call her name in the darkness, hoping that she answers me.

The next day and the day after that, she still isn't home, and now my nerves are shot to shit. I'm on edge, having only slept maybe six hours in three days when I call Becca again. "Hey, did you try to find out where she was?"

"Yeah," she says, "but I hate to say it, I have no idea."

"This is fucking bullshit!" I shout. "She has to be somewhere." I sit on the couch and pull the hair on my head. "She has to be somewhere," I say again, my voice almost a whisper.

"I don't know what to tell you, Ralph," Becca says, and I hang up and toss my phone on the couch. I feel like my whole body is on alert. Bernadette has been coming in every single day, and I leave, but I just go and sit at Candace's house. Sitting on her porch, I plead for her to come home. Hoping that she walks in the door, and I can see her even for a second.

I'm rubbing my hands over my face when I hear a car drive into the driveway, and I swear my heart has never beat so fast in my life. "Candace," I say her name only to see Nico get out of his car.

"Hey," I say, surprised to see him. He is wearing aviator glasses, so I can't see his eyes.

"Hey," he says when he gets in front of me.

"What are you doing here?" I ask, and he takes off his glasses.

"No." He shakes his head. "The question is, what are you doing here?"

"I . . ." I start to say, and I try to come up with a story that I'm waiting for Candace.

"I got a call today," he says, and my neck tingles and my shoulders go back. "You can't be here."

"Who called you?" I ask, and he just looks at me. "Who the fuck called you, Nico?"

"Doesn't matter." He avoids my eyes, looking around. "What matters is that you don't come back here because next time, they won't be calling me."

"Who the fuck is calling you?" I ask, my heart pumping. "Is it Candace?" I wait for him to answer, and when he doesn't, I ask him another question. "You know where she is?"

"I need you to promise me that you won't come back here," he says, and I answer him without thinking twice.

"No." I shake my head. "I need to talk to her."

"Ralph," he says. "She doesn't want to talk to you."

"You know where she is." I don't ask him the question now. Instead, I tell him. "Tell me where she is."

"It's over, buddy," he says, and the pain in my chest starts again. "You need to go home and be with Ariella and just move on."

"How?" I ask him. "How do you expect me to move on when just the thought of not seeing her again has my chest hurting so bad that I think I'm having a heart attack? How do you expect me to move on when she's not with me?" I walk away from him. "You tell Evan that I'm not going anywhere until I talk to her."

"You want to start a war with Evan?" he asks, and I shrug.

"I don't give a fuck if I have to go through the whole fucking family to get to her." I walk to my truck. "You tell him that." I get in the truck and pull out of the driveway. Taking my phone out, I send Justin a message.

Me: Tell Evan to call me.

That is all I do as I toss the phone on the side and drive home waiting for the phone call.

THIRTY-THREE

CANDACE

"AUNTIE CAN." I hear Zoey as she walks outside. "You crying again. You have boo boo?" She crawls onto the outdoor couch that I'm lying on with a cover over me. The air is still hot, but with the shade, it's a touch cooler than I thought it would be.

"Yeah, I have a boo boo." I kiss her head when she lies beside me, and even though I don't want the tears to fall, they do. I wrap her into the blanket, and she watches her iPad.

I've been here for over a week, and every single day when I get up, I think the pain will be less. I think that the burning in my stomach is going to go away, but it doesn't. I hear the dogs bark and look up to see that Zara is coming out of the house carrying two cups of coffee. "You forgot your phone inside." She smiles as she hands me a cup of coffee and my phone and then sits on the big chair facing the couch.

"Thank you," I say, ignoring the phone in my lap. The phone that gets heavier and heavier through the day. "I didn't even notice."

"You were too busy trying to pretend you were okay to your brother to notice that your phone was left on the kitchen table when you escaped outside." She takes a sip of her coffee.

"I thought it would get better day by day," I say. "I mean, is this normal?"

She looks at me. "The thought of losing your brother would cut me off at the knees. I don't know how I would go on," she says and blinks her own tears away. "I know that what he did was horrible."

"Horrible." I laugh bitterly, but the tear rolls down my cheek anyway as I sit up. Zoey's not even a bit concerned about what is going on around her as she starts dancing back and forth. "He called me Cassie."

"Yeah," Zara says, looking at me. "I know but—"

I shake my head. "No, there is no excuse. None. And even if there was, I don't want to hear it. We want different things out of life. I want a family with children. I want to be woken up at five a.m. because my baby is sitting on my bladder. I want to feel my child move in me. I want to give birth to my child, knowing I made this. Knowing that the love that we have together made a miracle. I want that, and I'm not going to sacrifice it for anyone."

"And you shouldn't have to," she says. "You'll find someone out there who will give you everything that you want," she says, and my heart hurts, thinking that this person isn't going to be Ralph. I close my eyes and see his smile, and just when I'm about to open my eyes, I see Ari smiling at me. "So what are you going to do?"

"I don't think I can go back to Dallas," I say the truth. "I don't think I can be in the same town as him and not think of what he is doing at that moment. Fuck, I'm in New York, and there hasn't been an hour that I haven't thought about him."

"Does that mean you are actually going to move here?" she asks me, smiling. "Not going to lie. Evan is going to be over the moon."

"Why not?" I say. "There is nothing for me there." I take a sip of my coffee. "I have to go back and pack up the house."

"We can get movers that can do that," Zara says. "Say the word, and you never have to go back there."

I shake my head. "No. I'm going to go back and pack up the house, put it on the market, and say goodbye to Layla. Meet with my clients to tell them what is going on." I look over and see Evan coming out, and I can tell he's pissed. The vein in his head is bulging, and I see him charging toward us. "What has gotten into him?" I motion with my head, and Zara turns to watch him, and she must see what I see.

"Oh, fuck," she says and smiles, getting up. "Hey there." He just shakes his head.

"That did not go well at all," he says, sitting down in the chair that Zara was sitting in and then pulling her down to sit on his lap.

"You didn't say anything you are going to regret,

right?" Zara says, and he looks at her.

"Oh, I said plenty of shit," he says, looking at me. "But I don't regret anything. Pussy ass bitch."

"Daddy," Zoey says. "Pussy ass bitch is a bad word, right, Mama?" she asks, and I roll my lips.

"Honey, let's go play in the playhouse," Zara tells her, getting up and holding out her hand for Zoey. "Listen to your brother and remember that he did it because he loves you," she says, and I tilt my head to the side. "And if it helps in any way, just think, my brother is Matthew."

I laugh at her and watch her walk away.

"What happened?" I ask him.

"I called Nico," he says, and my neck starts to get hot. "Sent Ralph a message."

"What kind of message did you send him?" I ask him, glaring at him.

"Just that the next time he went into your house, you're calling the cops." He folds his hands over his chest. "It's creepy as fuck watching him walk into the house and sit on the couch for hours."

The day after I got here, I finally opened my phone and saw all the missed calls from Ralph and that my voice mail was full. I was going to listen to the voice mails when my phone alerted me that my garage door was opened. I watched him walk into my house and sit on my couch. The pain in my chest coming out tenfold and it was like someone was stomping my chest with heavy boots. I started to dry heave, and that is how Evan found me and then picked up the phone.

"You didn't have to do that." I look down at my coffee

cup. "He would have given up eventually."

"Not according to the phone call I just had with him," Evan says, and I sit up now.

"You spoke to Ralph?" I ask, and he nods his head. "What? How?"

"He sent Justin a message that he wanted to talk to me." He grabs the arms of the chair. "Gotta say the guy has some balls."

"I want you to stand down," I say.

"Absolutely not. You're my baby sister," he says, and I roll my eyes at him. "It's my duty. Fuck, when I got with Zara, I had Matthew and Max on my dick." He mentions his two brothers-in-law. "I have to set rules."

"Rules?" I look at him. "You are out of your mind. I don't want you to do anything, please. Just, it'll fade away."

He laughs at me now. "I can tell you right now he's not going away." I look at him, and my heart speeds up. "No matter how much—" I hold up my hand.

"You need to stop." I wipe the tear away with my thumb that is going to escape thinking about Ralph. "I'm asking you to stop."

"Would you choose him?" he asks, and I just look at him. My head is shouting yes, and my heart is telling me that there will be no one else but him. "Answer me, Can. Would you choose him over me?"

"I choose Ari," I say, and now I don't even have time to wipe the tears that come blurring my vision. "I choose Ari, and I would not want to hurt her ever."

"You are too good for him," he says. "But if you ask

me, you're too good for anyone." His voice goes soft. "He wants me to give you a message."

"I don't want to know," I say, getting up. "I don't want to hear. I don't want to know. It's over and done with."

"Are you sure about that?" he asks me softly.

"It is what it is. I just don't want the drama. So I need you to just let it be," I say.

"That doesn't answer my questions, Candace." He looks at me, waiting.

"I can't change the past, and he can't see the future." I grab my phone off the table. "I'm moving here," I say, making it official. He nods his head. "We have space for you here."

"I'm not moving in with you," I say. "I'm going to rent Viktor's place from him." Mentioning his brother-in-law who has a place in New York City. "I have to go home and sort my shit."

"You think that's a good idea?" He gets up. "We can come with you."

"You have to get back on the ice, Evan. I know that you don't have time," I say. "I'm giving myself one week."

"It'll be good to finally have you close," he says, and I nod my head, ignoring the lump in my throat.

"I'm going to make a list of things I need to do," I say, walking away from him and going inside. I walk up to the bedroom that I always use when I'm here and close the door behind me. The drapes are still closed, so the room is dark. I slip under the bed covers and close my eyes. I feel like I haven't slept in a week, but I know that isn't the truth since all I have been doing since getting here is sleeping. It's my way to escape; it's also my way to see Ralph and Ari. It's the time I get to laugh and smile and grab his face and kiss him over and over again. It's the time I get to rock Ari to sleep. I wonder if she misses me? She probably doesn't even notice; she probably will never know how much I love her.

The tears don't stop; in this room, I can cry for however long I want. The door opens softly, and I see Zara stick her head in. "Hey," she says. "Can I come in?" I nod my head, and she comes in and sits on the bed. "Are you okay?"

"No," I say. "Not in the least."

"Evan told me . . ." she starts to say, and I just sob.

"I don't want to know," I say. "I don't want to know because it's going to hurt me, and I can't handle the hurt. I can't handle it. My heart can't."

"I'm going to come with you," she says. "To help you close up the house." I shake my head.

"You have Zoey, and Evan goes back to work," I say. "It's okay. It's okay, it will be fine."

"It's not even going to be close to fine," she says. "But you are strong." She gets up.

"You also need to eat something. Evan hasn't noticed yet, but you've lost a good ten pounds, and you didn't have ten pounds to spare to begin with." She walks to the door, closing it softly behind her.

"Today," I say to myself. "I give myself today to cry it all out and then tomorrow." I take a deep breath. "Tomorrow will be better."

THIRTY-FOUR

Ralph

FOURTEEN DAYS. IT'S been fourteen days that I've been in this hell. Three hundred and thirty-six hours of hell. Three hundred and thirty-six hours of living the memories over and over again. I call her every hour, and it goes straight to voice mail.

I step off the ice, sweat pouring down my face as I walk to the locker room. I unsnap my helmet and put it on the shelf with my name on it. I don't bother showering here. Instead, I change and make my way back home. When I get there, Bernadette is rocking Ari, and I kiss her on her cheek and head for the shower.

I'm about to step into the shower when my phone rings, and I see it's Evan.

"Hello," I say, hoping it's Candace instead.

"Yeah," he says, his voice low. "I have to ask you something," he says, and I just wait for it. "Is she it for you?" I think about his question.

"You think I'm going to tell you how I feel about her before I tell her?" I laugh. "Nice try but this isn't fucking high school." I wait to hear the hang up signal or for him to tell me to fuck off when my voice goes low. "Listen, you don't have to like me. Not now, not ever. But Candace, she is the only one that matters."

I wait for it, wait for anything, and then he shocks me. "I thought you'd like to know that Candace is back in town." My heart speeds up so fast and so loud I don't think I heard it properly.

"What?" I ask him again.

"Don't make me regret this," he says and hangs up the phone. It pretty much sums up the first time we spoke.

He called me, and it was tense and to the point. Basically, I wasn't good enough for his sister, and I didn't even argue that. I know I wasn't; fuck, I will never be good enough for her. The whole conversation lasted a whole two minutes. I didn't argue with him. I didn't tell him my side of things. I wanted one thing and one thing only, and that was for him to tell Candace that we missed her. That I missed her. I wondered every single day if she got the message. Every single night, I would say good night to her, closing my eyes and seeing her smile.

I shower as fast as I can and slip into shorts and a shirt, and right before I walk out of the house, I go to kiss Ari. "I'm going to try to get our girl back." I nod at Bernadette who just smiles at me.

I play my speech over and over in my head. When I finally pull up to her house, my heart almost shatters. The for sale sign is in the middle of her lawn, making it almost official I've lost her.

I get out and look at the house, my heart speeding up faster and faster. The last time I was here, Nico told me never to come back. I want to say I listened, but I didn't, I would drive by at night with Ari, slowing down just to see if there were any lights on. I walk up and press the doorbell, not knowing if he was lying to me or not, but I couldn't not take the chance.

"Come in." I hear her voice yelling, and I open the door and walk in. My heart speeding up, my hands sweaty, and I suddenly want to fall to my knees and thank whoever for bringing her back to me. I walk in and see the boxes everywhere, and I stop in my tracks. The heart that was beating so hard and so fast now sinks into the pit of my stomach. "Hi." I turn, and she doesn't expect that it's me. The minute her eyes meet mine, she takes a step back.

"What are . . .?" I take her in. She looks thin, too thin. She stands there in jeans and a shirt and her hair piled on top of her head, but I see that her eyes are red as if she's been crying, and I want to wipe away the tears from her face. She, without a doubt, owns my heart.

"What is all this?" I ask, looking around at the place where we spent so many days wrapped in each other. Boxes and boxes are all over the place, and some are even labeled. "Are you leaving?"

"Yeah," she says, avoiding my eyes. "I, um . . ." She moves away and picks up a bag by the door. "These are Ari's things. I thought maybe you would want them."

"Baby, please," I say, and she shakes her head furiously.

"Don't do this," she says, almost begging. "Please don't do this. I can't do this." She sobs and puts her hand to her mouth to stop it from roaring out. I start to walk to her, and she puts up her hand. "Please, I need you to just leave."

My lips tremble, and my hands shake as I lift one arm up and put my hand to my heart. "Candace, please, you have to give me a chance."

"There is nothing to explain," she says, wiping her tears with the back of her hand. The same hand that I held that night and every night before going to bed. The same hand that I brought up to my lips when we would just be near each other. The same hand that held my daughter with all the love in the world.

"There is everything to explain," I say. I know that I am going to get one shot at this, just one, and I know that if I don't, I am going to regret it my whole life. "I didn't want kids, I mean." I look at her face while I tell the story. "That night, listening to you say how much you couldn't wait to have kids. Well, you see, I heard it before." I swallow as I finally let go of the biggest secret I have. "I was trying to process everything, and the only thing I heard was Cassie's voice. It brought me back to the time I heard Cassie talking to her co-workers about finally having her own kids." I look up and then let go.

"I can't say for sure, but I'm pretty sure that Ariella was not an accident like we thought she was." I wipe away the tears. "That doesn't change the fact that I love her with everything that I have. Let's be honest, I didn't exactly have the best experience with father figures. I didn't know if I was good enough to even be a father to a child, let alone have more than one." My voice trails off.

"When you left me, I thought I was having a heart attack. I collapsed on my knees in the middle of the driveway, and all I could do was think I was going to die, and I never told you that I love you. I was going to die, and I was never going to be able to say I'm sorry. I was never going to look you in the face and beg you to forgive me." I can't stop my feet as I walk to her. She stands there in the middle of the room, and her whole body shakes from the sobs. "Being with you was so much more than I can ever explain." I hold her face in my hand. "When Cassie died, it hurt. I can't deny that it hurt, but it hurt because of Ari. It hurt knowing that she is going to miss out on our beautiful girl. But . . ." I want to bend and kiss her lips. "Being without you, my heart stopped. It stopped in my chest. I'm a shell of a man without you. I'm existing when all I want to do is live. I want to live, and I want to do it with you and no one else. I can't do it with anyone else but you. I feel it now, what love is. It creeps into you without knowing. It's the air that makes your lungs breathe. It's the beat of the heart. It's the feeling that you want to do whatever you can to make the other person happy."

"Ralph," she whispers.

"I love you, Candace," I say. "I love your smile and your laugh. I love the way you take care of everyone without asking twice. I love your loyalty. I love your stubbornness. I love all of you." I smile now. "Every single piece of you was made for me." Then I ask her the only question I actually want the answer to. "What would it take for you to stay?"

THIRTY-FIVE

Candace

"WHAT WOULD IT take for you to stay?" he asks, and his forehead hits mine. His hands cupping my face make my heart finally beat normal for the first time in fourteen days.

I knew coming back here would be hard. I knew it would hurt, and I was expecting the hurt, but what I wasn't expecting was the hurt to be so bad that I would have trouble breathing. I stepped into the house in the darkness, and the minute I did, I could still smell him here. I cried the tears as I relived the memories. I refused to even sleep in my bed and instead camped out on the couch. It was only going to be for a week anyway. I had everything already lined up, and the realtor had my house on the market. The boxes were waiting to be filled. I just had to fill them, and in two days, I would be out of my house.

"I need you to stay," he says, and I want nothing more

than to say yes. I want nothing more than to give into him, but I can't.

"I can't," I say, and his eyes close as the tears fall. "I can't be the one who forces you to be someone who you aren't." His hands fall from my face now. "You don't want the whole white picket fence thing and the screaming kids. And that is okay." I hold up my hand when he is going to say something.

"This has nothing to do with you calling me Cassie. If I'm honest, it hurt, but it hurt more knowing that you will never allow yourself to see what an amazing father you are." I wipe my nose on my sweater. "You're stuck thinking that you don't deserve the happiness that you have. I can't be the woman who forces you to be that person either. It isn't fair to you, and it isn't fair to me. I love you," I say this because he has to know. "I love you with every single fiber of my being. I love you with everything, but I can't forgo what I want." He puts his hands to his chest.

"I want to get married. I want to have a whole big wedding or small wedding, but I want to stand with the man I love and promise to love him through everything. Good and bad. Then I want to get my white picket fence, no matter how stupid that sounds. I want to carry a child and give birth to that child. I want to breastfeed my child and help it grow. I want to read them stories and then tell them stories about our love story. I want to cry when the kids go off to school. I want to be there for them when they fall and scrape their knees. I want it all, Ralph. I want it all."

"I don't know if I can give you that," he says what I already knew.

"I know," I say, "which makes this that much harder because I just know how amazing you would be at all that." I walk to him now. "I hope you find it." I try to say the words without crumpling to the floor. "I hope you find whatever it is that will make you see what I see." I get on my tippy toes, and I kiss his cheek. "Goodbye, Ralph," I whisper the words, then turn and walk out of the room. I walk into the bathroom and close the door behind me and sink to the floor. I put my hand in front of my mouth to stop the sob from echoing out. The sound of the front door slamming making it final. I wanted closure, and now I got it. I peel myself off the floor and wash my face, but I know the tears are not going to go away.

Walking out of the bathroom, I look around the room, and my eyes go to the bag that I packed not too long ago. All of Ari's things, I packed it, not even able to see through the tears. "Fuck." I bend to pick it up, and the door opens again and slams, and I stand here looking toward the hallway when he comes back into the room. His face is streaked with tears, his hair looks like he just pulled it. "Ralph?" He stands there in front of me with a wild look on his face.

"What if I gave you all that?" he says. "What if I said I want to give you all that?" My heart speeds up in my chest, and I don't have time to say anything else because he walks toward me. " What if I said that I want to unpack my boxes. I want to take your boxes and then take mine, and I want us to unpack the boxes together." His hands on my face again, and this time, I put my hands on his hips. "I want to buy you a house," he says softly. "Build you a fence and make babies with you."

"Ralph," I say with trembling lips.

"I left here thinking, she's right, I can't give her that," he says. "Then the thought of you doing that without me made it unbearable to breathe. The thought that my life would be without you, it just . . ." he says, smiling. "It's unimaginable." He comes closer. "So stay with me, Candace. Stay with me and help me make a home for Ari."

In all my life, I could never expect to be given a man who I would love so unconditionally, and with that he would come with a beautiful baby girl, that I would give my life for. "Okay," I say the word in a whisper. "Okay, I'll stay."

"What?" he says almost as if he didn't hear me.

"I'll stay." I say the two words that make my heart soar. His lips finally touch mine, and we fall into each other. He holds me up as his tongue finds mine. I wrap my arms around him, and then he picks me up, and my legs wrap around his waist.

"I've missed you," he finally says when he pulls back from my lips. "I've missed you so much." I'm about to answer him when he continues. "Ari, she's missed you, too."

"She must have gotten so big," I say as he wipes the tears streaming down my face. "Where is she?"

"She's home," he says, "with Bernadette."

"Can we go get her?" I ask him. "I mean, I love this with you, but . . ." I look down. "I've missed her so much, and I just don't want her to think I forgot about her."

"I used to call you and make her hear your voice," he says, killing me. "She would smile."

I'm about to kiss him when there is a knock on the door, and I look at him. "Those must be the packers," I say, getting off him and going to the door. "Hi," I say to the four people who are standing there. "Um, I'm so sorry, but I am going to have to reschedule."

The woman smiles at me. "No worries, just give us a call when you are ready." She turns, and the four women walk away. I close the door and then walk back into the living room and see him sitting there.

"Can we go?" I ask, and he smiles and gets up.

"I sold my house," he says. "Last week."

"What?" I ask, shocked.

"I hate my house, and after spending time here in your house, I want this. Not what I had."

"Where are you going to go?" I ask him, and he shrugs.

"I have to decide in seven days," he says. "I have to be out of the house next week."

"Have you even looked at other houses?" My mind is reeling.

"I have not," he says, getting up. "I didn't want to do anything without you."

"Move in here," I say the words before I even get a chance to think about it. "It's not a big house, but it's the right size for the three of us, and then we can see if maybe we want to buy another one."

"You would be okay with us living here?" he asks,

and I look around.

"I mean, technically we were kind of living here before," I say. "But we can talk about it after we get Ari."

"Let's go get our girl," he says, and my heart literally skips a beat. He holds my hand the whole way there, and when I finally walk into the door and hear her voice, the tears just come.

I walk into the living room and see her sitting on the floor with Bernadette. "Hello, baby girl," I say, going to her, and she smiles so big but then pouts and starts to cry.

I look over at Ralph, who laughs. "That's her way of telling you that you are taking too long to pick her up. She started doing it last week." He walks to her and picks her up, and I'm expecting her to stop crying, but she doesn't. "You want Candace?" Ralph asks her. I hold out my hands to her, and she flies into my arms.

"Hey there, pretty girl," I say, hugging her as she lays her head on my chest. I kiss her head. "I missed you, baby girl," I say and look at Ralph. "I missed you both."

"Welcome home, baby," Ralph says to me, and for the first time in fourteen days, my tears are happy tears.

THIRTY-SIX

RALPH

"GOOD NIGHT, BABY girl." I place her down in the middle of the crib and walk out softly, closing the door just a touch. Walking to the kitchen, I put the empty bottle in the sink and head back to the bedroom. Wearing a smile on my face, I see her sitting in the middle of the bed. Her hair is wet from the pool and tied up on top of her head as she reads something on her phone. "She's out."

She looks up from her phone. "You're suing me?" she asks, shocked, and I laugh. "Don't you laugh, Ralph. I just got a notice from Becca."

I lean over and kiss her lips. "I had to do something to see you," I say, and she throws her hands up.

"So your first thought was to sue me?" She gets on her knees, and I see that she is only wearing a white T-shirt. Her nipples showing through the shirt, and she walks over to me on her knees. "You know that I could have just sent my lawyer, right?" she says, wrapping her hands around my neck, and my hand comes up and grabs her ass.

"I have to make a phone call," I say, and she looks at me.

"Now?" She leans in and kisses me. "Like right now. It's been two weeks."

"Trust me, I know." I kiss her again. "I won't be long," I say and slide my tongue into her mouth and then smack her ass. "Don't shower without me." I walk out of the room because if I stood there for another minute, I wouldn't have left her.

I walk outside to the backyard and sit down, dialing the number. "Hello," he answers right away.

"It's me," I say. "I just wanted to let you know that I spoke with your sister."

"I know," he says and I look up at the sky as the stars twinkle like diamonds.

"I'm moving in with her," I say and he stays quiet. "And I'm going to marry her. I don't know when, and I don't know how, but at the end of the day, she's going to have my last name."

"Is that a fact?" Evan says, laughing.

"Just stating the obvious," I say. "Thank you for giving me the heads-up."

"You going to tell her I told you?" he asks me.

"If she asks, I will. I'm not lying to her," I say. "Not now, not ever."

"You're a good guy, Ralph," he says. "As long as she's happy, you don't have to worry about me."

"Glad we are on the same page." I look out.

"Just because you're dating my sister doesn't mean I'll go easy on you on the ice, though." I laugh now.

"Good to know," I say and hang up the phone, getting up and going inside. I lock up and walk to the bedroom, seeing that she isn't in the bedroom. I hear talking and walk down to Ari, and I see her rocking Ari as she talks to her.

"I missed you so much." She holds her sideways with Aria's face on her chest. Ari holds her finger tight while Candace kisses her. "Did you miss me?" I lean on the doorjamb and listen to her. "Did you make friends?" She looks up now and sees me and smiles. "She woke up."

"I love you," I say.

"I love you, too," she whispers. "Who did you have to call?"

"Evan," I say, and she stops rocking.

"What?" she asks, shocked. "Why would you call Evan?"

"To tell him that I'm moving in," I say, and she starts to rock again.

"You know that it's my house, right?" she tells me. "He doesn't get a say about who lives here and who doesn't."

"I let him know that we're together." I walk in now and squat down next to the chair, seeing Ari's eyes getting heavier and heavier. "I want to meet your parents and get to know them."

"Okay." She looks at me and then looks down. I see a

tear roll down her cheek and put my hand under her chin and raise it. "It's okay. I'm okay."

"Then why the tears?" I ask her, not sure, and she shrugs.

"I'm happy," she whispers, and another tear falls. She sniffles, and I look down and see Ari sleeping. "I'm so happy."

"Put her down," I say. "Let's go shower."

She gets up, kissing Ari's head before putting her down, and the two of us walk out of the room with her holding my hand. "Did you really talk to Evan?" she asks me when we get into the bedroom, and I turn off the lights. I grab the baby monitor with one hand while my other hand holds her and drags her into the bathroom.

I don't turn on the light in the bathroom, putting the baby monitor down on the sink and turning around to face her. The moonlight gives me just a touch of light, enough to see her, and I pull the elastic from her hair. "I really called Evan," I say softly. Grabbing her face, I lean in and kiss her. "I had to set some things clear." I let her go, walking over to the shower and turning on the water.

"Like?" she asks me, standing there, not moving. I walk over to her, taking off my shirt and tossing it on the side.

"Like the fact that you are mine." I grab the bottom of her shirt and rip it over her head. Her nipples pebbled. I grab her breasts in my hands and roll her nipples. "I am here to stay," I say, bending down and taking a nipple in my mouth. "That one of these days." I switch to the other nipple, sucking it deep into my mouth. "You are going to have my name." Her head falls forward as she watches me.

I pull my shorts off, and my cock springs free. I slip her panties off, bending while she steps out of hers. I kiss her mound, slipping my tongue along her slit. "Ralph," she says, and I stand, grabbing her hand and walk into the shower with her. The hot water hits my arm as I turn around to kiss her. Her hands go to my hips and then straight to my cock as she jerks it.

My head falls back as I close my eyes. "Fuck, that feels good," I say, and then I feel her mouth on my cock head as water pours over her head. "Baby." I fuck her mouth slowly as she swallows me. Her hands cup my balls, and I get lost in her mouth. My balls start to get tight, and I know that I'm going to blow any second.

"Going to come," I say, looking down and moving so the water hits my back as she looks up at me and swallows my come. Pulling her up, I go sit on the bench she has in the shower.

"Come here," I order her, and she comes over to me. She starts to straddle me, and I turn her around to sit on my lap with her back to my chest. "Missed you." I kiss her neck as my hands reach around to tease her nipples. "Spread your legs open for me." She opens her legs for me, and my hand moves from her breast all the way down to her pussy. My finger slips into her dripping wet pussy, and her head falls on my shoulder.

"Going to fuck you with my fingers and then you're going to ride me until you come all over my cock." I take my finger out of her and play with her clit now, one hand still rolling her nipple. Her moans fill the shower as I stick my two fingers in her.

"I hope you know." I bite her neck and feel her pulse under my tongue as I lick down. "That I'm going to spend the rest of the night fucking you." My fingers slide in and out of her, then bring her wetness to her clit and go around and around in a circle. "Fuck you so hard." I stick two fingers back into her as her hip arches up to meet my hand. "You won't be able to stand without feeling that my cock was in you."

"Right there," she says, and I feel her pussy getting tighter and tighter. "Oh, God, right there." She licks under my chin. My fingers pound into her over and over. "Oh, God," she chants. "Oh, yeah." Her legs start to shake, and I know she's so close. "I want your cock."

I want my cock in her and now. "You want my cock in you, baby?" I ask her. I take my fingers out, playing with her clit and then rubbing back down. "If you want my cock, you have to come on my fingers." I rub her clit back and forth, harder and harder. "That's it." I stick two fingers in her, and she comes.

"Come on my fingers." She groans out her orgasm. I wait for her to finish coming, then take my fingers out. I don't give her a chance to recover before I grab her by the hips. "Put my cock in you," I say, and she puts her hands between our legs, holding my cock up as I slam her down on it.

"Fuck," we both say at the same time. I wait for her to start moving before I move my hand to her clit. "Ride me, baby," I say and let her control it. "Your pussy is heaven," I say as her head falls back. "Play with your clit," I say. "Let me fuck you." Her finger moves mine out of the way, and my hands go to her hips. I grip onto them as I pick her up and slam her on me over and over again. She comes too soon and then again when one of her hands starts to pinch her nipples. "I'm there," I say, and she winds her hips, helping me move her up and down. "So good," I say right before I slam her on me and feel her pussy contract over and over again, and I come inside her.

Her hand stops moving between her legs, and she falls on me like a limp noodle. "Rule number one," she says, trying to get her breathing back to normal. "You give me your cock every night."

"I can do that," I say, kissing her neck, and she turns and slips her tongue into my mouth. Her hips go around and around. "Are you really ready to go?" I pinch both her nipples, and she moans.

"I'm ready to go, but first," she says, "I want to suck your cock again." She gets up and turns around to get on her knees. She sucks my semi hard cock back into her mouth, tasting both of us now. "Missed doing this." She takes her mouth off my cock and licks my shaft all the way up, then twirls her tongue around the head. "Rule number two." She bobs her head down my cock. "I get to suck your dick every day."

My head rolls back and forth on the tiled wall. "Only if I get to eat that pussy whenever I want, however I want." Hmm, she moans, and the vibration makes my cock come alive again. "Sit you at the table, spread your legs, and eat you for my meal." She starts to suck faster now, and I watch her hand disappear between her legs. "Be nice to my pussy," I say. "I'm planning on destroying it later," I say right before I come again down her throat.

THIRTY-SEVEN

CANDACE

"DADDY'S HOME," I say, clapping my hands as soon the sound of the front door slams. Ari copies me with a huge smile on her face, showing off her two bottom teeth. I grab her and walk out of the bedroom to the kitchen in time to see him put down his overnight bag.

"There are my girls," he says, coming over to us. He kisses me and then Ari. "I missed you."

"You were gone two days," I say, shaking my head. "But we missed you also." The preseason has already started, and this was the first road trip of the year.

Ari reaches for him, and he takes her in his arms. "Gotta say, Weber." I wink at him. "A man in a good suit with a baby in his arms. That, right there, that'll get you the ladies." We both laugh.

"It's a good thing I'm off the market," he says, and my heart literally pitter-patters in my chest. It's been two months since they moved in. Although his boxes are still in the garage unpacked, there are a couple of touches from his house. The picture of Cassie is now in Ari's room. I didn't even bat an eye when I put it up. She was Ari's mother, and she will never be brushed aside.

"I got a call today." I fold my hands over my chest, and he just looks at me. "Do you know from who?" I wait for him to say something, but he just kisses Ari. "My bank called to tell me the transfer went through."

"Oh, good," he says. "That took longer than I thought."

"Well, it's going to take even less time to send it back," I say, and he stops kissing Ari and looks at me. "You can't pay me for my house," I say of the money he transferred to me. "My house is not for sale."

"I'm not living here for free," he says, glaring. "That is a rule."

"You sent me five hundred thousand dollars." I throw my hands up. "My house is worth less than that."

He shrugs. "Oh, well."

"I'm putting the house on the market," I say, and he just looks at me. "I want to get a house that we both love. I want to get maybe another bedroom so we can do a playroom for Ari, and I want to have a guest room for when Zoey comes to town," I say. "If that's okay."

"I think I found a house," he says, and now I look at him shocked. "I spoke with Evan."

"Nothing in the past two months has ever started good with I spoke with Evan," I say. My man has stepped up his alpha tendencies, thanks to my brother whispering in his ear. I have panties that I can only wear with him because if something happens, he's there to make sure no one sees them. I have jeans that have gone "missing" along with some shirts.

He ignores what I just said. "Becca set me up with a realtor, and I showed him pictures of this house, and I said I wanted this but bigger."

"So it'll be our house." I put my hands on the counter in front of me as he nods. "So fifty-fifty."

"If you mean you are paying for the house." He looks at Ari. "That is a no." He smiles at her. "Is Candace talking crazy?" he asks Ari, and she claps her hands again. "Yeah, I think so, too." Then he looks at me. "It'll be our house that I buy for us," he says, getting up and coming around the counter. "And you can do whatever you want to it." He puts one of his arms around my waist and pulls me close. "Now I've been without you for two days," he says. "I need to get Ari down for a nap so I can get my welcome home bj." He winks at me. "Rule number—"

I put my hand up. "You can't use rules that I say during sex," I say, and remember when I made the rule up right before he left. His face was buried between my legs. "It's called temporary insanity." He laughs, and when Ari rubs her eyes, he smiles.

"Give me ten, maybe twenty and be naked and ready," he says.

Just so he doesn't get the last word, I ask, "Do you want me to get really ready and break out the—"

He doesn't let me say the word vibrator before he flips me the bird. "I'm just asking." I shrug.

"I'm throwing that thing out," he says, walking down the hallway to Ari's bedroom. I pick up his bag and bring it into the bedroom and unpack it for him, and I get sidetracked folding Ari's laundry when he walks back into the room ten minutes later, and he's throwing his jacket on the desk. "Why aren't you naked?" I laugh. "It's been two days."

"It has not. We had sex yesterday before you got on the plane," I say. "My parents are on their way."

"Now?" he asks, kicking off his shoes. "Like, this minute?"

"No, not now, but they are coming down for the home opener," I say, and he nods his head. He has yet to meet them face-to-face, but we talk to them on FaceTime each week. "Are you nervous?"

"I mean, a little bit." He takes off his pants. "But I've spoken to your father and let him know my intentions."

"Excuse me?" I ask, shocked. "Did I wake up, and it's nineteen fifty again?" He grabs me by the hips and takes the shirt out of my hand and tosses it back in the laundry basket. "I mean, I guess you would want the same when Ari moves in with a man," I say, and he stops.

"Ari's becoming a nun," he says, and I laugh when he picks me up and carries me to the bathroom. "Shower sex, it is." We stay in the shower until the water runs cold and I've came at least a dozen times. During which I conceded to him buying us a house.

The next night, he heads off to the arena to prepare for the big home opener. "Are you ready for the big night?" I ask Ari as I dress her in black tights and then slip the baby jersey that I had made for her with Ralph's name on the back. "Look at you," I say, grabbing the headband I also had custom made with a huge bow in the middle with the team logo. "Are you the most beautiful?" I say to her, and she claps her hands. I pick her up and snap a picture of us dressed the same, minus the big bow.

"Let's go prepare your bag," I say, packing her diaper bag while I put her in the walker that she zooms around the house in. Once I have everything done, I pick her up and get her in the truck. I go through the players' entrance, showing them the badge that Ralph got me. I grab her bag and buckle her in the stroller, and head to meet my parents, who gush all over her.

I get us settled into the players' box when I hear the cheers and see that they are taking the ice. "Are you ready to go see Daddy?" I ask, taking her from my mother, who wants to grab her back. "Let's go see Daddy." I walk down the steps to the arena where the other players' kids are standing. Manning's son waves his hand at me, and I wave back while his mother glares but smiles at the same time. *God, she's horrible*, I think to myself. I walk to the glass and point out things to her as she looks all around, taking in the lights. She jumps a bit when the puck hits the board, and then I spot Ralph skating over. His helmet not tied, and he smiles when he sees Ari. "Look at Daddy." I point, and she smiles at him as he taps the blade of his stick on the window. "You want to show Daddy your outfit?" I say, turning to the side so he can see that his name is on the back, and then he throws his head back when he laughs at "is my dad" down the back of it instead of his number.

"What does yours say?" he asks me, and I turn to show him that it's just a plain jersey, and he winks at us. "Love you," he says and skates away, and Ari starts to cry for her father.

"It's okay, baby girl," I say, turning around and walking away. We get back to the box, and my mother tries to take her out of my arms, but Ari is having none of it. She wails louder, and for the whole game, she sits in my lap never once letting anyone touch her. We leave before the third period ends with my mother kissing her and my father helping to bring us to my car. We make plans to meet the next day for a late lunch.

We get home, and I take off her outfit and place her in her comfy pjs, then grab a bottle and settle with her in the rocking chair. "Are you ready for our story?" I ask her, and she just lies in my arms. I grab the storybook that I made for her and only her. "Once upon a time, there was a baby girl named Ariella." I start the story, and she drinks her milk. "She had a mommy in heaven who loved her so much." I show her the picture of Cassie. "She had a Daddy named Ralph." I show her the picture of Ralph holding a small Ari in his arms. "The two of them loved her more than anything in the world." I show her the picture of the two of them together. "Then one day, Daddy met Candace." I show her the picture of Ralph and me. "And Candace fell in love with Ariella." I smile at her as her eyes get heavier and heavier. I don't finish the story because the bottle slips out of her mouth, and she is out like a light.

I get up and place her in the crib, covering her with her favorite blanket and setting the book back right next to her other ones. I look at the picture of Cassie, and just like every other night, I thank her for giving me Ariella.

EPILOGUE ONE

Ralph

One year later

"Mama," Ari says as she walks in the sand, one of my hands holding hers as we walk down the beach. "Mama," she says again, and I laugh because that is all she says all the time. I still remember when I waited for her in bed after she spent the past thirty-six hours holding Ari because she was feverish and teething at the same time, and she was miserable. But Candace just held her and spoke to her; fine, she shed tears because she couldn't take away her pain. Even when Ari would fall asleep, I tried to get her to sleep, but she refused to put her down. I sat Candace down and asked her if it was okay for Ari to call her momma. She collapsed in my arms in tears and nodded her head. From that day on, she was Mama and not Candace.

"Yeah, Mama is coming." I smile as the water washes

over her feet, and she squeals. Another thing that changed is Bernadette went from full-time to just a babysitter when needed. It happened when Candace missed Ari's full first step and cried for two days. The next day, she informed me that she was going to let Bernadette just be here on Sunday if I wasn't here so she could work, and when she needed extra help. Other than that, she was a stay-at-home mom, and she couldn't love it more. "You think she's going to be surprised?" I ask Ari who just looks up at me, smiling and scrunching her nose like Candace does. "Let's go and get things set up." I grab her and pick her up.

"There you guys are." I hear Candace when we walk closer to the house I rented for the week in Turks and Caicos. Right on the beach, just the three of us with one girl waiting on us and a chef.

This past year has been the best year of my life. My game was better than ever and the sponsorships were rolling in thanks to all the social media that Candace has been doing. We just got eliminated from the playoffs, and none of us were surprised. Fuck, we were shocked when we beat New York during the first round. Something I will be throwing in Evan's and Justin's face every single time. She sits up in the chair, her skin a nice bronze. "I missed you guys." She gets up and walks over.

"Mama," Ari says. "Ook," she says, pointing at the water. "Wawa."

"Is that the water, pretty girl," she says, taking her from me. "Do you want to go into the water with me?" Ari nods her head. "You coming with us?"

"I have to talk to the chef about dinner," I say. "It's a surprise."

"Oh, a surprise," she says and leans up for a kiss. "I like this surprise. Is the surprise going to include your tongue and a couple of fingers later?"

"I can do that," I say, slapping her ass when she walks away. I keep waiting for us to be tired of each other. Waiting to get into that groove that happens when you are with each other too long, but with her, it's like it was the first day. She puts Ari down as they walk into the water a little bit, and I hear Ari squeal. I turn and walk inside, making sure they have everything they need for tonight's big surprise.

"I'm going to go and dress Ari," I say to Candace, grabbing Ari from her. "You get dressed and meet me outside."

"Wait," she says. "Don't dress her in a dress. I think I saw a mosquito."

"Your mother has lost her mind," I say, walking to the bedroom that is right next to ours and grabbing the special outfit that I had shipped here. "Your mama is going to be so surprised," I say, dressing her in a little blue and gray tutu dress that I know Candace will love. She dresses her up all the time, and the shirt says it all. A matching headband makes her whole look. "You ready to go see Mama?"

She claps her hands. "I'm going to wait for you outside," I say, popping my head into the room and seeing that she's putting her panties on. "I'll wait for you there."

"But I'm almost done," she says. "Let me see Ari."

"No," I say. "We'll meet you outside," I say, rushing away and making Ari laugh when she thinks it's a game. I step out of the house and walk past the in-ground pool that has floating flower lights tonight and see the canopy set up in the middle of the way down the beach. The soft wind makes the white drapes blow, the tea trees lights hanging from them giving it a glow and candles are all lit up in a path toward the table. "Are you ready, baby girl?"

I look up and see that Candace is coming out, and she is wearing a white dress with thin straps and the way the wind blows, it flows all around her legs. "There she is," I say to Ari who spots her and calls her name. "It's Mama," I say when she gets closer.

"This is so pretty," she says when she gets close enough, and I see she's barefoot also. "You look handsome," she says of my blue linen shorts and white linen shirt. "And don't you look so pretty with that flower," she says, and Ari leans down and kisses her lips. "What is she wearing?" she asks, and I put Ari down in front of me and finally let her see her outfit.

"Mommy, will you marry Daddy?"

"Oh my God." She puts her hands to her mouth when she sees the shirt, and I get down on one knee right next to Ari, and now Candace sobs out and puts her head down and then back up again.

"Candace," I say. "I never thought I was capable of love." I start to talk, and I have to wipe away my own tears when I think about her. "Then I had Ari, and I knew I could love. It was a love that you couldn't explain."

"Me," Ari says, pointing at herself when I say her name.

"Then I met this woman who was a gift from heaven

really. You came into my life with your sweetness and your gentleness. You came into my life without even blinking an eye or shying away. I love you with everything that I am. I love your smile and your frown. I love the gentle way you hold my hand. I love the way you kiss me just because. I love the way you let Ari bake with you, knowing that she is going to make more of a mess than anything else. I love that you love our daughter with everything that you have." I look down. "I want to walk down the aisle with you. I want to promise to love, honor, and cherish you for the rest of my life. I want to have a baby with you. I want to sit down and tell them stories about how much I love you. I want to hold your hand now and for the rest of my life." I grab the blue square box in my pocket and open it. "Will you marry us?" I ask her, and she still has her hands over her mouth, and she nods. "She said yes, Ari," I say, getting up and grabbing Candace's face and kissing her. "I love you," I say, and I'm interrupted by Ari, who sneaks in the middle of us and holds her hands up to Candace.

"Yes, I'll marry you both," she says, kissing Ari who lays her head on her shoulder.

"I've dreamed about this moment for my whole life, I think," she says. "Felt it in my heart that you were the one for me. Felt it in the very first kiss. It's stupid. I know it is."

"No, it's not. All it took was one kiss for me, too. I thought it was strange, but all it took was," I say, "only one kiss."

EPILOGUE TWO

Candace

Two years later

"THAT'S IT; YOU can do it," Ralph says, pushing my hair back. My eyes close as I try to breathe through the contraction. "You are doing so good," he says, and I open my eyes now as the pain subsides. Rubbing my swollen stomach, we've been in the hospital for three hours now. My water broke at home while I was picking up Ari. Needless to say, he wasn't thrilled with that either. For the past eight months, he's treated me like I was glass, and every single time I moved or had a pain, he was on the phone with the doctor. He even had my mother fly in when he was going to be gone for more than two days.

"That one was hard," I say, and he nods and gets up to press the button again. "What are you doing?" He stands there dressed in shorts and a polo, his hair showing how nervous he is by the number of times he's run his hands through it. "You seriously need to relax," I say and look over at the monitor that shows the baby's heart rate. "I'm fine; the baby is fine." He ignores me, waiting for the nurse to come in.

Sandy, the nurse, comes in, and this time, she is less in a rush than she was the first ten times. "What is the problem, Mr. Weber?"

"She said the last one hurt and was a hard one," he says to the nurse, and she rolls her lips, trying not to laugh. "I'm sure it was, but I checked her five minutes ago, and she was at three centimeters."

"But what if," he says and looks at me and then at her. "Are you sure she's okay?"

"I can tell you one hundred percent that all her vitals are good." She puts her hand on his. "We've got her." She turns and walks out of the room, and I look at him.

"What?" he says, throwing up his hands. "You can never be too safe." If I didn't love him with every single beat of my heart, I would now.

"Why don't you go and call my mother and check on Ari for me?" I try to change his mind, and he nods, walking out of the room, but I can see him standing in the hallway. I look down at the engagement and wedding ring on my left finger, actually two wedding rings. The day of our wedding was the day I officially adopted Ariella. She was mine before the piece of paper was signed, but on the day of our wedding, he slipped an extra ring on my finger for her.

"Who let you in?" He looks down the hall and then

over his shoulder, smiling at me. "Take off that fucking shirt."

"Not a chance in hell," my brother, Evan, says. "What does this say?" He stops in front of him. "I'll help you since you look like you can't read. It says Stanley Cup Champions."

"It also says two thousand and fifteen," Ralph says, shaking his head, and Evan pushes him by the shoulder, walking in.

"Hey there," he says, coming into the room. "You are huge," he says of my big belly. He comes to me and puts a hand on my belly. "It's your favorite uncle," he says to the baby and kisses my cheek then sits on the bed next to me.

"Don't crowd her or my child." I look over at Ralph, who stands there with his phone in his hands. "She's having sharp pain."

"What's his problem?" Evan asks me, and I'm about to answer him when a stabbing pain hits me right in the stomach, and I yell out.

"Oh my God," Ralph says, rushing in. "Press the button." He rushes over and presses the button, and I'm trying to tell him not to, but he does, and she comes in. "She just yelled."

I wait for the contraction to pass me before I can talk. "It's normal. All of this is normal." I look at Evan. "Would you tell him?"

"You know what you should have done." Evan looks at Ralph. "You should have hired a separate private nurse to sit in the room and make sure she's okay." I look at both of them in shock. My husband actually thinking that was a good idea.

"If you don't stop, I'm kicking you out of here," I say to my brother and then look at Ralph. "I'm fine." I wince. "Okay, maybe not fine, but this is my body getting ready for what is to come." I smile at him and hold my hand out to him. To say I was thrilled to be pregnant was the understatement of the year. We had officially started trying, and by the next month, I was pregnant. I had the easiest pregnancy that you could have. I was not sick, I was only tired at the beginning, and I swear every single time I felt him or her kick, I would cry.

"I don't know if I can take this," Ralph says, and for the next five hours, he paces the room every single time I'm done with a contraction.

"Okay," Dr. Brown says when she comes in. "Let's see what is going on with the baby." She sits on the stool and rolls over to me, putting my feet in the stirrups. "How is dad doing?"

"Worse than mom," Sandy answers for us, and I have to roll my lips but not for long because another contraction comes. "Looks like someone is ready to push."

"Is that safe?" Ralph says from beside me. "Wouldn't it be easier to have a c-section?"

"I want to have this baby natural if possible." I look at Dr. Brown, who looks over at Sandy.

"Get everything ready," she says. Sandy presses the button, and a nurse comes on the intercom.

"We are getting ready to push in room seven," she says and then looks at Ralph. "Do you need a chair?"

"No." He hisses at her and then grabs my hand, bending to kiss it. A tear escapes his eye, and I just look at him.

"I'm going to be okay," I say. "We are going to be okay."

He comes to me now, putting his forehead on my temple. "I can't live without you," he says softly. "Don't leave me." He kisses my cheek, and I want to tell him that I'm not going anywhere. I want to tell him that it's going to be okay; it's going to be fine.

"Okay," Dr. Brown says. "We are going to count to ten, and I want you to bear down and push."

I nod at her, and she starts counting as I hold my breath and push. At the end of ten, I let out a big breath. "That was good," she says. "Let's go again." I don't know why I thought it would be right away. I was wrong, so wrong. I push for thirty-nine minutes. Sweat is now forming at my hairline, and I'm exhausted.

"I don't think I can do this." I look at the doctor and then back at Ralph. "I'm tired."

"You can do this," Ralph says, kissing my lips. "You can do this."

"Okay, go," the doctor says, counting, and I close my eyes and push. "Stop pushing. Daddy," she calls for Ralph, "come and see your baby's head." He looks down and then looks up at me with tears welled in his eyes. "Another big push like that one, and you can meet your baby." It happens so fast when they get to six, I hear Ralph cheer out and then look down when the doctor places the baby on my chest.

This overwhelming feeling rips through me, and all I can do is sob. "My baby," I say over and over.

"It's a boy," the doctor finally says, and I look at Ralph, who is crying beside me.

"Our baby," I say, kisssing our son's head. The nurse rubs the baby's back and then takes him from me, and I look at Ralph. "Go to the baby."

He shakes his head. "I'm not leaving you until the doctor tells me you're okay."

"She's fine," the doctor says. "Perfectly fine." Our son's crying now fills the room, and I start to panic.

"Why is he crying?" I ask the nurse who is weighing him and putting a diaper on him. "Is he okay?"

"He's perfect." She comes over with the baby. "Nine pounds, five ounces. Time for skin to skin, Mommy."

I lower my hospital gown and place my baby on me. "Hi," I say and feel Ralph sit on the bed beside me, his arm around us. "I'm your mommy, and this is Daddy," I say, and all he can do is look at us. Blinking and looking around, his mouth opening and closing. "We have a son."

"We have a son," Ralph says. I put my head back exhausted. "You are so brave."

I look over at him. "Is it too soon to tell you I want another one?" I smile at him, and he just shakes his head.

"I'll give you however many you want." He bends and kisses me and then kisses our son. "Whatever you want." My husband has given me my white picket fence, he's given me a daughter, and now he's given me a son.

He's made all of my dreams come true, and it all started with only one kiss.

www.ingramcontent.com/pod-product-compliance
Lightning Source LLC
Chambersburg PA
CBHW072043190726
48294CB00005B/1388